OTHER BOOKS by KASSANDRA LAMB

The Kate Huntington Mysteries
Psychotherapist Kate Huntington helps others cope with trauma, but she has led a charmed life...until a killer rips it apart. (10 novels)

The Kate on Vacation Mysteries
Even on vacation, Kate Huntington can't stay out of trouble. (4 novellas)

The Marcia Banks and Buddy Cozy Mysteries
Marcia Banks trains service dogs for veterans, and solves crimes on the side, with the help of her Black Lab, Buddy. (13 novels/novellas)

The C.o.P. on the Scene Mysteries
Eight days into her new job as Chief of Police in a small Florida city, Judith Anderson finds herself one step behind a serial killer. (spinoff from the Kate Huntington series; 2 novels–more to come)

Romantic Suspense
written under the pen name of Jessica Dale

FATAL ESCAPE

A C.o.P. on the Scene Mystery

Kassandra Lamb

a misterio press publication

Published by *misterio press LLC*

Cover art by Melinda VanLone, Book Cover Corner

ISBN: 978-1-947287-40-2

CHAPTER ONE

As usual, I was awake before the sun. But the grim reaper had also risen early today.

I roust myself out of bed predawn so I can get in some exercise, before that day's quota of defecation hits the ventilation system.

Not happening this morning, though. I was only on my ninth push-up when I got the call. Shoving myself up off the floor, I grabbed my police-issue cell phone. "Chief Anderson," I barked.

"Good morning, Chief," an undaunted Bradley replied. "We've got a scene on the Sofki Bridge that I thought you'd wanna see before the body's transported."

"Homicide?" I stepped into the bathroom, got the shower running.

"Not sure. Looks like a suicide on first blush. Of course, the medical examiner will make the final call, but..."

"...something looks suspicious."

"Yeah."

I could've pushed for more info, but that would've only slowed me down. Sergeant Bradley, my second in command, would not be calling without good reason.

"Be there in twenty minutes." Ten to shower and dress, ten to get to the scene. Ours was not a big city and there would be little traffic on a Sunday morning.

Eight minutes later, I had donned my least favorite black pantsuit—crime scenes can be hard on one's clothes—and I was stuffing badge and phone into the jacket pockets. My Glock slid smoothly into its middle-of-the-back holster. I glanced in the mirror over my dresser.

Dark hair, still damp, stuck out in places. No time for a comb, I used my fingers to smooth it down into what my mother had called a pixie cut.

I growled softly under my breath. *I'm no damn pixie, that's for sure.* But the short hairstyle was easy to maintain.

The Sofki Bridge, named after the tributary of the St. John's River that it spans, is the smaller of two bridges linking our city of Starling to Jacksonville, where at least half of our residents work. It's only one lane in each direction, with a center lane that reverses direction depending on the time of day.

Despite being Sunday, some cars were already lining up on the Starling end. I pulled off on the shoulder and called Bradley as I hoofed it the rest of the way to the crime scene. "I'm here. What have we got?"

"Two locations," he said. "Abandoned car up here on the bridge and a body pulled out of the river that's on the pier below."

I spotted an ambulance ahead, with two paramedics, looking bored, beside it. Beyond was yellow crime scene tape, stretched between two trees on either side of a dirt path leading down to the pier.

"Who's lead?"

"Cruthers," Bradley said, "but I assigned Patterson to help out, until we know what we've got."

"Be up top in a minute." Disconnecting, I nodded to the paramedics and trotted toward the crime scene tape on the dirt path. I should've grabbed my sneakers instead of the low-heeled pumps I usually wear to the office.

Two men stood silhouetted by the streetlights along the pier, their backs to me. Beyond them, a woman's bare legs stretched across the wooden planks, one shoe missing.

A uniformed officer, dripping wet, sat nearby on the side of the pier. He shivered under a shiny silver blanket draped around his shoulders, no doubt provided by the paramedics.

"You called her?" one of the standing men said to the other.

"Nah, Bradley did," the other answered.

The dripping officer turned his head. His eyes went wide when he saw me.

"Better him waking her up than me," the second man continued. "He's got his nose so far up her butt..." He trailed off when the uniform cleared his throat.

The man turned, the lights overhead revealing the face of Detective Patterson. He faked a smile. "Good morning, Chief."

"Good morning." Not sure what to do about the disrespectful comment, I opted to pretend I hadn't heard it, for now. "I'm going up top to check in."

The other man had also turned. He was in uniform, my newest sergeant, Armstrong, recently promoted to watch commander. His expression was grim.

"In the meantime," I said, "how about getting some more tape up around this part of the scene." I glanced meaningfully up to the road above, where some folks were getting out of their cars, trying to see what was going on.

Armstrong's cheeks flushed, but Patterson's bogus smile hung on. "Sure thing, Chief."

"Come with me," I said to the seated officer. He jumped up and followed me.

I glanced at his name tag. *Dulles. Shouldn't be hard to remember, like the airport in Washington, D.C.*

"You were first on the scene, Officer Dulles?"

"Yes, Chief." His teeth chattered. "It was called in as an abandoned vehicle. But when I ran my flashlight beam over the river, I spotted a clump of clothes, caught in the grasses on this side, downstream some. I came down here to the pier to get a better look." He jerked his head toward the river. "Turned out to be her."

"So you went in after her?"

"Yes, ma'am, in case she was still alive." He shook his head mournfully.

"Describe her." I'd get a better look at the body eventually, once the ME's people arrived, but I wanted to hear his impressions.

"Short, petite, except she's curvy." He gestured with his hands to indicate a voluptuous figure. Then grabbed for the edges of the blanket as it attempted to slither off his shoulders.

"Long black hair. Light tan skin. I think she's...uh, was Hispanic. Tight red dress, short. But her shoes are black sneakers—or should I say, shoe. She's missing one."

We'd reached the official entrance to the crime scene, where another uniform was keeping the crime scene entry log. He noted my entry and tilted his head to one side. "The detectives are over by the car, Chief."

I nodded my thanks and headed that way, Dulles dripping along beside me. "Did you call for the detectives?"

"Yes, ma'am. Couple of things felt off. One, I couldn't find any purse or wallet in the car."

"You searched the car?" My voice rose a bit.

"No, ma'am," he said quickly, his face anxious. "Only with my eyes. I didn't touch anything. But the driver's door was hanging open, the overhead light on, and the contents of the glove box were dumped out on the passenger seat and floor. No sign of a purse or wallet, that I could see."

"She might've taken it with her into the river." Although that would not be typical suicidal behavior. You don't need your possessions if you plan to be dead, and usually the suicide wants people to know who they are.

"Well, then there was..." We'd reached the front fender of the car. He gestured toward the guard rail along the side of the bridge. "On the railing, something's smeared there. I, uh, think it's blood."

"Good call." To Bradley and Cruthers who were now approaching us, I said, "You need this officer right now?"

They both shook their heads.

"Go home and change your uniform, Dulles."

Sergeant Armstrong had walked up.

"Is that okay with you?" I asked him. Technically, the uniforms were his province.

"No problem. Uh, Chief, could I speak to you for a moment?"

"Does it relate to this case?"

"No."

"Then later, my office in an hour." My tone was more terse than I'd intended. I decided I was okay with that.

"Got it." Armstrong turned away.

"Did you all know the corpse is missing a shoe?" I asked.

Cruthers nodded his shaggy dark head. He was a big guy, always reminded me of a bear. "It probably came off in the water."

"Maybe, but she's wearing a sneaker, so less likely to have come off on its own. And it's out of sync with the rest of her attire."

Cruthers nodded again and beckoned to a couple of uniforms nearby. "Look for a sneaker." He glanced my way.

"Black."

"But don't touch anything inside the car until the CS team gets here," Cruthers was saying as he walked away with them.

Barnes suddenly appeared at my elbow. I jumped a little.

"Sorry," my short but sturdy assistant said. Even at this hour, she was meticulously turned out, in a well-pressed uniform, her dark hair up in a sleek bun. "I didn't mean to sneak up on you, Chief."

"How'd you know I was here?" I asked.

She grinned. "Heard the calls for an ambulance and detectives on the radio. Where else would you be?"

"Can you help with the search, we're looking for–"

"A black woman's sneaker. I heard." Barnes jogged off to join the other uniforms.

"CS guys are on their way with a warrant," Bradley said, "to take the car back to our lot." He skimmed slightly-too-long brown hair out of his blue eyes. Like Barnes—his sister—he was impeccably dressed, only his "uniform" was a navy business suit.

I scanned the scene. More looky-loos were getting out of their cars. "We need to get one lane open as soon as possible." I could imagine the mayor yelling about inconveniencing the citizens, as if that took precedence over investigating a woman's death.

"Yeah." Bradley said, a grimace on his handsome face. "Otherwise, we're gonna need the auxiliary people for crowd control."

"Actually, that's not a bad idea. Call them in."

Bradley grimaced again. He apparently shared the opinion of quite a few officers regarding the recently formed auxiliary group—that the "wannabe cops" were a hazard as often as they were a help. But Mr. Mayor was constantly searching for ways to save money. The word *volunteer* was a favorite of his. And the auxiliary folks were able to lighten the load at times like these.

"We don't want to open the bridge though," Bradley was saying, "until the CS guys see those." He pointed to the road in front of the car.

The sun was still below the horizon but the predawn sky revealed black streaks on an angle in front of the abandoned car.

"Looks like someone may have veered in front of her and then slammed on their brakes," Bradley said. "There are skid marks behind her car as well. Two sets. One belongs to the commuter who almost rammed into the car's back end. He called 911."

I nodded.

"Have you seen the body yet?" he asked.

"Not up close."

Bradley made an after-you gesture. We walked to the end of the bridge, ignoring the questions some drivers were throwing our way.

The ME's van was now parked behind my car. Bradley and I picked up speed, jogging down the dirt path.

We got to the pier just in time to watch the assistant ME turn the body over.

There was a bloody gash on the back of the dead woman's head.

CHAPTER TWO

I sat at my desk, sipping my second cup of caffeine. I'd inhaled the first one.

It might be Sunday, but it wouldn't be a day of rest for us, not with a possible homicide to investigate.

My private line rang. *Officer Barnes*, the caller ID screen read.

"Found the shoe," Barnes said without preamble when I picked up. "And here's what's odd. It was tucked up under the driver's seat."

"What do you mean by 'tucked up?'"

"As in, very neatly placed there, up against one side. It didn't look like it could've ended up there because it fell off or even was kicked off."

"She put it there on purpose?"

"That's what we think, Cruthers, Danny and me." In her excitement, she'd forgotten to call her brother Sergeant Bradley.

"Who found it?" I asked.

"Officer Dulles. He's helping the CS guys with the evidence collection inside the car."

"He's back there already? I told him to go home and change."

"I carry a towel in my trunk," she said.

Of course, you do, I thought. Out loud, I said, "Were you a Girl Scout, by any chance, Barnes?"

"Ma'am?"

I swallowed a chuckle. "Never mind. You were saying?"

"Another odd thing, that was probably in the glove box originally—it was on the floor of the passenger side. A bar of soap, with a phone number printed on one side, and some scrape marks above that. And get this..."

I tapped my fingers on my desk.

The sound of air being sucked in. "The guys dusted the exterior of the car before having it towed, and there are no fingerprints on the outside of the doors."

My heart rate kicked up a notch. "None?"

"Nada. Why would someone about to commit suicide stop and wipe down their car?"

"Not likely. We have to wait for the official word from the ME, but we're handling this as a suspicious death in the meantime."

"That's what Detective Cruthers and Sergeant Bradley already assumed. Do you mind if I stick around here awhile, in case I can help..." She trailed off.

I smiled at the phone receiver. I was beginning to get it that my assistant was a bit of an adrenaline junkie. Not a bad thing for a cop, as long as one learned to channel the rush.

"That's fine." I disconnected and sat back in my desk chair. My cell phone pinged. Bradley had texted me some of the crime scene photos.

I stared at the close-up of the woman's face. She couldn't be more than mid-twenties. My throat and chest tightened.

Who are you, sweetheart? And who the hell tossed you off that bridge?

———◆———

My door was open, but Sergeant Armstrong knocked on the frame.

"Come in and close the door." I stood and twisted the blinds closed over the glass walls of my fishbowl office.

I gestured toward one of the two uncomfortable visitors' chairs I'd inherited from my predecessor. A well-padded, comfortable chair, for visitors I like, sat off to one side.

Armstrong glanced at that chair—the one he was normally offered—and raised an eyebrow, then sat on the edge of the chrome and vinyl one. He was a little over forty, a fifteen-year veteran, with a rugged face and a shaved head.

"I do not," he said, "in any way, shape or form, agree with Detective Patterson."

"About what?" I asked in an innocent voice, knowing full well he meant Patterson's comment on the pier earlier.

"About just about anything." His tone was mildly disgusted.

Patterson was the detective that I knew least well. He tended to keep to himself, rarely sought the limelight. When we'd been chasing a serial killer a few weeks back, he'd quietly taken over the pending cases of the other detectives, so they could work that bigger one.

"Is that kind of comment common," I asked, "coming from him?"

"Not common, but not out of character either." Armstrong squirmed some. Because of the chair or the topic of conversation?

"Not much respect for authority, huh?"

Armstrong sighed. "May I be honest, Chief?"

"I would certainly hope so." My tone was somewhat acerbic.

"Only my opinion, but I think he doesn't like women in general, since his divorce. I'm not sure he's happy about having a female boss."

Nor perhaps having Bradley promoted over him. Bradley had less time on the force, and he was gay. *Could Patterson be a homophobe?*

I reminded myself not to jump to conclusions. With only two months on the job, I was still learning the personalities and foibles of my people.

"So, have I earned my way back into..." Armstrong glanced sideways, toward the comfy chair.

I hid a smile. "Your preferred status has been restored."

Armstrong gave me an impudent grin. "Thanks, Chief."

The macho male brass I'd worked with through the years might've taken offense at the grin, but I found Armstrong's mildly irreverent attitude refreshing.

And he never questioned my authority, which was the bottom line.

———◆———

While waiting for more info on the case, I dug into the perpetual incident reports. I'd reviewed a few of them, when my personal cell phone rang. I pulled it out of my laptop case and checked its screen.

Ah, Sheriff Sam. My insides got a little warm and melty. "Hey there," I said into the phone.

"Hey, yourself." I could hear the smile in his voice.

I sighed. We were supposed to have brunch together. Something else not happening today. I opened my mouth.

But he spoke before I could. "Afraid I've got some bad news." His tone was now sober. "Did you know we have several properties that cross the border between your city and my county?"

"No, I did not know that." I wasn't quite willing to let go of the warm feeling, thinking maybe he was teasing me with a local history lesson.

"You know how most county lines are determined by rivers or creeks. Well, when Starling incorporated as a city, they followed a creek that's since dried up."

His matter-of-fact voice finally cooled my mood. I wondered where he was going with all this.

"A developer bought up the land that creek used to run through and built a bunch of houses, and guess what?"

My hand tensed around the phone receiver. "What?"

"We've got a home invasion and homicide in one of the houses that straddles the line."

"Damn!"

"My sentiments exactly. You wanna come out and take a look before we decide on jurisdiction?"

I blew out air. "Yeah, I guess."

A soft chuckle. "Such enthusiasm for your job, Chief."

I laughed. "Bite me!"

I was discovering that the reward for enduring a relentless Florida summer was a long, beautiful autumn. Today, the temperature was in the seventies, with low humidity. A perfect day for a drive in the country, if a murder scene weren't my destination.

The nineties-era clapboard rancher sat on a third of an acre. It was well maintained with a manicured lawn and neat flower beds along the front walk. The sun glinted off a relatively new metal roof.

Sam stood—tall, lean, and handsome in his khaki uniform—in the open front doorway. "We've got to stop meeting like this."

I gave a feeble smile for the feeble joke.

He snorted softly. "Tough audience."

One side of my mouth quirked up, despite myself. "What've we got?"

"Victim is the homeowner, Caroline Baumann, forty-nine," Sam said, as we walked toward the kitchen. "Lives alone. Widowed five years ago, moved down here a year later, from Michigan. Signs of forced entry via the back door. Bludgeoned with a blunt object, although no murder weapon has been found."

We'd reached the doorway between the kitchen and some kind of recreation room. The corpse lay a few feet away.

Sam stopped, his expression grim. He sucked in air, and I acknowledged internally what his neutral tone cost him. His was a small and rural county. He knew pretty much every citizen in it.

"She's been gone at least nine hours." He nodded to the assistant ME who was hovering over the body.

I glanced at my watch. It was barely nine a.m.

"So around midnight," I said.

"Or earlier in the evening." Sam ran his hand through thick sandy hair, sprinkled with gray.

Pressure against my right ankle. I jerked my foot away and looked down—saw nothing but the terrazzo floor.

Pressure against my left ankle. I swooped down to catch the elusive source of the pressure. It was a kitten. I held it up at eye level, and almost dropped it when I realized what was discoloring one side of its white coat.

Blood.

CHAPTER THREE

I was still holding the creature, trying to figure out what to do with it, when Barnes stepped up beside me. I jumped a little.

"Sorry. I heard we might have another case out here." She deftly lifted the kitten from my hands.

A tugging sensation in my chest. I opened my mouth to protest, not sure why. Then I closed it again.

Barnes and the cat melted away. I shook my head to clear it.

Sam and I sparred good-naturedly over jurisdiction, neither of us particularly wanting it. I always laugh when I see TV cops fighting to *keep* jurisdiction of big cases. Most of us would just as soon let them be someone else's headache.

"But you have more resources than we do," Sam said, with a fake whine in his voice.

I chuckled. "Yeah, you've got sixteen people. I've got twenty-three."

"I was thinking more along the lines of crime scene techs and such."

Still with some humor in my voice, I said, "I'll lend you one of my dynamic duo, once they've finished going over the car they're working on now."

"You talking about the one abandoned on the Sofki Bridge?"

I nodded, my mood sobering. "We've managed to keep the rest of the story under wraps for now, but that won't last. The media will get wind of it soon." I filled him in on the suicide that might be a homicide.

"You know," he said, "you've got enough on your plate with that. I'll take Caroline."

I'd known he would eventually. He played the role of the retired detective from up north, now trying to take it easy as a rural sheriff in Florida. But he took his job seriously, and someone had messed big-time with one of his citizens.

Barnes was standing next to my car as Sam and I exited the house. "Dinner later?" he asked in a low voice.

My chest warmed. "We'll see. The day is young."

He gave me a half smile and a mock salute, then turned away.

As I approached my assistant, a faint purring sound came from one of her hands. "Didn't you call Animal Services?"

She looked at me, her big brown eyes wide. "Clover County doesn't have an animal shelter."

I sighed, knowing what she would say next. The Starling Animal Services Center was *not* a no-kill shelter. If the deceased's family didn't claim the kitten...

"So you're taking it home?" I asked.

"Can't," she said, her expression a combination of anxious and hopeful. "No pets allowed at my new apartment."

We stood frozen in a silent tableau for a moment. Finally, it dawned on me what she was hoping for. I started shaking my head.

"I cut off and bagged the bloody fur as evidence. I'll give it to the sheriff." She thrust the now partially bald kitten at me.

I should've kept my hands at my side, but they rebelliously accepted the animal.

"You've been thinking about getting a cat," she said.

"Not all that seriously." The kitten snuggled against my chest and purred.

Barnes's face fell. "I'll find him another home, as soon as I can. But could you keep him in the meantime?"

I gently lifted the kitten in front of me and examined its belly and under its tail. "I guess, but it's a she, not a he."

Barnes flashed me a relieved smile, which I assumed had nothing to do with the kitten's gender.

My assistant had found a box—what didn't she have in that trunk of hers? Now, said box was mewling at me from the passenger-side floor of my car.

What was I thinking when I agreed to take the kitten? I didn't need to be tied down by a pet. Not that cats were all that high maintenance, but still.

The mewling rose in volume, became a full-blown yowling, angry and screechy. Then it fell silent. Excuse me, *she* fell silent. Maybe she was cleaning herself.

Or maybe she's somehow hurt herself.

I am not pulling over to check on her, I told myself, as I pulled the car onto the shoulder.

The kitten was fine. She climbed up my blouse sleeve, made it almost to my shoulder before I could grab her with my other hand.

Now there were tiny prick marks in the satiny fabric of the sleeve. *I never liked this blouse all that much anyway, too shiny and girlie-girl.*

The cat resisted going back into the box, flailing its little legs. "Okay, you can sit on the seat, as long as you behave."

As soon as the car was moving again, she crawled onto my lap. But she stayed there, purring, until we pulled into the Starling municipal parking lot. I somehow managed to get her back inside the box for the trip to my office.

The car from the bridge was already there, in a section of the lot fenced off by ten-foot chain link, with a beefy padlock on the gate. I walked over to the fence, the cat scrambling around in the box, making it hard to carry.

"What've ya got in there, Chief?" Ernie Mansfield asked.

Ignoring the question, I nodded a greeting to him and the senior member of the team, Bert Deming. Yes, they were Bert and Ernie, and their builds matched the Sesame Street characters as well. Bert was tall and slender with thinning blond hair. Ernie was shorter and more squat, with thick dark hair. He wasn't the brightest bulb in the package, but he did his job.

"Anything from that shoe?" I asked.

Bert's face lit up. "Yeah! There was a slit in the side of the sole, and a plastic key card inside."

"Interesting place to keep your hotel room key."

"This one's a little smaller than those usually are. Only writing on it is," he made air quotes, "'You prize it; we protect it.'"

"Property management? Or private security?" I speculated.

Bert shrugged. "The detectives are researching it."

I tilted my head toward the car.

"No prints on the outside of the doors," Bert said. "Plenty elsewhere but most too smudged to be useful. A few partials. Detective Cruthers is running them."

"No clear ones on the steering wheel?" I asked.

He shook his head. "That was wiped clean too, as was the front of the glove box."

I caught my jaw before it dropped open. More evidence that our Jane Doe was not a suicide, unless she had some reason to want to slow down the identification process.

"We're gonna go over it again," Bert said, "make sure we didn't miss any. Oh, and the tags are from a different car, that had been junked. VIN number has been filed off in both places on this car, so no idea where it came from."

I looked skeptically at the car. It was an older model, with faded splotches in its navy paint.

"Ford Taurus," he added. "Late 1990s vintage. I'll look it up on the computer once we've finished going over it, try to nail down the year."

"It runs great," Ernie threw in.

I nodded.

"Aren't ya gonna tell us what's in the box?" he asked, watching the thing rock and roll in my hands.

"A cat." The box bounced hard in my hands. I almost lost my grip on it.

An eerie yowl made Ernie jump. "Uh, ya need us to do anything with it?" His expression was now wary.

"Nope. Related to another case, on which I need your help. One of you needs to go up to the county line and help process a scene there for Sheriff Pierson."

"Wanna flip for it, boss?" Ernie said hopefully.

"Sure." Bert tossed an imaginary coin in the air, faked catching it and slapped his other arm. "You lose, you go."

Ernie's face fell. "Aww, boss, you always do that."

On the third floor of the municipal building—home to the Starling Police Department and not so affectionately referred to as 3MB—Barnes had a bag of litter, a disposable roasting pan, two small dishes and several cans of kitten food on her desk.

I stopped abruptly when I spotted the supplies. "You did not have those in your trunk, did you?"

She gave me a confused look. "Only from the dollar store to here. Why?"

I shook my head, not about to explain how I've come to think of the trunk of her car as "the magic trunk"—that seems to produce whatever is needed, no matter how obscure.

"Bring them in here." I marched past her and into the tiny bathroom off of my office, still juggling the squirming box.

Detective Cruthers's large form loomed in my doorway. I left Barnes to get the cat settled and motioned for him to lead the way back to his desk.

He gestured toward the bar of soap, now in a clear evidence bag, lying in the middle of the chaos of his paperwork.

"Any prints on it?" I asked.

"A couple of partials. They're running now. No hits so far. I called the number on the side. Woman answered, just said, 'Hotline.' Hung up when I identified myself."

He sighed. "And before you ask, it's probably a burner phone. No matches in the reverse phone directory."

"That's curious. Why would a hotline use the number from a burner phone?"

He shrugged.

I glanced around the bullpen. Only Patterson was at his desk on the other side of the room.

I pulled out my personal cell, which I had set up to block caller ID on the other end. Cruthers held up the bag so I could read the number. I punched it into the phone.

"Hotline, how can we help?" A woman's voice, warm and kind-sounding.

"Hello?" I said, making my tone tentative.

"Whatever you need," the woman's voice had softened even more, "we can help."

"Um, I'm not sure...what I need." I tried to sound young, and scared. No way of knowing what kind of hotline this was, but most likely all of their callers were scared of something.

"Would you like to meet with us, at our office? It's safe. We keep the location secret. Or we can meet you somewhere, at a coffee shop, maybe?" A pause. "Or we can just keep talking on the phone now, whatever you're comfortable with."

"Uh, I guess... I mean, I could come to your office. How do I find it?"

She mentioned a street corner in downtown Starling. "Do you know where that is?"

"Yeah."

"One of our volunteers will meet you there and lead you to the office."

I paused trying to decide if there was anything else a frightened young woman would ask or say.

"My name's Cheryl," the woman said, again in the soft voice. "Can you give me your first name?"

"Uh, Judy."

"Okay, Judy. When do you want to come in?"

"Um, I can get there in about an hour. I have to take the bus."

"An hour will work fine. A woman named Nancy will meet you at that corner."

I waited. The line stayed open. She wasn't going to hang up, in case the scared young woman she thought was on the other end had anything else on her mind.

I disconnected, then blew out pent-up air.

"Good acting, Chief," Cruthers said, a smile lighting up his broad face.

A few minutes later, the cat now closed inside the bathroom, Cruthers, Barnes and I stood by my desk, plotting my disguise.

"Whatever kind of hotline it is," Cruthers was saying, when Bradley appeared in the doorway, "they'll probably be expecting a young woman from the streets, homeless if not a prostitute."

"It could be a pregnancy hotline," Barnes pointed out. "Those would get women from all walks of life."

I'd already ditched my jacket on the back of my desk chair. Now I was glad I was wearing the satiny blouse. It wasn't as stiff and cop-like as most of my shirts are.

Bradley had an eyebrow crooked in the air. "Fill him in," I told Cruthers.

Barnes handed me a pair of gold hoop earrings, about an inch wide. Not garish, but a bit more hip than my small pearl posts. I started switching out the earrings.

In her other hand she held a tube. "Lemme work on your hair."

I gave her a don't-make-me-look-ridiculous glare and leaned my head down.

She rubbed some gel into my hair and tugged gently here and there.

"Done." She held up a hand mirror as I lifted my head. Not severe spikes, but again, a hipper style than my usual cap of hair.

I hate purses, but I kept one in my desk drawer, in case I needed it for more formal appearances. Most of the time, I carried whatever I needed in my leather laptop case.

Now I was deciding what to put in the purse. Twenty-dollars' worth of cash, in fives and ones. Some coins. Not my driver's license but a department store credit card that had only *Judith Anderson* on it. A key from my key ring that I'd long since forgotten what it opened. I transferred a packet of tissues from my laptop case to the purse.

Barnes handed me a lipstick, bright red, and held up the mirror again.

I grimaced, but dutifully applied the stuff to my lips, then dropped the tube in the purse.

Last but not least, Cruthers held up a button that was really a tracking device.

I glanced at my watch. It was a rather masculine style, not what a girl on the street would wear. I took it off, but noted that twenty minutes had passed already. No time to sew the button somewhere. We wanted to get to that street corner before whoever was meeting me arrived.

I nodded toward the purse. Cruthers dropped it in there, along with a small cell phone. "Burner," he said.

"You need backup," Bradley said to him.

"Not Patterson," I said, my voice a little too adamant.

Bradley's eyebrow went up but he didn't respond.

"I've got him working on the card key," Cruthers said, "that was in our Jane Doe's shoe."

"I'll come along myself," Bradley said.

"And me." Barnes's face was hopeful.

I started to tell her to stay and take care of the kitten. But part of the deal when I'd pulled her rookie butt off of street duty to be my assistant was that she'd go out into the field with me, to learn how to be a detective at my side.

As she so often did, Barnes read my mind. She went over to the bathroom door, cracked it and peeked in, then quietly closed the door again. "She's curled up in the shower stall, sound asleep."

"Okay. Let's get this show on the road." I led the way out of my office, patting my small back-up gun, a .32 five-shot snub nose revolver, in one pocket of my loose-fitting suit pants.

CHAPTER FOUR

I stood on the street corner. It wasn't hard to fake being nervous. I'd never been fond of undercover work, and it had been a long time since I'd done any. Even if this wasn't a particularly dangerous situation, it was still nerve-wracking, playing a role, pretending I was someone that wasn't real.

My three-person back-up team was in Bradley's burgundy car on the other side of the street and down a half block, so they had a clear view of the corner.

A nondescript white sedan pulled up beside me and the passenger window whirred down. "Are you Judy?"

The forty-something woman had a mop of dark curls and intense blue eyes. She reminded me of Kate Huntington, an acquaintance—well, a friend really—in Maryland.

"Yeah," I said, trying to seem skittish.

"I'm Nancy. You can either ride with me, or we can walk. It's not far."

I looked around quickly, as if afraid of being seen with her. Then I opened the passenger door and hastily got in.

She went around a corner and pulled up to the curb again.

"Boy, that was close by."

She laughed slightly. "No, we're not there yet. Can I ask you to turn your pockets out, please?"

I gave her a startled look that wasn't faked. I turned out my left pocket, while surreptitiously sliding my right hand into the other pocket and palming my small pistol. I pinched the inside of the pocket between index and middle fingers and managed to turn it out without revealing that the gun was in my hand.

Nancy nodded, a pleasant smile on her face. "Can I see your purse for a minute?"

This I had expected, thus the careful decisions about what to put in it. I handed the bag over.

She gently poked through its contents, then pulled out the button and the lipstick tube.

Suddenly another woman was at the driver's window that was whirring down. I caught myself before drawing my gun up on her. It was still cupped in my hand.

"This is Cheryl," Nancy said. "You spoke to her on the phone. She's going to hold onto these two items for you until we get back." She started to hand the items over.

I grabbed her arm to stop her. "Why?"

"In case they are listening or tracking devices. We sometimes get some nasty characters who try to find our office." She tried to tug her arm loose, but I held on.

"Nope, you're not handing those over to anybody else." In the short tussle, I turned my other hand, unintentionally revealing the pistol. "I'm the chi–"

I was interrupted by a scream from Nancy. Cheryl took off.

Nancy pulled harder on her arm.

I hung on. "Drop the button and I'll let go, but if you try to leave the car, you'll be arrested."

"Arrested? You're the one who's about to be arrested. Cheryl went to get a cop."

I glanced over my shoulder and almost burst out laughing.

Cheryl was jogging back toward us, with Barnes in tow.

"I don't have my badge with me," I told Nancy, "but I'm the chief of police." I tilted my head toward Barnes's face, which had just appeared in the open window. She was not trying to hide her amusement.

"Officer Barnes here will vouch for me."

"Yup, she's the chief," Barnes said, finally managing to swallow her grin.

Cheryl, with some encouragement from Barnes, climbed into the backseat. Barnes followed.

"Now, Nancy," I said in a reasonable tone, "what exactly does your organization do and where is this secret office of yours?"

She shook her head. "We're not doing anything illegal, but we have to keep the office location secret."

"And if you truly are not doing anything illegal, we will gladly keep your secret."

She didn't move.

"Enough!" My tone was no longer all that reasonable. "Start driving, or we'll arrest both of you for obstruction of justice."

The "office" was a storefront. No signs anywhere giving any hint to the nature of the organization within.

We stepped out of the car. The heavily-tinted plate glass windows bounced our reflections back at us.

Nancy unlocked the door and pulled it open, made an after-you gesture toward me and Barnes.

I shook my head, held up an index finger in a wait-a-minute gesture.

Barnes had her service weapon in her hand, down by her leg. "Keep it down there unless you need it," I whispered. No doubt she already knew that, but she was a rookie. Didn't hurt to remind her of such things.

Cruthers and Bradley trotted up behind us.

"Stay out here for now," I told them, "unless you hear shouting or shots."

I nodded to Nancy who stepped through the doorway. Cheryl followed.

My .32 still mostly hidden in my palm, I went in quick and to the right. Barnes went to the left.

Three women of varying ages and one young man sat at metal desks, several of them with phones to their ears. Were the small, clear partitions between the desks for privacy, or were they residuals of their Covid precautions?

I glanced down at an empty desk, a little away from the others. Among the papers strewn on it were several with letterhead that read *Magdalene Repurposing Center*. Was that the organization's name?

At the back of the large room, a tall, big-boned woman stood by an open door, arms crossed, frowning.

"What's going on?" she asked Nancy as we approached.

"This is Judy," the latter said, then whispered, "Only she's a cop."

I glimpsed a Spartan office beyond the open door and gestured toward it, not eager for an audience.

The furrows in the tall woman's forehead deepened. She turned and led the way, stark light from the overhead florescent tubes glinting off silver threads in her blonde hair, which was pulled back in a tidy bun.

I'm not a short woman, but this gal had at least two inches on me. And with that scowl and the hard glare in her ice blue eyes, she only needed a horned helmet to be a Viking warrior.

Behind her desk, she turned but didn't sit down.

Barnes had followed me into the office. She closed the door in the faces of the other two women, then leaned against the doorjamb, pad in hand.

"We found a bar of soap," I said, "with your hotline's number on it, in an abandoned car."

The woman's eyebrows went up slightly, but otherwise she didn't react.

"The woman, whom we believe had been driving that car, was pulled out of the river."

The ice-blue eyes softened some. Her jaw clenched, even as her shoulders sagged.

"We're trying to ID her." I reached for my pants pocket, where my phone would normally be. But of course, it wasn't there.

"Barnes, you got the crime scene photos on your phone?"

She handed it over.

The woman's face crumpled. "Crime scene?" she said in a shaky voice.

I gestured toward her desk chair and she sank into it. I took the visitor's chair across from her. "Let's start over. I'm Chief of Police Judith Anderson." I nodded toward Barnes. "This is my assistant, Officer Barnes. And you are?"

She stared at me for a beat. "Mary Striker," she finally said.

I found the least horrific shot of the victim's face, laid the phone on the desk and slid it toward her. "Sorry that we don't have a better photo."

Her already fair skin blanched to pure white. "I know her," she said carefully. "She goes by Tatiana Gomez."

"Why do you say 'goes by'?"

"Most of the women we work with started out running away from something, so they rarely use their real names. And sometimes their pimps give them another name, something they think is sexier."

"You help prostitutes get out of the life, then?" I had been thinking either that or they helped battered wives disappear. Personally, I approved of either venture, but the latter would be more problematic, since it often involved helping the woman break the law by kidnapping her own kids.

"Yes, but it's more complicated than that." She took a deep breath. "Are you going to keep our location, indeed our existence, a secret?"

"Probably, but only if you're straight with me."

She stared at me again, for a couple of seconds. "There's a human trafficking ring that operates out of Jacksonville. We've told the Jax Sheriff's Office about it. They tell us they'll take care of it. Then nothing happens."

"But you're here in Starling. Why?"

Mary Striker stared at me some more.

After several beats of silence, I said, "Because they have women here as well. Did you report this to the Starling PD?"

More silence.

Considering what I'd come to learn over the last few weeks about my predecessor, the silence didn't surprise me. Chief Black had a reputation, well deserved, as a sexist and a bigot.

"So you help the women get away." More statement than question.

"Yes," she said. "We get them a new ID, give them...several choices for transportation out of the city. We have a couple of safe houses where they can go initially, until their pimps have stopped actively looking for them."

"This ring, it only operates here in Starling and Jacksonville?"

Mary Striker shook her head. "They're all over Florida, best we can tell. We're not sure where they get their victims. Most are women, some are teenage boys. Many are Latina, some are white or African-American."

"Okay, tell me more about Tatiana Gomez."

"We lost contact with her about three days ago." She shrugged. "It happens sometimes. The woman gets spooked and takes off early. All we can do then is pray for her."

"Was she in a safe house?"

"No, she was supposed to go into one, but she never showed."

"Was her car from you all?"

Striker was silent again, stone-faced.

"Do you have an address for her?"

She tapped keys on her computer, read off an address. Barnes plugged it into her phone.

"Most of the women live together," Striker volunteered. "In two houses. We don't have addresses. The women won't tell us much. But Tatiana was one of the lucky ones. She has, *had* her own apartment. It was paid for by one of her rich johns. It's small, but at least she had some privacy."

"Why the special treatment?"

She shrugged. "I guess she made a lot of money for her pimp. She's...she was quite beautiful."

I changed tacks. "You call this place the Magdalene Repurposing Center?"

She nodded, with a flicker of a smile. "That's our cover, that we're a charity and we repurpose stuff people give us to help the poor. What we're really repurposing are these women, from a life of prostitution to a normal life."

"And Mary Magdalene was the most famous prostitute ever."

She nodded again, flashed a full smile for a moment.

I smiled back, then changed tacks again. "Why would a pimp work so hard to find these women when they get away? Most of the time, if one of their girls leaves town, they just go to the bus station and pick up some new runaway."

The hardness was back in the woman's eyes. "These women did not enter prostitution willingly, nor were they enticed and groomed like most pimps do. Some are illegal immigrants who were kidnapped and sold to the highest bidder. Others were picked up the usual way, at the bus station and such. But they weren't seduced into the life, they were forced. They are sex slaves!"

I caught myself as my mouth began to fall open. I was about to ask how she knew that, when another door in the back of the office swung open.

My hand flew to my pocket where my pistol was.

A man stepped into the office. "Honey, I can't seem to get this–" He stopped abruptly when he saw me. "Oh, sorry." He turned to Striker. "You didn't lock the door."

She waved a hand in the air. "She's not a client."

"Oh." He left as quickly as he'd entered, pulling the door shut behind him.

He was handsome, in a boyish way, maybe late thirties, and the grease smudged on his tee shirt and hands told me that Tatiana's car probably did come from these people.

But I didn't press that for the moment. "Who was that?" I asked instead.

"My husband."

I nodded, surprised and yet not. The 'Honey' had implied a relationship, but the man was at least ten years younger than Mary Striker, and way out of her league appearance-wise.

But then again, not all men are hung up on looks, only most of them.

———— ❦ ————

In Bradley's car, I rode shotgun with Cruthers and Barnes in the backseat. I repeated the interview to them.

"Who's Tatiana's pimp?" Cruthers asked.

"Mrs. Striker didn't know. She said Tatiana never told her, and that isn't unusual. Apparently, the women are threatened with all kinds of dire consequences if they tell anyone about the operation."

Bradley nodded. "They just want to get away from them."

Cruthers's phone rang. He answered and listened for a minute. "Thanks," he said and disconnected.

"That was Patterson. He hit pay dirt on that card key. It's for a self-storage company in the Jax suburbs, but get this. It's very high end. Climate controlled and all that jazz. Tight security 24/7. They cater to rich people who have too much stuff, even for their big houses."

"So we have two addresses to check out," Bradley said.

"Which would you prefer, Chief?" Cruthers asked.

"Storage place, but it's your call." As lead detective, he got to say who pursued what.

He nodded. "Patterson's already headed there. I'll send the address to your phone. We'll drop you back at 3MB, and Bradley and I will check out our gal's apartment."

"Sounds good," I said out loud, while thinking that my earlier tactic of avoiding Patterson was about to shift. I'd play things by ear with him, see how he acted.

Cruthers's phone rang again. He answered, then put the phone on speaker. "It's the ME's office, the pathologist on our case."

"Hi, Doctor," I said.

"Hi, Chief. I thought you'd want to know this right away. Full autopsy is tomorrow, but the preliminary assessment is that this is a homicide. There may very well be river water in her lungs. But the way her skull has been fractured, it's highly likely that she was unconscious and possibly already dying before she hit the water. Drowning only sped things up."

I asked, "Could the head wound have been caused by her slipping and banging her head on the railing? It's metal."

"Unlikely. She'd have to hit it awfully hard to do this much damage."

Cruthers thanked her and disconnected.

"Okay, folks," I said, "we've got a murder investigation on our hands."

Patterson was waiting in the storage facility's parking lot. Dark-haired, he was very average—in pretty much every way—and he rarely smiled. His forehead puckered slightly when he saw me climb out of my car, but otherwise his expression remained neutral. "Hey Chief, where's Cruthers?"

"Checking out another lead. We have a name, although it's likely to be an alias—Tatiana Gomez—and a home address."

Inside the low rectangular building, the air was downright frigid. I was glad for my suit jacket. Barnes, in her short-sleeved uniform shirt, shivered beside me.

We approached a counter that could have been the check-in desk of a high-end hotel, with a marble top and gold, silky-looking fabric across the front. A tall, painfully thin young man, wearing a black suit, stood behind it. His dark hair was pulled back in a short ponytail.

"You the manager?" Patterson asked as he flashed his badge.

"I am the concierge. How can I help you, Detective...?"

"Patterson. This is Chief Anderson and Officer Barnes." He held up the card key, in a clear evidence bag. "We need to know what unit this goes to and who is renting that unit. And we need to search it."

The young man's eyebrows went up to his hair line. "Do you have a warrant?"

Patterson pulled the folded papers from his inside jacket pocket. I mentally gave him kudos for having gotten the search warrant so fast.

The young man looked down, scanning the page. "This says you can only visually view the contents of the unit, and only take what is specifically relevant to the case." He looked up, met Patterson's eyes. "What's the case?"

"We'll get to that. First, which unit does this go to and who's renting it?"

The man gingerly took the bag by one corner, as if it might bite him. He laid it on the counter, then squinted at a six-digit number on the card key and tapped on his computer keyboard.

"Guadalupe Martinez rents that unit, number 108. Nice lady." He sniffed. "Although her dresses tend to be a bit too tight."

Hmm... I'd bet my next six paychecks that Guadalupe Martinez wasn't our victim's real name either.

The concierge slid the key, in its bag, back to Patterson, then just stood there.

"Can we see the unit, please?" I asked.

"I'm not allowed to let anyone into a client's unit. Tight security is very important to our clientele."

Patterson picked the warrant up off the counter and shook it.

"I know, but I'd rather call Ms. Martinez first."

"You can call," I said, "but she won't answer. She's dead."

The blood drained out of the young man's cheeks, and I flashed to a line drawing in one of my books as a kid, of Ichabod Crane.

Without another word, he led the way down a long corridor to a pull-up door made of polished mahogany. It contrasted nicely with the cream-colored stucco walls.

Patterson donned latex gloves and took the card key out of the bag. It slid smoothly into the card reader next to the door and a soft click announced that it had unlocked the door.

The concierge tapped a button beside the reader and the door slid soundlessly up.

A rustling noise.

What? Surely this place doesn't have mice.

The concierge glared at the contents of the unit, apparently seeking the source of the noise. But nothing moved.

Several boxes were stacked three high, creating a low wall across the center of the unit. At one end, the top box was open, with several plastic toys spilling out of it.

Barnes, Patterson and I spread out. I headed for the toys. Why would our young female victim have a box of plastic trucks, cars, and blocks?

When I was close enough to see over the barrier of boxes, I got my answer.

A small boy lay on a blanket, clutching a teddy bear, his thumb planted firmly in his mouth. His light tan skin was ashen under the surface.

And his eyes were full of terror.

CHAPTER FIVE

"What the hell?" Patterson said.

The concierge stood, open-mouthed and gasping. He took out an inhaler and sucked on it.

The little boy sat partway up and scrambled backwards, crab-like against the far wall of the unit.

Barnes, in between Patterson and myself, leaned forward slightly. "*Buenos días, niño.*" She pointed quickly to the three of us. "*Amigos de tu mamá. Mi nombre es Gloria.*" She pointed to herself, then to the boy, who was now watching her with a mixture of fear and fascination. "*¿Cómo te llamas?*"

My assistant's accent wasn't perfect, but she was doing better than my rusty high-school Spanish would be.

The boy opened his mouth, then seemed to remember that he needed to remove his thumb before he could speak. "Alejandro," came out along with the thumb, so soft I almost didn't catch it.

Barnes leaned a little farther over—trying to get closer to his level, I suspected.

Again she spoke in Spanish, too fast for me to translate.

"*¿Dónde está mi mami?*" the boy asked.

Barnes gave a rapid response.

"*¿En el hospital?*"

Barnes waggled her hand back and forth. "*Algo como eso.*" I translated in my head, *Something like that.* What was she telling the boy?

More rapid-fire Spanish. She put one hand behind her back and made a shooing gesture.

I took the hint and backed up almost to the door, waving Patterson back as well.

While still talking, Barnes moved down the row of boxes and slid the toy box and those under it out of the way. She crouched down and held her arms wide.

The boy hesitated for a long moment, then jumped up and ran to her. She stood up, holding him tight. She started to turn away, but the boy leaned over, almost pulling himself out of her arms. "*¡Osito!*"

I pulled out my phone and began snapping pics of the bear *in situ.*

Barnes was trying to soothe the boy, but he kept asking for his teddy, tears now welling.

I grabbed it up and gave it to the child.

Patterson scowled. I was messing with the evidence.

But I'm the Chief, I thought, hiding a smirk. And I seriously doubted that one ragged teddy bear would end up being all that important to the case.

At least not as important as it was to this little boy.

Back on the third floor of the municipal building, the boy still clung to Barnes like a tick. She stared at me over his shoulder with a soulful look.

"Kittens are one thing, Barnes," I declared emphatically. "Rug rats are another."

"I know," she said. "DCF is on its way."

Department of Children and Families, the Florida version of Maryland's Child Protective Services.

My vision clouded.

The woman on the floor, not moving, despite the efforts of the paramedics hovering around her.

The social worker at my elbow. "So sorry, hon. We'll get you into a foster home."

I shook my head hard, to clear it.

Barnes gave me a quizzical look.

Damn it to hell! Yet another case that was stirring demons from the past. I'd had enough of that last month, when a serial killer who liked to strangle women had triggered old memories.

Barnes had managed to get the little boy to let go of her and sit in my comfy visitor's chair. She perched on one of the less comfortable, chrome-and-vinyl ones nearby.

With her acting as translator, I questioned him, trying to be as gentle as possible. "When was the last time he saw his mother?"

She asked the question and the child rattled off a rather long answer. I caught the word for *dinner*, but that was about it.

"She brought him a burger and fries for dinner last night," Barnes reported, "then told him to play very quietly on his blanket and she would be back soon."

Through the open blinds of my fish-bowl office, I spotted Cruthers and Bradley entering the bullpen. I'd texted to tell them about the boy. Now, I held up my hand in a wait gesture. Too many people crowding into my office might shut the child down.

The men headed for Bradley's office instead.

"Ask him how long he was there," I said.

Barnes did so. The boy gave her a blank look. She rephrased the question and again I caught *cena*—the word for dinner.

His expression was thoughtful, then he held up three fingers.

That jived with the info from the concierge. Tatiana had rented the unit three days ago.

"Ask him where he lived before that." She did so and got another lengthy answer.

Alejandro's voice went up slightly at the end. He had asked a question. His stomach rumbled.

Barnes's eyes were shiny when she turned toward me. "He wants to know when his mom is coming. She usually takes him to the park midmorning, and they get hot dogs and ice cream after he plays for a while."

I nodded. "What did he say about where they lived?"

"He just called it their apartment. Doesn't sound like anybody else lives there. But he said he sometimes stayed with his *Abuela* Donna, when his mom was working."

"*Abuela*, grandmother."

The boy was watching us, his gaze flitting from my face to Barnes and back again, his expression intent. He rattled off some words.

"She's not really his *abuela*," Barnes translated. "His mother told him to call her that. She lives down the hall from them. Any other questions?"

"Yeah, what does he like on his hot dogs?"

Barnes grinned, asked the question in Spanish. "Ketchup and mustard."

I looked at the boy. "*Me también*." My own stomach grumbled. I'd never had breakfast.

The boy giggled and I smiled.

Barnes jumped up. "Three hot dogs coming up. Should I take him with me?"

I nodded. "But hang onto him tight. And send the guys in so I can brief them."

A minute later, she had stopped in the doorway of her brother's office, then was walking out of the bullpen holding the child's hand, her head down chatting away with him. The kid was a talker for sure—not particularly shy, thank heavens.

Bradley, Cruthers and Patterson paraded across the space and into my office. Cruthers raced to the comfortable chair. Bradley gave him a mock glare.

"Hey, age before beauty," Cruthers said with a grin.

An accurate statement. Cruthers had at least a decade on his superior, and he was big and hairy, wearing off-the-rack suits that were usually wrinkled. Not anyone's idea of a beauty, and a sharp contrast to fashionable and handsome Bradley.

Patterson, by comparison, was somewhere in between—he wasn't hard to look at but wasn't really handsome either.

I filled them in on what the boy had said.

Cruthers checked his notepad. "There was an older woman, a Donna Glaser, two doors down from the apartment. She said she didn't recognize Tatiana, didn't know the name."

"In other words," Patterson said, "she lied."

Cruthers shrugged his broad shoulders. "We'll talk to her again."

"I left a uniform to go through the storage unit more thoroughly," Patterson said. "But I didn't spot anything that would likely be all that useful. Most of the boxes were empty. I guess they were only there to create the wall, to help keep the boy hidden. Two boxes were clothes and one of toys. Plus there were two sleeping bags."

"The apartment's pretty small," Bradley said. "Only two rooms and a bathroom. Queen-sized bed in the front room. Small kitchen area off to one side. The smaller room must have been the boy's, only a twin bed in there."

"Place was neat and clean," Cruthers said. "A few clothes in the closet and a half-dozen books and some small toys on the shelves. Now that we know she'd moved out a few boxes of stuff, I'd say she left just enough there to make the place look lived in."

"She didn't want her pimp to catch on that she was leaving town," I said. "Any luck figuring out who that is?"

Shaking heads. "We'll ask our CIs," Bradley said.

Confidential informants—how could any police force operate without them? They knew the little tidbits of info that only those on the streets would be privy to.

Speaking of which... "Ask Sarge to talk to the patrol officers, see if any of them recognizes Tatiana and knows anything about her."

"Aren't we going to a lot of trouble for what might be a suicide?" Patterson said.

"We got unofficial word from the ME," I told him, "that she was hit hard on the head before she went into the river. And even without that, I would be doubting that Tatiana killed herself. She wouldn't leave her child in a storage unit where he'd eventually starve."

"But she hid the key to that unit in her shoe," Bradley said, "and then intentionally took off that shoe and put it under her seat. She wanted it to be found."

"And yet," I added, "she did *not* want whoever she encountered on that bridge to be the one to find it."

While we waited for someone from DCF, I tried to review some reports in my office, but I couldn't concentrate. Alejandro and Barnes were ensconced at an empty desk in the far corner of the bullpen, happily chowing down on hot dogs and French fries.

My personal phone pinged, indicating a text message. It was from Kate Huntington, in Maryland.

Just touching base. How are you dealing with what happened?

I grimaced. A downside of being friends with a psychotherapist, they were always asking how you were *dealing* with things and how you were *feeling*.

The "what happened" she referred to was almost becoming another victim of the serial rapist/killer I'd been chasing last month.

I texted back. *I'm fine. In the middle of a new case at the moment. Talk later?*

As an afterthought, I added, *Thanks for asking.* And hit send, then had another afterthought. I typed in, *Hope you and the family are well.*

As I hit send again, movement across the bullpen caught my eye. A woman had entered and stopped, looking around. She was a little plump, with salt and pepper hair, cut short. Probably late forties or early fifties.

She made a beeline for my office, but changed tacks when she spotted the boy.

I jumped up and got there barely before she did.

"Is this the child?" Her tone made me want to snap, *No, we have another child locked in a closet.* Of course, this was *the* child.

"Chief of Police Anderson," I said, my tone equally brusque. I did not offer my hand. "And you are?"

"Ellen Hudson, Department of Children and Families." Her pinched face said she'd rather be elsewhere.

Burnout? I'd seen it all too many times in social workers. Like police work, the heartache of it all took its toll, until you had to stop caring or get out. Or build a really thick wall around your heart. I'd gone for the wall.

Ms. Hudson shifted as if to step past me. I moved into her path.

She looked over my shoulder. "Come on." She gestured for the boy to come with her.

Instead, he scrambled onto Barnes's lap, smearing mustard on her uniform shirt. She gave him a reassuring squeeze and glared at the interloper.

A rapid-fire exchange between the boy and Barnes. I caught the word *policía*.

"His mother told him to never, ever go to strangers," Barnes translated. "I asked him why he came with us. He said she told him he could trust the police."

Say what? Even in Baltimore County, a sanctuary county, undocumented immigrants feared the police, mainly because all too many of them were corrupt in their home countries. But that was assuming Tatiana was undocumented.

Be careful of those assumptions, Anderson!

"Even *female* strangers," Barnes added. "She emphasized not to trust other women either. She told him to only trust herself and Abuela Donna, and a Señor P. Not sure who he is."

"Well, the boy needs to come with me." Ellen Hudson again moved to get past me.

Again, I blocked her. "Slow down! This kid's been through a lot. And he doesn't even know that his mother isn't coming back for him."

"You didn't tell him she's dead?" Hudson's tone was incredulous.

I winced. We'd been trying to avoid any words along the lines of *dead*, not knowing how much passive English the boy might understand. And I definitely didn't want anyone saying the word *murdered*, which was way too close to the Spanish word for dead, *muerte*.

I swallowed a sigh. "He's been through a lot," I repeated. "We figured it would be better to wait until he was settled with a foster family, before telling him."

And why do I have to tell this to a social worker?

"We need to know where he's placed," I added. "We'll have more questions."

The woman snorted. "Foster care placements are confidential."

"*Not* from the police department!" My tone broached no argument.

Barnes stood, the boy in her arms and fire in her eyes. "Permission to accompany Ms. Hudson to her vehicle, to assist with the transfer?" She then said something to Alejandro. I caught the word that I was pretty sure meant *safe.*

I nodded.

They were no sooner out of the bullpen than I was on the phone, requesting, not all that politely, to speak to the director of DCF for Starling, Florida.

"I don't care that it's Sunday. I need her to call me back, right away!"

Ten minutes later, my phone rang. Ellen Hudson's boss turned out to be a much more reasonable person.

CHAPTER SIX

Barnes and I went with Cruthers to talk to the neighbor again. And I wanted to check out Tatiana's apartment for myself.

I was surprised to find that the building was in a decent neighborhood. No hookers, no druggies, no homeless sleeping in doorways. Just young women out for a mid-afternoon walk, some with strollers, others with elementary-age children. Their clothes weren't fancy and the cars parked along the curb were older models. A working-class neighborhood, but relatively safe and stable as city neighborhoods go.

Tatiana's apartment was as described, small and neat. If one didn't know better, the assumption would be its owners would be back soon.

Cruthers traipsed down the hall to another door, Barnes and I following behind. "Maybe you ladies can get more out of Ms. Glaser than I did," he said over his shoulder as he knocked.

I didn't take offense at the "ladies." Cruthers was a bit old-fashioned, and the reality is that women are often more willing to talk to other women.

Donna Glaser was not what I'd expected. My mental image had been of a short, plump old lady in a house dress. The woman was early sixties, with some dark streaks remaining in her silver hair, and only a few wrinkles. She was a little shorter than me, and while she had some extra padding, she carried herself like a woman who knew she was attractive. She wore a slim pair of black slacks and a sleeveless cotton top the same blue color as her eyes.

Once Cruthers had introduced us to her, he stepped back.

"I'm sorry for your loss, ma'am," I said. "I understand you and Tatiana were close."

Glaser stared at me for several seconds, probably trying to decide whether to deny that statement. Finally, she muttered, "Thank you." She shuffled to one side of the doorway. "Come in."

Her apartment was slightly larger than Tatiana's, with a picture window in the living room that overlooked the street below. A sofa—that had seen better days but was scrupulously clean—sat across from the window.

The woman waved us toward the sofa and made a cursory offer of drinks, which we all politely turned down. Cruthers and I sat, but Barnes remained standing, off to the side, pad and pencil at the ready.

"Alejandro seems to be fond of you, Ms. Glaser," I said, as she settled into an overstuffed armchair.

"He's okay?" She tried for a nonchalant tone, but her eyes were clouded with worry.

"Yes. A little disoriented. He's in foster care for now." Most likely for the rest of his childhood, actually, but I wasn't ready to say that out loud to her, or to Barnes for that matter.

"Do you think I could go see him?" Now she was clasping her hands in her lap. The knuckles were white.

"I'll see if I can arrange that," I said. "Um, did you know what Tatiana did for a living?"

Ms. Glaser sucked in air through her nose. "Yes." Her tone said, *What of it?*

"We're not here to judge her, ma'am," Cruthers quickly said.

"Do you know how she came to be in that situation?" I asked.

"She had no choice."

When she didn't elaborate, I said, "Because she didn't have any other way to support herself and her boy?"

"No," the woman said impatiently. "She literally had no choice. Whoever was in charge, her pimp, I guess, used the boy as leverage."

"He threatened to harm Alejandro?" I asked.

She nodded.

"Do you know where they were from?"

"Mexico. She came over with a group of families, mostly women and children, some men. They crossed the Rio Grande at a shallow spot, and were no sooner across the border when a truck pulled up. Men with guns started forcing the women and children into the back of it. The few men who were with them were shot."

She paused, cleared her throat. "In front of their families. She and a half dozen of the women were brought here. She was the only one of that smaller group with a child. He was two at the time."

"She must have trusted you very much," I said, "to share all that."

"She swore me to secrecy, said that if I told anyone and it got back to the man she worked for, he would hurt her or the boy, or both." Ms. Glaser made eye contact with me for the first time. "She said if anything ever happened to her, I should tell the police and ask them to protect me."

"Excuse me, ma'am," Cruthers spoke up, "but why didn't you tell us all this earlier?"

She turned toward him. "Two men come to my door and flash badges, asking about Tatiana, saying she was dead. I didn't know if you were legit or sent by that *animal* who forced her to sell her body." She pointed to me. "But her, I know she's the chief. I've seen her on TV."

Ha, at least one good thing's come out of all those damn press conferences. I loathed them, but they were a necessary evil when you were police chief.

"She also told me," Ms. Glaser continued, "that if a man ever came around asking for her, to pretend I didn't know her, that she didn't live here, and then let her know as soon as possible."

I glanced sideways at Cruthers. His wrinkled brow said he was as confused as I was.

"Did she explain any further?" I asked.

She shook her head. "Oh, and she told me I should hide Alejandro from him."

So maybe her pimp? But no doubt he already knew where she lived. Pimps did not usually let their girls wander far.

"If this man who controlled her..." Cruthers said, "I mean, how did she live here if he was keeping her on such a short leash?"

Ms. Glaser sighed. "She told me that she and the boy were forced to live with some other women when they first got here, and a couple of men lived there, to guard them, I guess. But Tatiana is, *was* quite beautiful. She said she had several regulars who were wealthy. One of them insisted on renting this place for her."

"Did he come here?" Cruthers asked.

Ms. Glaser glared at him. "Not the way you think. She wouldn't expose her boy to that. She would go to them, either their homes, if they were single, or to a nice hotel room."

"Do you know a Señor P?" I asked.

She rounded on me, obviously startled, and began to shake her head.

"Alejandro mentioned him," Barnes said.

"I was beginning to wonder if you even had a voice, young lady." The older woman's tone was sharp, but my guess was she was trying to divert us, maybe buy time to come up with a lie.

"Was he one of her rich clients?" I asked.

Ms. Glaser closed her eyes. Then she nodded. "He was the one paying for her apartment. He came here a few times, but only to pick Tatiana up. She didn't have a car, at least–" She paused. "But I was never told his name, just Señor P. That's what Alejandro called him. Sometimes Tatiana would take the boy with her to his house. She said he'd set up a playroom for him."

She sighed again. "She was afraid she was abusing our friendship, she said, because I usually babysat for her in the evenings, while she was working."

"Did you know she was planning to leave town," Cruthers asked, "to get away from her pimp?"

The woman's body stiffened.

"She'd contacted an organization," I said, "that helps women in her situation disappear."

Ms. Glaser was still for a beat before she gave a small nod. "I didn't want them to go, but I knew they had to."

"And the organization gave her a car," Cruthers said, more a statement than a question.

"Yes, but Tatiana didn't give me any details of where they were going or how it was all supposed to work. She said the less I knew, the safer I would be."

"Can you describe this Señor P?" Cruthers asked.

Ms. Glaser looked him up and down. "About your size, Detective, but not in very good shape. I always thought of the Pillsbury Dough Boy when I saw him. Sandy hair, medium length. I think he has brown eyes but I couldn't swear to it. I mostly caught glimpses of him going or coming. And he was a little...not sure what to call it...*nerdy* I guess would be the best word."

"And the car, ma'am?" Barnes asked.

"I never saw it. Tatiana parked it several blocks over. She didn't want anyone to realize it was hers."

"Can you think of anything else that might be helpful?" I asked her.

She shook her head, then said, "Alejandro didn't witness...you know?"

A moment of confusion, until it dawned on me what she was asking. "He wasn't with her. You didn't know about the storage unit?"

"What storage unit?"

"Tatiana had rented one," I said, "climate controlled, and she had the boy there. I guess to keep him out of her pimp's reach."

Her eyes were now shiny with tears. "He was there by himself?"

I nodded.

Her hand flew to her mouth. "That poor baby. He must've been terrified." She jumped out of her chair. "Please, I've got to see him."

I stood, patted her arm. "I'll do my best to make that happen." I handed her my card and so did Cruthers. "Again," I said in a soft voice, "we're very sorry for your loss."

Ms. Glaser bit her lower lip and a couple of tears broke loose.

"We can show ourselves out," Barnes said, barely above a whisper.

Once out on the sidewalk in the afternoon sunshine, Cruthers blew out a long and loud sigh. "I looked into Glaser's background. No criminal record, not even parking tickets. She's a retired schoolteacher, divorced. And her ex-husband apparently had a better lawyer than she did. He pays her alimony, but it's a pittance. And schoolteachers don't make very good money in Florida. Their pensions aren't great either."

I gestured toward the apartment building we'd just exited. "Thus the modest abode."

Cruthers nodded, his expression grim.

———⋄———

Back at 3MB, Detective Foster of the Jacksonville Sheriff's Office was lying in wait. As we entered the bullpen, he rose from a seat behind one of the empty desks and stepped in front of us.

"Chief, a moment of your time." His tone was neutral but his eyes were hard, his face tense.

What's his problem?

"This about our current investigation?" I asked.

"Yes."

"Conference room." I turned on my heel and walked away. The others trailed after. I detoured slightly to Bradley's open doorway and signaled for him to join us.

Foster took two long strides to catch up with me. "I meant alone."

"Cruthers is lead on the case. Bradley's my second in command." I didn't bother to explain Barnes. Foster knew she was my shadow. And I wasn't in the mood for politics nor for having to repeat what Foster had to say to the others.

Once inside the smaller of our two conference rooms, where Cruthers had set up the murder board for Tatiana's case, I gestured toward chairs. "Everyone here can be trusted to keep to themselves whatever you have to say."

I turned to Barnes. "You want to add what we learned today on the white board over there?"

"You want me to get some coffee for everyone first?" she asked in a low voice.

"That depends." I turned to Foster, who was still standing. "What is the purpose of this meeting?"

"I need you to back off from trying to find Tatiana Gomez's pimp."

"Don't bother, Barnes. Detective Foster won't be staying long."

I gestured again to the chair across from Cruthers and Bradley. Foster sat and so did I. Barnes went to the whiteboard and started writing notes, consulting her pad occasionally.

Foster sighed, ran a hand through salt and pepper hair. "A cup of coffee from your personal stash would've been nice."

I didn't respond.

"Why do you want us to back off?" Bradley asked in a mild tone.

"Can't tell you that, other than the FDLE is involved." The Florida Department of Law Enforcement, the state's version of the FBI.

Bradley cocked an eyebrow at him.

I swallowed a snicker. Bradley has very expressive eyebrows.

Foster sat forward. "Look this guy is not your average pimp. This whole thing is a lot bigger than that."

I gave him a knowing smile. "As in this guy buys women who were captured at the Mexican border after they crossed it illegally."

Foster's eyes went wide. "How long have you known about that?"

Cruthers glanced at his watch. "About fifteen minutes."

"*Where* did you hear about it?" Foster demanded.

"Not telling you that," I said. "It would jeopardize someone's safety."

Foster took a deep breath and blew it out, loudly.

We all remained silent.

Finally he leaned forward again. "There are branches of this trafficking network all over the state." His voice was low, barely above a whisper. "Bringing them down, it's a huge operation that we've spent months setting up."

And why am I only hearing about it now?

I managed to maintain a neutral expression, but anger was tightening my chest. "Tatiana's pimp is a prime suspect in her death."

"It's definitely been ruled a homicide then," Foster asked, "not a suicide?"

"Not officially yet," I said. "But her skull was bashed in before she went into the river."

Foster winced.

"Yeah," I said. "Now, do you know who her pimp is?"

A knock on the conference room door postponed what would no doubt become a major tug of war. I nodded to Barnes who went to answer it.

"Uh, Sarge said y'all were discussing the Gomez case." Bert Deming's voice. "Well, I may have something for you. And something weird just happened."

I gestured to Barnes to let him in.

"Two sets of fingerprints on the key card," Bert said, still standing near the door. "One is the victim's and the other belongs to the concierge at that storage place."

I frowned at him. Why was he interrupting us for that?

"But we found a couple of prints from the car," he quickly added, "that might be helpful." He kept his gaze on me, obviously trying to ignore Foster, who was scowling at him. "We went over everything again, including the parts that were apparently wiped down—the outsides of the doors, the steering wheel and the front of the glove box."

Now Foster's eyebrows were in the air. "Wiped down? So the killer didn't care if y'all figured out it wasn't suicide."

Cruthers nodded his shaggy head. But I ignored Foster, signaled to Bert to continue.

He handed me two photos, pointed to the top one. "We found a partial on the inside of the driver's door handle. No matches came back when I ran it. The other one was on the underside of the glove box handle. You know how you..." He pantomimed opening a glove box with his index finger. "But the thing is, when I ran it, the inquiry was blocked by the FDLE."

All eyes but Bert's swiveled to Foster. I ground my teeth.

After a short staring contest, I said, in an exaggerated sweet voice, "Would you be so kind, Detective Foster, as to run these fingerprints for us and confirm or deny if either belongs to Tatiana Gomez's pimp?" I handed over the photos.

CHAPTER SEVEN

Jenny Coleman, Director of the Department of Children and Families for Starling and Clover County, sat next to me and Barnes at the kitchen table of Alejandro's foster home. In Spanish, his foster mom was explaining to him that we had some questions to ask him.

I begrudgingly gave the absent Ellen Hudson credit for having placed him where at least one person spoke his language. Or maybe Jenny had intervened.

"Alejandro, who is Señor P?" I asked, nodding to Barnes to translate.

But Ada Johns, the foster mom, beat her to it. "*¿Alex, quien es Señor P?*"

The boy's eyes went wide. He let out a short, rapid-fire string of Spanish, starting with *Señor P* and ending with *Alex.*

Barnes turned slightly toward me. "He says that Señor P is the only one who calls him Alex."

Another rapid string of Spanish from the child.

Barnes's eyes were clouded as she translated. "He wants to know if he can go live with Señor P, until his mom comes back for him."

"Ask him if he knows where Señor P lives." It was a long shot that a four-year-old would know that, but worth a try.

The boy shook his head after Barnes translated. Then he spoke a few words.

Her face brightened. "No, but he can show us."

We had to drive to Tatiana's apartment building first—in two vehicles since my compact wouldn't hold five people.

From there, the boy started out on foot. He led us five blocks, to a much swankier neighborhood, and pointed to the top of an eight-story building.

Jenny Coleman had tagged along. She was a petite woman, early forties, with dark, shoulder-length hair, hazel eyes and fair skin. Ada Johns, a blonde thirty-something, had also insisted on coming with us, after calling her husband to pick up their children at school.

Ada shaded her eyes with a hand while staring upward. "Do you think he means the penthouse?"

Barnes asked the boy that, and he answered.

Jenny Coleman whistled softly. "He says the very top." It was the first indication that Jenny understood Spanish.

We entered the building and were stopped by a polite but determined security guard. "Names, please. And who are you here to see?"

Then he looked down and his eyes brightened. "*¡Alejandro! ¿Cómo estás?*"

"*Bueno, gracias,*" the boy answered. "*Estamos aquí para ver al Señor P.*"

"Is Mr. Pirolnik expecting you?" the guard asked the adults.

I flashed my badge. "No, but I think he'll see us."

The guard nodded, went to his desk, and spoke quietly into a phone. He hung up and gestured toward a row of elevators. "One on the far end takes you to the penthouse."

The man who met us at the elevator was indeed a life-sized version of the Pillsbury Dough Boy—about five-eleven and husky. His face was pasty and his pale blue eyes red-rimmed.

"My Tater, she's gone, isn't she?" he said in a mournful voice, before we could introduce ourselves.

A beat of silence. "I'm sorry for your loss, sir," I said.

He nodded, blinked. "Which of you is the police chief?"

I pointed to myself, then introduced the others.

The man crouched down to Alejandro's height. "Hey little man," he said in a falsely bright voice. "How about you go play in your room for a while, okay?"

The boy scampered off through the open door behind the man.

"Come into the kitchen," he said, leading the way. He wore baggy jeans and a tan tee shirt bearing the logo of a video game. Without asking if we wanted anything, he got a coffee maker started and brought mismatched mugs to the table. "Please, sit down."

Three of us sat, but Barnes hesitated. He gestured to the remaining chair and pulled a stool over from the counter for himself.

Barnes sat beside me, her pad on the table.

"Pirolnik," I said, "is that Russian?"

The man snorted. "Heck no. Polish. It used to be longer."

I nodded, the ice officially broken. "Sir, can you tell us how you came to know Tatiana Gomez and her son?"

His cheeks pinked. "Please, call me Gabe." Then he cleared his throat and the pink shaded toward full-blown red. "I, uh, called an escort service, asked for a young lady to go to the movies with me. They sent Tater—Tatiana." He looked away, staring into space. "When she got here, she immediately started taking her clothes off. I told her no, I really did want to take her to the movies."

He chuckled softly, but still looking away. "'Like a date?' she said, all surprised. She has this lovely rich accent. I love to listen to her talk...*loved* to listen to her."

He swiped at his eyes with the back of his hand. "We went out a few times a week after that."

When he didn't add anything else, I said, "You paid each time, for her services?"

"Yeah." His face brightened. "She's so beautiful, and friendly and kind. I fell in love with her."

His gaze finally met mine. "I like to think she was fond of me as well. Then one day, I saw her on the street, with her little boy. She tried to pretend that she hadn't seen me, but I caught up with them, introduced myself to the boy. Alex has great manners, for such a little guy. Tatiana seemed nervous at first, kept looking at this guy who was standing at a street corner, watching us."

I was about to ask for a description of the guy when the coffee maker made a pinging noise, and he jumped up. Coming back with the pot, he said, "Anybody need cream?"

We all shook our heads. He poured coffee into the mugs.

"Can you describe the guy who was watching her?" I asked.

"Not really, he was far enough away I couldn't see his face all that well. Light-skinned African-American, a little shorter than average, but a husky build. I got the impression he was young."

So probably not her pimp, but his employee maybe.

He sat down again on the stool. "Where was I? Oh, yeah... Well, after that first time I met Alex, I asked her where she lived. She wouldn't tell me the address but said it was with other women. I asked if I could rent her a place, no strings attached. She shook her head no, but the next time she came here, she said it would be okay to rent a small place for her and the boy. I started meeting them sometimes, in the park near the place I rented. And after a while, she'd let me pick her up there, to go out. Then some days, after I met them at the park, they'd come back here. Alex and I played video games and Tater took a nap, in the guest room." He blushed again.

"She didn't get much sleep at night, you see." His blush deepened.

He swallowed hard. "Then I told her I didn't want her going out with other men, that I wanted to marry her and have her and Alex live with me. I, uh, thought maybe she would laugh at me, but she didn't." He smiled a little. "She said, in that gorgeous voice of hers, 'Oh, Gabriel, that is so sweet, but it can never be.' That's when she told me that she belonged to the man who owned the escort service."

He shook his head at the memory. "What do you mean by *belong to*, I asked her. And she said, 'He owns me.' Then she told me how she and Alex and a bunch of other women were captured at the border and brought to Florida and forced to become prostitutes for this man. I wanted to report him to the police, of course, but she went crazy, started crying, said he would kill her and the boy, and maybe me too."

He sucked in air, let it out on a long sigh. "I couldn't report the guy anyway because she wouldn't tell me who he was."

"What's the name of the escort service?" I asked.

He shook his head again. "I never knew. I only had this phone number, and when I called it, a woman answered with 'Escort service,' and I asked for a date with Tatiana."

"Where did you get the number?" Barnes asked.

"From some guy online, a gamers' chat room."

"Do you remember who?" I asked.

"Not really, but I remember which chat room. I could go in there again and hang out, see if any of the usernames jog my memory. But that's all we'd have, a username."

"That might be enough," I said. "We have some good tech people." I didn't want to admit that it was only one person, not *people*. Derek the Geek was it.

"How do you make a living, Mr. Pirol–"

He waved a hand in the air. "Gabe."

"Gabe," I finished with a small smile.

He pointed down at the front of his tee shirt. "You've never heard of Raider Boys, Chief Anderson."

"*Chief* will do, and no, I'm afraid I haven't."

"It's really popular. And I designed it." He ducked his head a little. "It's made me tons of money, but..." He trailed off, his face sobering. "Money doesn't mean much when you don't have anyone to spend it on. I was so happy when I had my little family to take care of." He sighed.

"How did you know she was gone, Gabe?" I asked. "Did you hear about the incident at the bridge this morning?"

"What incident?"

I waved my hand in a never-mind gesture. "How did you know?" I repeated.

He leaned forward, clasped his hands together on the table in front of him. "When Jerry—that's the guard—when he said that Alex and three women, one of whom was the police chief, were asking for me, I knew..." His voice caught. "I knew she didn't make it."

I shook my head slightly. "Tell us, all of it." It wasn't ideal, interviewing him in front of Jenny and Ada, but he might clam up if I tried to take him to 3MB. I'd just have to trust the two women to be discreet.

Gabe sucked in a big breath. "About a week ago, Tater changed, became more anxious. When I pushed her to tell me what was wrong, she said there were two men now that she had to get away from. I asked who, but she wouldn't tell me. I assumed one was the owner of the escort service, and I wondered if maybe the other was..." He looked over his shoulder toward the open doorway into the living room, and dropped his voice. "Alex's father."

Jenny Coleman's eyes widened.

"I told her we'd go away somewhere, the three of us, where no one could find us. But she said I couldn't go, that a Latina and a little boy could blend in, but not a Latina with a boy and a big, strappin' white man in tow." He sat up straight, his chest puffed out. "That's what she said, a 'big, strappin' white man.'" A quick grin that faded fast.

"I begged her to let me take her away, to someplace safe. But then a couple of days later, she said she had a plan, that she had a way to get a car and papers for a new identity, and would I give her some money to help them get away. Again, she said I couldn't go but she was real sweet about it. Told me she cared too much about me to put me at risk. I begged some more, but finally got it that she wasn't going to budge."

He shook his head slowly. "You know the saying about loving something and setting it free. I knew that's what I had to do. I knew she wasn't exaggerating the danger. Tater was always really practical, down-to-earth. And she always had a plan. So I knew she and the boy would probably be okay without me. But it broke my heart to say goodbye."

He fell silent for a couple of beats. I leaned forward. "When's the last time you saw her?"

"Last night, around midnight. She came to get the money I'd collected for her. I had to go to a bunch of different ATMs and take out a few hundred at a time, over the course of several days. She didn't want me going to the bank to withdraw a large sum, said that the escort guy would suspect me when she disappeared. It couldn't look like I had helped her. She kissed my cheek and I hugged her..." His voice broke.

"She thanked me...for being so kind to her and Alex." Tears were now rolling down the man's pale cheeks.

Suddenly he shoved himself to a stand. "Lemme take a quick look in that chat room. I think I remember that guy's username." He bolted from the kitchen.

The other three women and I sat quietly for a few seconds. Ada Johns had tears in her eyes. Barnes was huddled over her pad, scribbling notes. Quite possibly her eyes were shiny too, but she kept them down.

"Ladies," I quietly said, "this is all confidential, by the way."

Jenny and Ada nodded.

"Mommy Ada..."

We all whirled toward the doorway. Alejandro stood there, his ratty teddy in one hand and a newer looking stuffed polar bear in the other.

"*Sí*, Alex." Ada gestured for him to come to her.

His steps were hesitant, but when he reached the table he scrambled up onto her lap. "*¿Dónde está mi mami?*"

"We'll talk about that later. *Luego*, okay?" She smoothed his hair back from his forehead.

Jenny Coleman leaned forward. "*¿Alex, sabes dónde está tu padre?*"

The boy shook his head. Then he muttered, "*Papi...*" followed by something unintelligible.

"Papa loves me," Ada translated softly.

An arrow of pain in my chest and a flash of my father, across the dinner table, laughing at something I'd said. I'd always known, on some level, that he'd loved me, despite everything else.

"He's using present tense," Barnes whispered to me.

I nodded slightly.

"Of course he does," Jenny said. "*¿No tienes una idea de dónde está?*" *You don't have any idea where he is?* I translated in my head.

The boy's face sagged. "*Papi está muerto para nosotros.*"

"Papa is dead to us," Ada said, barely above a whisper, her voice a little choked.

"Odd choice of words," Barnes muttered out of the side of her mouth.

Another small nod from me.

"Alejandro," I said, "what did you do during the time you were in the storage locker?"

He gave me a confused look even after Ada translated. She said something else in Spanish and outlined a big box shape in the air in front of her.

The boy spoke for several seconds, his face puckered like he was trying not to cry.

Ada translated, "His mother brought him meals. She would stay for a while, then tell him to play very, very quietly so the bad men didn't hear him."

My stomach twisted. No wonder the kid was struggling not to cry. He must've been terrified. But what choice did his mother have? If men were after her to kill her, she had to scare the boy to keep him safe.

"Last night," Ada paused, swallowing hard, "she told him again to stay very quiet, and she would be back by morning. Then they would go away, to someplace safe where the bad men would never find them."

Gabe came back into the room and handed me a slip of paper. "Phone number for the escort service, link for the chat room, and the guy's username."

"Thanks." I handed the slip off to Barnes, who tucked it inside her notepad.

Alejandro jumped down off Ada's lap and threw his arms around Gabe's legs. He babbled something in Spanish.

Ada opened her mouth, but Jenny held up a hand. "Don't translate that." Her voice was firm, almost hard.

Gabe didn't seem to notice them. He picked Alex up, sat back on the stool and put the boy on his lap. "I don't know what you said, little man, but I hope you know I love you. I'd love to be your daddy."

Ada looked at Jenny who gave a slight shake of her head.

An awkward beat passed, then Ada said, "Out of curiosity, Gabe, how did the boy come to call you Señor P?"

Gabe smiled. "Pyrarolnik—P-Y-R-A-R-O-L-N-I-K—was my family's name back in Poland, before my great grandparents came to the U.S. It literally means *potato farmer*. Alex and I were joking around one day, and I told him my name meant that. He called me Señor Potato, but his mama thought that sounded disrespectful, so it got shortened to Señor P."

Ada chuckled. "That's why he kept saying Señor Potato. I thought he meant the toy, but when I took the Mr. Potato Head out of the toy box, he wanted nothing to do with it."

Good job of lightening the mood, Ada.

"You said you told him about your name," I said. "How do you communicate with him?"

Gabe scratched his neck. "Sometimes Tater would translate. Sometimes he just seems to understand. What is it they call that?"

"Passive language." Jenny gave me a look that said, *Are you done?*

I nodded, and both of us stood. "Thanks for your help, Gabe." I handed him my card and gave him the "if you think of anything else" speech.

He had risen as well, and Ada took the boy from him.

Gabe turned to Jenny. "Can I keep in touch with him?" The anguish in his voice made my chest hurt.

"We'll see what we can arrange," Jenny said, her tone sympathetic.

We trooped out of his apartment, and no one said a word on the elevator ride down to the lobby.

Once out on the sidewalk, Ada blew out air. "You can't buy happiness, but that guy sure tried."

"And succeeded, for a while," Barnes said, her voice sad.

Jenny and I made eye contact but said nothing.

———◄○►———

Jenny asked me for a ride back to Ada Johns's house—where she had left her car. It would've made more sense for her to ride with Ada and Alejandro, but I agreed, wondering what she really wanted.

Once we were underway, she said, "We need to track down the father, see if he's still alive."

"No, *we* don't," I said.

Her head jerked around in response to my somewhat sharp tone.

"My department will do our best to find him." I glanced her way and softened my voice. "There's a lot going on in this case, and you could get hurt if you talk to the wrong people."

Her expression morphed from annoyed to surprised. "Why are the police even involved? I thought his mother drowned."

I drew in air, trying to decide how much to tell her. The longer we kept the fact that Tatiana was murdered under wraps, the easier our jobs would be. But this woman seemed pretty level-headed.

"She did drown, but it's likely she was helped into the water, after being knocked unconscious. And keep that to yourself, please. It's not official until the ME report is finalized."

She nodded slowly. "So if the father is alive, he's a suspect."

"Yes, especially since the boy's wording was *papi is dead to us.* Not just dead, but dead *to us!*"

"You think the father was the second person she was running from," Barnes said from the backseat, "besides her pimp?"

I glanced up at the rearview mirror, made eye contact. "He may very well be the *first* person she was running from. The reason she left Mexico in the first place."

CHAPTER EIGHT

When I opened my office door, I was greeted by a tiny arched back of white fur standing straight up. The kitten, perched on top of my bookcase, hissed at me.

"How'd you get out?" I demanded.

"Maybe the bathroom door wasn't latched tight," Barnes said from behind me.

I looked around the room. Nothing seemed disturbed so I decided to let the creature live.

As I walked past it...her...she jumped onto my shoulder.

I jerked a little in surprise, then turned my head. I was staring into tiny bright blue eyes. "You ruin this jacket and you're going to the shelter."

Barnes lifted her off, carefully disengaging her claws from the fabric. I took off the jacket and hung it from the back of my chair.

Cruthers appeared in my doorway. I gestured toward the comfy visitor's chair.

"Foster got back to me," he said as he settled into it with a sigh.

Barnes put the kitten down on my desk so she could take notes. Not that I needed her to. Whatever Cruthers had to say would also be in his report. But she'd told me once that taking notes helped her process and remember things.

Cruthers eyed the cat, bushy eyebrows in the air.

When I said nothing, he cleared his throat. "Foster confirmed the partial on the glove box was her pimp's, but he wouldn't identify him. Said he might be able to tell us more tomorrow. Apparently the case is at a 'delicate place.'" He made air quotes.

I grunted.

"He didn't have any luck with the other print either. Apparently it's not in the system anywhere." The expression on his broad face was skeptical.

I let out a short laugh. "Cruthers, there are a few law-abiding citizens out there."

"Not many," he said. "Where'd the cat come from?"

"Long story. Barnes, tell the detective what Pirolnik told us."

She flipped back a few pages in her pad and repeated Gabe's sad story.

As she spoke, I eyed the kitten. She was now washing herself, including her butt. *Charming.* But I caught myself smiling in spite of myself.

Patterson knocked on my ajar door. "Tracked down the license plate," he said to Cruthers.

I gestured for him to come in, pointed toward one of the uncomfortable chairs.

He made a face. "I'll stand."

I chuckled. "Maybe we should get a second comfy one," I said to Barnes.

"The plate was for a car that the DMV was told was junked," Patterson reported. "They received the title back, but the plate never arrived. I called the junkyard, and the owner swears he sent the plate, that it must've gotten lost in the mail."

"Where's this junkyard?" Cruthers asked.

Patterson checked his pad. "In Clover County, just over the line. Harry's Salvage. It's open today, until six p.m."

Cruthers pushed himself up out of his chair. "Worth checking out." He gestured for Patterson to follow him.

Tiny needles jabbing my arm. I looked down. The kitten was climbing up to my shoulder.

"Cat!" Barnes jumped forward to grab her, but I held up a hand.

"It's okay. The blouse is already ruined, and I didn't like it anyway."

"Hey, Sheriff," I heard from across the bullpen. Cruthers greeting Sam as they crossed paths. The good sheriff was carrying a large brown paper bag. As he approached my office door, the fragrance of Chinese food preceded him.

My stomach rumbled.

Sam stepped into my office, and the cat hissed at him from my shoulder.

I held up a finger and gently tapped her head. "Hush, pipsqueak. He's friend, not foe." I stroked her tiny ears and she settled down, even purred softly.

"Judith Cat-Whisperer Anderson," Sam said with a grin.

I snorted.

He lifted a smaller bag in his other hand, gave it to Barnes. "I brought you some supper too, on the condition that you eat it out there." He jerked his head toward her desk.

"It's a deal." Barnes grabbed the bag and left, closing the door behind her.

Sam glanced around, checking that the mini-blinds were closed, then settled into the comfy chair. "I figured odds were good you'd cancel on me, so I brought supper to you."

"Thanks," I said, as he pulled cardboard food boxes out of the bag. He handed over chop sticks, and we dug in.

After eating in companionable silence for a few minutes, I said, "So, how's your day been?"

"Boring. The techs—thanks for the loan of your guy, by the way—they found a dozen different sets of prints. One belongs to the victim, four of the others to neighbors. I've spent all day chasing down friends and acquaintances. I've still got three sets unaccounted for, and no hits from AFIS on any of them."

"Did you find whatever she was beaten with?"

"Nope." Sam sat back, wiped a napkin across his mouth. "The assistant ME said it was straight, slightly rounded and smooth. But too narrow to be a baseball bat." He picked up the remaining half of a spring roll and popped it into his mouth, chewed and swallowed. "But unlikely that it's a pipe. As much damage as was done, it would've been worse with a metal pipe or crowbar or something like that."

I chuckled. "Only law enforcement would sit around talking about bludgeoning instruments while eating."

"Are you sayin' I'm callous, lady?" he said in a mock drawl. He was from New York State, his accent as northern as mine.

"No more than any LEO."

He blew out air, his expression shifting toward grim. "I'll be wishing for even tougher callouses on my soul tomorrow, during the autopsy."

I dropped my chopsticks on a napkin. "I've got a confession to make. I've never been able to watch one without feeling nauseous, even after all these years. I try to go into them with an empty stomach. Fewer cookies to toss that way."

"Good idea. I'll postpone my lunch until after."

Internally, I again acknowledged how hard this must be for him, since he seemed to have known the victim.

I changed the subject and told him about my day, leaving out the info about the organization helping women get away from sex traffickers. I trusted Sam, but the fewer people who knew about them, the safer their secret was.

Sam leaned forward, his elbows on the corner of my desk. "You know what I think? I think we should go to a movie, put all this gore out of our minds for a while. Maybe get some ice cream afterwards."

"You're only trying to get me alone in the dark," I quipped.

He wiggled his eyebrows. "Is it working?"

I tilted my head to one side, amazed that I was actually flirting.

Judith Anderson did not normally flirt. But then again, I was toying with the idea of doing other things with this man that I didn't normally do.

"Hmm, I'd need to swing by my place and get the kitten settled." Said kitten was still sitting on my shoulder. I was a little surprised she hadn't tried to get any of my food, although she had batted at the ends of the chopsticks a couple of times.

"You got a name for her yet?" Sam asked.

"Nope."

He gave me a lopsided grin. "How about Pipsqueak?"

I returned the grin and went back to eating.

———◆———

Cruthers and Patterson waylaid us before we got out of the bullpen. Sam was carrying the bags of cat supplies that Barnes had packed up before she'd gone home.

I had the cat in her cardboard box, mewing pathetically and making the box rock back and forth with her movements. I needed to get her a crate.

That thought took me by surprise. I had no intentions of keeping this cat. Barnes had promised she'd find a home for her—if Caroline Baumann's family didn't want her—a home *other* than my apartment.

The bullpen was empty at the moment, so we settled around Cruthers's desk, rather than reopening my locked office.

Bushy eyebrows in the air, Cruthers eyed Sam. I gave a slight nod, indicating it was all right to talk in front of him.

"We got to the junkyard just as it was about to close," he said. "The owner swears he mailed in the license plate, and has no idea how it got on somebody's car."

"But," Patterson added, "he was antsy as all get out."

"Did he explain why he mailed things separately?" I asked.

"Yeah," Cruthers said. "He hemmed and hawed some, then said he forgot to put the title in with the plate. Had already mailed it when he noticed the title was still sitting on his desk."

"His desk *was* pretty messy," Patterson said.

Cruthers waved a hand at his own desk. "Mine's *pretty messy*. His was a rat's nest."

"So he mails the title separately," I said, "and it arrives at the motor vehicle administration, but not the plate. A clerk probably stuck the title in a file somewhere and never followed up."

"Plate *could've* gotten stolen in the mail," Sam said, sounding skeptical. "Or lost, like he claims."

Cruthers nodded slowly. "Maybe, but there were three cars off to one side of his yard. They were in better condition than the wrecks scattered about. Looked like he'd even washed them."

"Cruthers here saunters over and starts admiring one of them." Patterson's mouth crooked up on one end, the closest I'd ever seen him come to a genuine smile. "I thought the owner, Harry, was gonna crap his pants."

Cruthers was full out grinning now. "I asked how much he wanted for it, said I was in the market for a car for my daughter."

I snorted softly. His daughter was fourteen.

"While he was stammering," Cruthers continued, "trying to come up with a reason why he couldn't sell it to me, I got a good look at the VIN area through the windshield."

"Lemme guess," I said, "it had been filed off."

"Yup," the two detectives said in unison. Cruthers turned his phone toward me. On it was a photo of an older-model white car.

"Harry finally named a figure three times what the junker's worth, and I said I'd think about it." He scrolled a little, and showed me a pic of the junkyard owner—fortyish, dark beard and hair, with a beer belly that strained his overalls.

"I called Donna Glaser," Cruthers said, "asked if she knew anything more about the car. She said no. Tatiana always parked it several blocks away and walked to their building, taking different routes each time."

"How many boxes in that storage locker had stuff in them?" I asked.

"Only four," Patterson said. "The rest were empty. The concierge said that boxes were a free service provided by the storage company. She'd asked for a dozen of them."

I nodded. "But the other eight were only blocks in her little wall to keep the boy out of sight, if someone opened the door."

Cruthers head waggled. For a second I thought it was going to fall off. He had dark circles under his eyes. "Glaser said Tatiana took one box at a time to the car. There's a Goodwill store near them. She'd go in there and out the back, to the car, load the box in the trunk, then back through the store. But Glaser thought she was keeping the boxes in the car. She's still saying she knew nothing about the storage unit."

"Clever taking the boxes through the Goodwill store," I said. "She figured she was being watched."

"She *knew* she was being watched," Cruthers said. "Glaser had spotted the thug on the street who did most of the watching. She gave me a description and is coming in tomorrow morning to work with Derek, to come up with a sketch on the computer."

"Good work, guys." Putting my hands on the bullpen desk in front of me, I pushed myself to a stand. "Go home, hug your kids, and get some rest."

Patterson shook his head. "My seventeen-year-old's pissed at me right now because I backed her mother's refusal to let her go to a party. Gonna be a long time before she lets me hug her."

I rolled my eyes in pretend sympathy, having no idea what it was like to raise teenagers, and just as glad I would never find out.

Sam and I gathered kitten and paraphernalia and headed for the elevators.

"Speaking of Derek," Sam said in a low voice. "I forgot to mention that I brought in Caroline Baumann's laptop for him to take a look at when he has time. If you don't mind, that is."

"Don't mind at all, since you don't have a resident geek. I'll tell him it's second in line after anything he's working on for Tatiana's case." I paused, juggled the cat box into one hand to push the elevator button. "So, the perp didn't take her laptop. Why go to all that trouble to do a home invasion and then not take something of value."

"Her jewelry box had been raided, but none of the electronics were taken. I'm not sure I buy that it was a robbery, though." He shook his head as we exited the back door of the building. "From the condition of the body and the state of the scene, I think the perp chased her around and beat her for a while."

His face was grim as he helped me load my stuff into my car. "I'll follow you," he said.

I nodded, wanting to offer some upbeat thought, something comforting, but I couldn't think of anything.

As Sam turned away, his shoulders were sagging.

—◆—

I settled the kitten in the extra bedroom in my apartment. I'd intended to set it up as a study, but right now it only had one bookcase in there.

I'd hit the ground running when I'd started the new job in September and hadn't had much time to take a deep breath since. Maybe I'd do some furniture shopping next weekend, if we got this case tied up by then.

With that goal in mind, I turned to Sam as I pulled the room's door closed to keep the cat contained. "Would you mind..."

He put his arms around me, kept them loose. But still I jumped a little at the unexpected contact.

And I hated to admit it, but a tiny zing ran down from where his hands lay at the small of my back—to a part of my body I rarely gave much thought to.

"Lemme guess," he said gently. "You want a rain check."

"Um, yeah. I think I want to go interview a witness this evening."

"About that car your guys were talking about?"

"Yes."

Still loosely holding onto me, Sam chuckled low in his throat. Another zing ran through me.

Don't screw this up, Judith! He's a nice guy.

"How about if I ride along?" he said. "Wait outside, and then we get some ice cream."

I slowly shook my head, laughing softly. "You are one persistent man."

"And I really like ice cream." He let me go. "Your car or my truck?"

My back felt quite chilly without his warm hands. "Uh, yours. Mine's kinda cramped." Sam's truck was a small silver pickup—six-cylinder, no extended cab—but it was still a lot roomier than my compact.

"Why do you drive such a small car?" he asked, as we headed out the apartment door.

"If you'd ever seen what parking is like in the Baltimore area, you wouldn't ask that question. I've squeezed that little thing into many a nonexistent parking space."

Another low chuckle. He punched the down button for the elevator.

At Gabe Pirolnik's apartment building, Sam parked in the loading zone out front.

"I'll be as quick as possible," I said, as I climbed out of his truck.

"Take as long as you need."

I ran into my first obstacle at the check-in desk. The same guard was on duty and he admitted that he recognized me. "But Mr. Pirolnik asked not to be disturbed this evening."

I flashed my badge. "I'm afraid it's pretty important." I was just being stubborn. I could easily come back tomorrow. But having put off what would've likely been a lovely interlude with Sam, I was annoyed at being thwarted now.

"Tell ya what, I need to use the men's room. Can't help it if someone slips past while I'm in there." He sauntered away.

And I strode to the penthouse elevator. On the top floor, I stepped out into the foyer.

I hadn't paid much attention to it earlier. It was tastefully decorated with artwork and potted plants, all of which looked well tended. I suspected the building management took care of them. I couldn't imagine Pirolnik doing so, since his apartment resembled a frat house.

I knocked on the fancy oak door, polished to a rich sheen.

No answer.

I knocked again. "Mr. Pirolnik," I called out. "It's Judith Anderson, the police chief."

No response. I raised my hand to knock again, heard a faint shuffling sound through the thick door. Then silence for several beats.

"I'm sorry to bother you, sir, but I have a couple of questions. I won't take much of your time."

More shuffling noises, slightly louder.

"Mr. Pirolnik? Gabe? Are you okay?"

The door opened a few inches and doughy Pirolnik stood in the opening. "Oh, hi, Chief. I, uh, was in the back of the apartment, didn't hear you at first."

"No problem." I gave him a disarming smile. "May I come in for a few minutes?"

But the smile did not disarm. He visibly tensed and narrowed the door's opening. "Um, no, now's not a good time. I mean, my cleaning people haven't been here in a few days, and I'm a total slob." He laughed but it sounded forced.

Besides, I'd been in the apartment earlier, had already seen the mess.

On alert now, I said, "Let me ask you one thing. The car Tatiana had, do you know where she got it?"

"Um, no. I offered to buy her something nicer, but she said it was fine, and..." He trailed off, glanced furtively over his shoulder. "I really gotta go."

I reached around and put a hand on my holstered Glock, under my jacket. "Gabe, is something wrong?"

He shook his head vigorously, too vigorously. "No, nothing's wrong. I'm, uh, preoccupied, that's all." His tone was casual, but his eyes were wide with fear. "You know, thinking about Tatiana..." Suddenly he jumped a little, as if shocked—or poked with something.

I drew my Glock. *Jump back and get down*, I mouthed, gesturing with my other hand to make sure he understood the *down* part.

He remained frozen for a nanosecond, then jerked to his left, away from whoever was behind the door.

I shoved the door hard, just as it was yanked inward. Off balance, I started to fall.

A human boulder slammed into me, bounced me against the far wall.

The boulder had legs, wore a dark suit. He raced toward the fire stairs, the tails of his jacket flying out behind him.

I struggled to catch my balance, yelled, "Stop! Police!" But he was fast. He was through the fire door before I could take aim.

Gabe was kneeling on the floor in a fetal position, hands clasped behind his head. "I'm okay. Get him," he yelled, without moving.

Gun clasped in both hands, I gave chase, knowing the guy was at least two flights of stairs ahead of me by now.

My shoulder hit the fire door. A second's pause as I stuck my head around it, scanned the staircase. Nothing but white cement-block walls and the clanging of feet on metal steps. I took off.

I hit the first landing, started down the next flight. Shifting my Glock to my left hand, I pulled out my phone and called Sam.

My feet landed on concrete. I glanced at a big black 6 on the wall. Around the corner and down another flight.

"Judith?" Sam said. "Why are you call–"

"Guy's running down the fire stairs." I hit the next landing. "Can you get a good look at him when he comes out?" I ran down the next flight.

"I can do better than that."

"No, he's probably armed!" I rounded another corner and started down more steps. The clanging was a little closer. I was gaining on him, but not fast enough.

"Hey, I'm an LEO, remember?" Sam chuckled in my ear. "Guard," he called out, "I need your help. The chief wants us to catch a bad guy."

"No!" I screamed into the phone, leaping the last three steps to the next landing.

"All right!" The guard's voice, gleeful, in the background.

I ran down another flight and rounded the corner. Glanced over the railing and spotted the bottom door two flights below, swinging slowly shut.

Down more steps—while staring at a big black 2 on the wall—and around that landing.

A gunshot rang out.

My heart stuttered in my chest. I bolted down the last flight, my feet barely touching the steps, and barreled through the door.

CHAPTER NINE

I screeched to a halt, scanning the lobby, frantically looking for Sam. He wasn't there.

But the guard was across the lobby, clutching one arm, blood oozing between his fingers. "I'll call 911," he yelled over.

I ran for the glass front doors and burst out onto the sidewalk.

There, next to his truck, sat Sam. On the back of the thug—a slightly short but beefy guy in a dark suit. Swarthy skin, shaved head.

Sam pulled an arm up and handcuffed the guy's wrist. The thug flailed his loose arm around, trying to get a hold on Sam somewhere.

He grabbed that wrist and yanked it hard against his back. "Stop struggling or we'll be adding resisting arrest to the charges."

"Hey," the thug yelled at passers-by, his accent thick, "this guy iz mugging me. Help me!"

They eyed Sam's uniform, then gave our little tableau a wide berth. Some jogged a few paces to put some space between themselves and the panting lady doing a 360 scan—with a crazed look in her eye and a big gun in her hand.

"Don't see anybody who might be his backup," I huffed out.

"Good." Sam climbed off the guy and hauled him to his feet.

The thug's face was a bit bloody from where it had hit the sidewalk, but I could make out his features enough to know I'd never seen him before.

"What shall we do with him?" Sam tilted his head toward his truck. "It would be kinda cozy with all three of us in there."

I laughed a little. It sounded semi-hysterical.

I clamped my mouth shut, cleared my throat. "Some of my officers should be on their way."

Sam backed his prisoner up to a large tree. "Sit." The guy complied, sliding down to sit on the ground. Then Sam looked at me and grinned. "Never a dull moment around you, Anderson."

I worked hard not to give in to the urge to throw my arms around him. "I told you to just get a good look at him." My words came out harsher than I'd intended.

Sam's face sobered. "Yeah, we'll talk about that later. You better check on the guard."

I nodded and went back inside the building.

Gabe had come down from the penthouse. He was helping the guard over to his desk to sit down.

"I'm sorry you got caught up in this," I said to the guard.

"I'm not. Most fun I've had in years." He winced as his butt hit the chair, jolting his injured arm.

One side of my mouth quirked up. "Lemme guess. Retired LEO."

"Chicago PD. Jerry Cranston." He looked ruefully down at his arm. "I'd offer to shake but I'd get you all bloody. It's only a graze though. Bullet's in that wall over there." He tilted his head.

Gabe patted his good shoulder. "You're gonna get one hell of a Christmas bonus from me."

"Jerry," I said, "you ever seen that man before?"

The guard pursed his lips. "No, but... There was a delivery guy earlier, baseball cap pulled down. He was about this guy's height and build, and now that I'm thinking about it, I never did see him come down. And it was a little weird that he was wearing a suit. He had a big box, didn't say anything, just showed me the label. It was for a fifth-floor tenant, so I let him take it on up. He could've taken the fire stairs from there."

"Thanks." I gestured for Gabe to follow me across the lobby. "This place will be mobbed in a minute," I said. "Have you ever seen that guy before?"

"No. Don't know how he got through my front door. I came around the corner and there he was. Literally started pushing me around, bouncing me off the walls, saying I'd better tell him where the kid was if I knew what was good for me."

"The kid? He was after Alejandro?"

Gabe nodded, his pasty face going even whiter. "I need to know where his foster family lives. I need to go there and protect him."

"I'll take care of it." I called the watch desk at 3MB.

"Sergeant Armstrong."

"Sarge, I need you to dispatch two uniforms to this address." I turned my back on Gabe, whispered it into the phone. "It's the foster family of the boy we–"

"Found in the storage unit," Armstrong finished my sentence. "Two of my best are on their way. You need more officers where you are?"

"No, just contact Cruthers and fill him in. And send one of the techs to take some fingerprints. Thanks, Sarge." I disconnected.

The lobby was starting to fill up. Two paramedics were working on the guard's arm, while a uniform took down his statement.

Sam came in through the double glass doors. An officer there tried to block him. "It's okay. He's with me," I called over.

"Our guy's on his way to lockup," Sam said as he approached Gabe and me.

"Thanks." I gestured toward the elevators. "Let's go upstairs." It would be crass to send Sam back to his truck at this point.

At the top of the building, his gaze darted around the elegantly appointed foyer. Then he let out a soft grunt as we entered Gabe's more eclectic living room.

Expensive furniture was interspersed with gaming stations. By the picture window, which gave a panoramic view of the city, was a small computer desk. It had held a laptop earlier.

The room hadn't been particularly neat then. Now it was quite disheveled, with an end table and several lamps knocked over. The laptop was on the floor near the front door. Had the intruder intended to take it?

"Did the guy go anywhere else in your place?" I asked Gabe.

He shook his head and kept walking through to the spacious kitchen. Out came the mismatched mugs. He set them on the counter. "Regular or decaf?" he asked without turning around.

Probably trying to regain his composure after being attacked in his own home.

Sam and I exchanged a glance. Normally I wouldn't be taking in caffeine this late, afraid it would keep me up all night. But I had a feeling that was going to happen anyway.

Sam gave a small nod and said, "Regular."

"Coming up." Gabe busied himself with getting the coffee maker going.

Finally, he turned around. Some color had returned to his face, but his eyes were red-rimmed. He gestured toward the kitchen table and we all sat.

"Tell us what happened," I said, wishing Barnes was with me, my official note taker. She'd be pissed when she found out what went down without her.

Sam took out a pad and pen.

I gave him a smile.

Gabe had been watching the nonverbal interplay. He might be a geek but I suspected he was a people watcher by nature.

"You mind if I use you two as models for the main characters in my next game?"

"Uh..." Sam said, "what game?"

"I produce video games." Gabe waved a hand in the air. "That's what pays for all this. Next game's got a cops-and-space-aliens theme."

Sam and I exchanged another look. He shrugged ever so slightly.

"Sure, I guess," I said, not at all sure. "But I'd rather not be an alien."

Gabe smiled. "Don't worry. You'll be the cops."

Then his face sobered. "That guy must've picked the lock on my door. I came around the corner and there he was, standing in the middle of the living room. He was on me in a nanosecond, grabbed the front of my tee shirt. Tried to lift me off the ground, but big as he was...well, I'm not a light guy. I heard a ripping sound."

He pulled one side of his khaki-colored tee shirt around in front. The seam was gaping open.

"I'll need the shirt for evidence," I said, "but keep going. What happened next?"

"Guy started yelling, 'Where's the boy?' He had a strong accent." Gabe rubbed his forearm, where a bruise was forming. "He tried to punch my face, but I blocked him. Then he got me in the stomach. I doubled over and he shoved me across the room. Kept yelling, 'Where's the boy?' At one point, I said, 'What boy?' He got really pissed and slugged me again in the stomach."

he ends of his lips curled up some. "I got in a few good ones of my own, though."

Would our guy have bruises in the morning, or was Gabe embellishing some?

"He'd just tossed me across the room again, when I heard the ding of the elevator. The guy pulled a gun and held a finger to his lips. He came over and grabbed one arm, stuck the gun in my ribs, told me to be quiet."

"I have the gun," Sam said in a low voice.

Gabe licked his lips. "I thought for sure he was going to shoot me, or you. When it was obvious you weren't going to go away, he whispered something along the lines of 'get rid of them and don't try anything.' So I opened the door, and you know the rest."

The coffee maker pinged. Gabe got up to pour coffee into the mugs, brought them to the table. "Black, Chief, correct? Would you like cream, Sheriff?"

Sam shook his head.

"Had you ever seen the guy before?" I asked.

"Nope."

"He's not the guy that Tatiana's pimp had watching her?"

He thought about that for a moment. "I guess he could've been. Same build as one of them. I've never seen their faces up close."

"There was more than one?" I asked. Donna Glaser had only mentioned one watcher.

"Usually it was this one white guy. But there's another guy, off and on, over the weekends. Tatiana said they were spread thin then, trying to keep track of everyone who was out entertaining gentlemen. That's why she picked last night to disappear. She was booked to be with me all night."

He shook his head slightly. "I never saw either of their faces. They kept their distance. I guess they weren't supposed to spook the customers. I thought the weekend one was a light-skinned black guy, but he could be Hispanic."

I nodded. "You said Tatiana started acting differently about a week ago. Did anything happen around that time, anything at all unusual?"

Gabe thought for a moment, started to shake his head, then stopped. "Wait... One day, we were at the park, sitting on a bench and watching Alex play with another little boy. Everything was fine, but suddenly Tater tensed up and clutched her stomach, like she had a cramp or something. She ducked her head and kinda curled up, almost in a fetal position."

He paused, his eyes glassy and worried as he relived the experience. "I asked her if she was sick, thinking maybe she got a bad hot dog. At first she shook her head but then nodded. She asked me to go get Alex and take them home. She stayed bent over, her head down almost the whole way, 'cept she'd peek up every minute or so and look all around. I tried at one point to pick her up but she told me not to, then she looked around kinda frantic like and hurried on. But as we got closer to her place, she suddenly stood up straight and said we were going to walk around for a while. We went to this Goodwill store. She looked around inside for a few minutes, then led us out the back door."

He paused. "Alex was getting tired so I picked him up. But still she kept walking for a few more blocks, before we circled around to her place. Back there, she was fine. A little distracted but she said she felt better. She said I should go so she could rest. I thought the extra walking around was a little odd, but other than that, I never gave it another thought. I figured she'd just had a touch of a stomach bug or something, but..."

"But she may have seen someone in the park," I said. "Someone she recognized who represented some kind of threat."

"Come to think of it," Gabe added, "she didn't want to go to the park again after that, made excuses not to."

"Whoever she saw," Sam said, "must've at least gotten a glimpse of her too."

I nodded. "But she did manage to lose him, by going through the Goodwill store."

Otherwise, he would've gone after her sooner, I thought but didn't say out loud. It had taken him a week to find her.

I was trying to remember what else I should be asking. Even with the jolt of caffeine, my brain cells were fading.

Oh, the car.

"Tatiana's car," I said. "Do you have any idea where she got it?"

"She said some charity gave it to her. I bugged her to let me get her something nicer." He chuckled softly, but his face sagged with fatigue, and something else, most likely grief. "She gave me that stubborn look of hers. Put her hands on her hips and said the car she got from them couldn't be traced."

I nodded. That jived with the missing VIN number and mismatched license plate. "It's not safe for you to stay here right now. Get some things, and I'll get an officer to take you to a hotel."

He shook his head. "I'll be okay here. I'll be on guard now, and so will the guards downstairs. And I've got a gun, know how to use it."

Gabe, my boy, you surprise me.

My eyes must've gone wide despite my efforts to maintain a neutral expression. He gave me a lopsided grin.

"Got my first video game at age six. My grandma gave it to me for my birthday. It was called *Sharpshooters.*"

At ten of nine Monday morning, my private line rang. Caller ID read *Foster-JSO.*

"Detective," I said in a neutral tone, even though I was still pissed at him.

"Good morning, Chief!" His tone was *not* neutral, it was downright gleeful. "Guess what?"

Before I had a chance to reply, he continued, "We found out late yesterday that the head of the trafficking ring was having a breakfast meeting today, with all of his lieutenants."

"Oh, yeah." I sat up straighter in my desk chair.

"Rounded them up, including your gal's pimp. You got about an hour before the FDLE transports him to their place. How fast can you–"

"Be there in twenty." I was already out of my chair, grabbing up my jacket.

I bolted past Barnes's desk. "Come on!"

She ran to catch up. "What's going on?"

"Call Cruthers and your brother. Tell them Foster's got Tatiana's pimp."

In the parking lot, we both jumped into my compact. Barnes put her phone on speaker. Cruthers's gruff voice filled the car. "Hey, Barnes. What's up?"

She succinctly explained. Then I said, "I'm on my way to interview him now, before he's transferred over to the FDLE."

Belatedly, I realized I should've waited for him to join us, as the lead detective on the case. But that would've wasted precious minutes. "You wanna meet us there?"

A pause. "Not unless you need me to. I'm in the middle of something else... Uh, this guy is used to being in total control with women. Being interviewed by you could throw him off, which could be good or bad."

"I'm thinking good. I'm hoping he'll underestimate me."

CHAPTER TEN

At Foster's precinct, we took the fire stairs to the second floor. He stood beside his desk, looking at his watch. "Eighteen minutes. Impressive."

"Where is he?" I huffed out.

Foster held up a hand. "While you catch your breath, there are some ground rules."

I narrowed my eyes at him.

"Hear me out, Chief."

I nodded.

"His name is Conrad Butler. You can't ask who his boss is, nor where he gets his girls."

I ground my teeth, but nodded again.

"And you can't offer him any immunity or other considerations. We want the big guy and Conrad needs to flip on him."

"Great," I growled, "so I have no leverage."

"Only your superior wit."

"Kiss my ass."

Foster grinned. "I thought I just did."

He gave us a quick rundown on the prisoner, as he led the way to the interview room. Butler had a rap sheet from his youth, but no arrests in the last ten years.

Barnes went into the observation booth next door, her trusty notepad in her hand.

In the interview room, a man lounged in a metal chair beside a table. He slowly rose to his feet as I entered. He was somewhere between mid-thirties and forty, well groomed, his dark hair slicked back. He wore a tailored suit of black silk and a white shirt, open at the neck. "Excuse me. I was not expecting a lady."

And you didn't get one, I wanted to retort but held my tongue.

"Sit, please," I said in a pleasant voice, gesturing toward his chair. I sat opposite him. "You've been read your rights?"

"Yes," Butler said.

"And you understand them?"

"Yes," he said again, a slight smirk on his lips that made me want to smack him.

"I have a matter to discuss," I said, "that has nothing to do with why you were detained this morning."

His eyebrows went up.

"I'm the Starling Chief of Police, and I'm investigating the murder of a young woman there, Tatiana Gomez."

He shook his head with a rueful expression. "I don't know anyone by that name."

"Really? Because I was led to believe that you were her pimp."

A blatantly exaggerated look of surprise. "I'm a respectable business-man, not a pimp."

"Uh, huh. Tatiana died early Sunday morning. Somebody hit her over the head and dumped her in the river."

"So sorry to hear that."

He and I stared at each other for several beats.

"Your fingerprint was found inside her car," I said.

Again, the mock surprised expression. "I can't imagine how that could be."

I took my phone out of my jacket pocket, pulled up a crime scene photo of Tatiana and showed it to him.

He studied it for a beat, pulled a sad face and shook his head.

I let the silence stretch out.

"Why," he finally said, "would the pimp of this young woman kill such an attractive business asset?"

"He might, if he thought she was trying to get away from him."

He shook his head again. "There would be other ways to control her."

Such as hurting her kid! I gritted my teeth behind a thin smile.

"But what if those other ways had been removed?" I said.

He gave a nonchalant shrug. "It is not my field of endeavor, but as I understand it, such girls are relatively interchangeable."

My fists clenched under the table, but I managed to keep a neutral expression on my face. I picked up my phone and scrolled to the mug shots of the guy we'd arrested at Gabe Pirolnik's building last night. "You know this guy?"

He carefully perused the photo. "No, never saw him before."

I hated to admit it, but I was pretty sure he was telling the truth this time.

I scrolled on to the artist's rendition Donna Glaser and Derek had come up with first thing this morning, of a thin-faced white guy with stringy dark hair. I turned the phone toward Butler. "How about this guy?"

His eyes flickered. Too quickly he said, "No, never seen him either."

Liar!

"Word on the street," I said, "is that this guy was watching Tatiana's apartment."

He shrugged. "Don't know either of them."

"Uh, huh." Another staring contest.

I rephrased my questions, asked them again, pushing him some. His answers didn't change.

Then he asked, "You got something to offer me?" His tone was lackluster, as if he knew I was only the opening act.

"Sorry, afraid not." And I was truly sorry, but not for his sake.

I stood and left the room.

Cruthers, Bradley, and I conferred in my office, with Barnes leaning against the jamb of the closed door, pad in hand. Collins, our newest detective, was in a mandatory workshop today, but I wondered where Patterson was.

Barnes read her succinct notes from the interview with Conrad Butler.

Then Cruthers gave his report. "The guy you and the sheriff nabbed last night, his name is Pedro Juarez. And he swears he doesn't know Butler. No body-language reaction to the name or his mug shot. Same reaction to Tatiana Gomez's picture. Total stone-faced denial."

He shook his shaggy head. "And I'm afraid that's all I got out of him. He asked for a public defender, claims he can't afford a lawyer."

I furrowed my brow. "He was wearing a pretty nice suit for a poor guy."

"My guess is," Cruthers said, "he's somebody's underling, and he's afraid to call whoever sent him. Doesn't want to admit failure."

Bradley snorted softly. "If he's more afraid of his boss than of prison, his boss must be one mean s.o.b."

A soft knock on my door. Barnes straightened and opened it a crack.

"Can I see the chief for a minute?" Ernie Mansfield's voice.

I gestured to let him in.

He held two sheets of paper in his hands. "Studying the tire tracks we found, I think I've pieced together what happened."

"What, you know who the murderer is?" Cruthers said, in a teasing voice.

Ernie blushed. "No." He sounded mildly irritated.

I was catching on that Ernie had a limited sense of humor, and Bert, along with the detectives, found that an irresistible challenge.

"May I?" Ernie gestured toward my desk.

I nodded, and he laid one of the sheets of paper in front of me. The detectives rose and gathered around.

"There were multiple sets of tracks." He pointed to two lines of cross-hatches in the middle of the page. "That's Ms. Gomez's car. She slammed on the brakes, probably to avoid hitting the car that had just swerved across in front of her and stopped, blocking her way." He pointed to a diagonal set of tracks in front of the others.

"Her tracks are blurred some, because she tried to back up. But she didn't get very far because someone else had stopped behind her, blocking her in. Those tracks were much lighter. That driver didn't stop as quickly." He pointed to a set of tracks behind hers and straddling the center line, blocking both lanes.

"Couldn't those tracks be the commuter who almost hit the car?" I asked.

Ernie shook his head. "I'll get to him in a minute." He tapped a box lightly penciled around the far end of the straight tracks. "That's where her car ended up."

"She might have jumped out to run," Bradley said.

Ernie shook his head again. "She'd locked herself in. There are signs that a slim jim was used to unlock the driver's door."

Cruthers grunted. "Somebody from one of those cars ran to her door and jimmied it open."

"The guy who left the fingerprint inside the handle?" Barnes said.

I nodded. "Quite possibly. And someone from the other car probably stood next to the passenger side." My throat tightened. "So she had no place to go."

Ernie placed the second sheet on top of the first. It was tracing paper. The drawing below showed through. "There were three sets of tracks behind her car. One was the guy who blocked her in. He was in the middle of the road. Then another set of tracks directly behind her, and a third set partially obscuring the second set." He touched the marks on the tracing paper. "That third set matched the tires of the commuter who almost hit her car."

"So someone else was there," Bradley said. "Maybe between the time she was blocked in and when the commuter found the car and called it in."

I sat back in my chair and blew out air. "More evidence that two people were after her, or at least keeping track of her."

"One was probably Butler," Bradley said. "His print was on the glove box handle. I wonder if we can get an imprint of the tires on his car."

Ernie nodded. "If you're thinking his was the other car directly behind her, those tracks were partially obscured by the commuter's car. Only one side of them is visible. The tires are brand new."

"How can you tell that?" I asked.

"The tracks are too pristine, no cracks or indentations in the tread. Over time, the tread wears unevenly, gets marked up by stones and glass and such. These tires were probably purchased in the last month or so. Derek's helping us track down the brand and model based on the tread pattern."

"Good work, Ernie." I pointed to the papers in front of me. "Can I keep these?"

"Yeah, I've got the diagrams on my computer, but I thought it would be easier to show you on paper."

He left, and I handed the pages to Barnes. "Put these on the murder board. Then meet me downstairs."

She turned and followed Ernie out.

To Cruthers and Bradley I said, "It's also possible that those new tires belong to a rental car. Or at least one of those sets of tracks is somehow related to Alejandro's father."

"The hypothesis being," Bradley said, "that he was abusive and Tatiana left Mexico to get away from him."

Cruthers's expression was pensive. "Batterers will often go a long way to track down the woman that got away."

"Especially if she takes his kid," I said.

Bradley skimmed hair out of his eyes. "You're thinking he was the one Tatiana saw in the park."

"Yes, or someone else she knew in Mexico, and feared they would go back and tell him where she was."

"He may have come here," Cruthers said, "rented a car, and went looking for her. Or he could've hired somebody else to track her down, maybe Juarez."

I pointed at him and Bradley. "We need to find the father, for several reasons."

They both nodded, acknowledging that by "we" I meant "you two."

Standing up, I said, "In the meantime, I think Barnes and I will talk to Mary Striker again, and her happy band of do-gooders."

Cruthers's bushy eyebrows pulled together.

"It's may not be all that important, but I'd like to nail down if Tatiana got the car from them." I shrugged. "And see if anything else falls out when I shake that tree some more."

Patterson caught up with me by the elevators. "Cruthers said you were going to talk to Mary Striker. I've got some info on her."

I mentally took back my earlier assumption that he was goofing off somewhere.

"She's forty-nine, born Marianne Osborne, grew up in Wisconsin. Father died of cancer when she was twelve, and a couple of years later a stepfather came on the scene. A few months after he married her mother, Marianne accused him of molesting her."

The elevator dinged. When the doors opened, Bert and Ernie were in it, headed down. I waved them on. The doors closed again.

"No one wanted to believe her," Patterson continued, flipping through some papers in his hand, "but she kept insisting. She pressed charges and it went to trial. And the jury didn't believe her either. He was acquitted and two months later she ran away, ended up a prostitute in Miami."

"Ahh," I said, "so she's lived the life. No wonder she wants to help others get out of it."

"She got lucky after that. Married a rich guy a good bit older than her. He died four years ago, and two years ago, she remarried, only this guy is younger than her."

I nodded. "I met him in passing yesterday. Thanks for all the background, Patterson. Good work."

I expected a smile, or something. All I got was a slight nod back.

He walked away, and I punched the elevator button again.

<hr>

I went out the front of the building. During the still-hot-in-Florida months of September and October, I'd learned to go down the hall and out the back, to stay in the air-conditioning as long as possible. But now that it was finally cooling down, I took the sunnier route to my space in the parking lot.

I was almost to the corner of the building when a man abruptly appeared in my path. I instinctively stepped back, a hand flying to the butt of my gun behind my back.

"Chief Anderson?" the man said. He was average height, average build, wearing a light gray suit, but the way he carried himself said cop.

I kept my hand on my gun. "Who wants to know?" It came out snippy. I decided I was okay with that.

"Special Agent Grant, FDLE." He took a half step toward me, hovering on the edge of my personal space.

"Uh, huh. You got a badge?"

He took out a slim leather wallet, flashed it open in my direction, then started to pocket it again.

I took an exaggerated step back, and held out my left hand, palm up. I was trying to decide between kicking his knees out from under him or elbowing him in the face if he got anywhere near my personal space again.

He wisely did not move forward. Instead, he stared at my hand for a beat, as if he didn't know why I had it stuck out there.

"Everything okay, Chief?" Barnes's voice, from the corner of the building. She'd apparently gone out the back.

Several rude retorts crossed my mind—rude toward the state guy, not Barnes. I let them whiz on by and finally settled on, "Just peachy." My hand hadn't moved.

Finally, the man put his badge wallet into it.

I opened it and carefully examined it, then handed it back. "What can I do for you, Special Agent Grant?"

"You can keep your nose out of my case." His tone was authoritarian, but his expression said he knew he'd lost most of his power advantage.

"And what case might that be?"

"I'm not at liberty to say."

I snorted. "Well, that makes it damned hard to know which case I should stay out of, doesn't it?"

"You interrogated Conrad Butler, before we'd even talked to him."

"Yes. He's a suspect in a homicide here."

"Yeah, well, we got bigger fish to fry than your dead hooker."

A gasp. I glanced past Grant's shoulder to its source—Barnes. Her face was turning red.

Again, many things that I *could* have said came to mind, such as how did an insensitive oaf like you get assigned to a sensitive case like this.

Finally I settled on, "I was given access to the prisoner by the Jacksonville Sheriff's Office. The Starling PD has a *cordial* working relationship with JSO."

"Well, you're not getting access to him again."

I gave him a fake smile. "Thank you for saving me some time, then."

His brow furrowed in confusion. Apparently, that wasn't the response he'd expected. He grunted and started to turn away to his left.

"If I need access again," I stepped around him on his right, "I now know to go directly over your head."

CHAPTER ELEVEN

"Who was that?" Barnes asked, as we headed for my car.

"State cop who likes to throw his weight around."

I'd requisitioned two unmarked cars for my detectives to use, but they hadn't been delivered yet. There was some customizing required—a more powerful engine than was standard, for one. When you chase bad guys, you need more horses under the hood.

In the meantime, we continued to use our own cars, submitting mileage.

I had Barnes drive, and I sat back in the passenger seat, trying to focus my mental energy on what I wanted to achieve in the upcoming interview.

I hadn't called ahead, so it was possible Mary Striker wouldn't even be in. The desire for an element of surprise, though, outweighed the concern about wasted time if she wasn't there.

I'd had the feeling, when we'd last talked, that she was holding something back. Maybe several somethings. And I wanted to know how the "repurposing center" operated. I suspected it was not always strictly within the law. I would be willing to bend some rules, for a good cause, but others maybe not. And I expected some cooperation out of her in return.

Barnes pulled my car to the curb next to the storefront office.

"Follow my lead," I said.

"Always."

A woman was coming out the front. We ducked past her before the door could close and made a beeline for Mary Striker's door.

Several of the volunteers at the desks called after us. "Hey, who are you? Where are you going?"

"You can't go in there," one woman yelled as we reached the office door. I recognized her as Nancy from yesterday. It took her a little longer to recognize me, now dressed in a tailored black pantsuit and carrying myself like a cop, rather than a scared, desperate prostitute.

I knocked on the door and turned the knob. It wasn't locked. *Off to a good start.*

I peeked around the door. Mary was alone. "Sorry to bother you again, Mrs. Striker, but we have some more questions."

She took a deep breath, blew it out slowly through her nose. "Come in."

I did so and took the liberty of sitting in one of the two chairs across from her desk. Barnes lingered by the door. I looked at her, made a slight gesture with my head toward the door, then looked down at the empty chair beside me.

Barnes had become expert at reading my body language. She closed the door firmly in Nancy's face and sat in the other chair. Out came her pad and pen.

"We've found out quite a bit about Tatiana Gomez," I said, "since you and I last talked. Did you know she rented a storage unit and moved her son into it a few days ago?"

"No, but I'm not surprised. She said she had to get him out of harm's way, in case her pimp caught on to what she was about to do."

"As in, run away from him."

She nodded.

"You're sure she never mentioned her pimp's name?" I asked.

A head shake.

"Does the name Conrad Butler mean anything to you?"

She tilted her head to one side, as if thinking about that. Another head shake. "No, never heard of him."

She seemed to be telling the truth, or she could be a good liar. "Tell us more about how you provide cars for the women."

She hesitated.

"We traced the license plate on hers."

She sighed. "They're older models, don't cost us much. Very average cars that will blend in. We prefer to give them bus or train tickets, bought in someone else's name. But some are too afraid of even that much of a paper trail."

"And there's no paper trail with a car?" I feigned surprise. "Aren't they registered?"

Mary's face paled as she realized she'd painted herself into a corner.

I let her off the hook, for now. "You sure Tatiana never said anything about Alejandro's father?"

She began to shake her head, then stopped. "She said something one time that made me think he was a big deal, that he had a lot of power."

"What did she say?"

"I don't remember exactly. It was just an impression I got."

"Did she ever say anything more specific about where she was from?"

"No. Only Mexico."

"How about where she came across the border?" I asked.

"She said it was one of the more narrow spots, a popular place to cross the Rio Grande. And it hadn't rained in a while so the river was down some. She was able to wade across, with her son on her back."

I glanced sideways at Barnes, scribbling on her pad. Maybe we'd be able, with some research, to piece together where Tatiana had come across.

Then I glanced in the other direction, at the door Striker's husband had come through yesterday. Time to make my move.

I jumped up, startling Mary. "Sorry, but I really need a restroom." One long stride over to the door. "Is this one?" I yanked the door open.

On the other side was a large warehouse-type space. And the end closest to me had been decked out as a mechanic's garage. It held a lot of shiny equipment.

The handsome younger man of yesterday looked up from where he was working under the hood of an old car. And leaning against the car's fender, shooting the breeze with him, was the guy from Cruthers's photo.

Harry, the junkyard owner.

The office was now quite crowded, with Mary behind the desk and Barnes and myself in front—and Mary's husband, leaning against the jamb of the doorway leading to the garage.

The junkyard owner had taken off when I'd flashed my badge. Barnes started to give chase, but I'd called her back. "We know where to find him."

Now Mary's husband had his arms crossed. His blue eyes, in his scowling face, were more an icy gray today.

I ignored him, focusing on his wife. "Walk me through the process, when you're helping one of these women."

She sighed softly. "There are four phases. First is communication, the easiest. We give them two disposable cell phones, with plenty of minutes on them. Tell them to not share the numbers with anyone. Second, we look at the transportation options. As I said, we prefer to give them a bus or train ticket, but we'll provide a hard-to-trace car if that's what they want." She stopped, took a breath. "We give them as much opportunity to make choices as possible, since they've been stripped of their power for so long."

I nodded, mentally giving this woman kudos for her astuteness.

"Then we figure out where they're going to go. Some, like Tatiana, want to disappear on their own. The others, we try to pair them with sympathetic people in the town or city they are going to, someone who can help with getting a place to live, a job, etc."

"Magdalene's Repurposing is a statewide organization?" I asked.

"No. But there are similar organizations to ours, in several cities, and we've developed contacts around Florida, and even in some other states. Some are women we've helped in the past."

She paused, sucked in air. "Look, some of what we do bends the rules, but we don't really break them."

"You talking about the cars," I said, "or giving the women new identities? That's phase four, isn't it?"

"We can stop providing cars, only give them the train or bus options." Her voice was a little panicky. Her husband stiffened.

"And it's not illegal to live under an assumed name," Mary added.

No, I thought, *but as soon as you sign a lease or get a credit card, you're committing fraud.*

"It's exactly the same thing the government does," the husband finally piped up, "with their witness protection program."

No, not exactly. But I didn't pursue that right now.

"The bar of soap Tatiana had. Something had been scratched off above the number."

Mary nodded. "It just says, *Need help? Call us.* I guess she scraped that off in case her pimp found the soap. We put the bars in the bus station and train station restrooms, and some other places."

"Such as?"

"Any restrooms that the women on the streets might use, such as the ones in the city parks."

That was probably where Tatiana had come by the soap, while taking her son to the park.

"Do you only help prostitutes?" I asked.

Mary and her husband exchanged a look. His face had relaxed some, his expression now more worried than angry.

"We, uh," Mary said, "sometimes help battered women get away from their husbands, but only if they've run out of options."

Legal options, in other words. I let that go, for now.

"The cars, do you keep any record of who gets assigned which car?"

"Yes, to protect, uh, our source, in case any car is ever used in a crime and is tracked back to him somehow. The cofounder of the organization keeps the list, in a protected file. And she only uses the woman's initials."

"Thanks." I stood. "That's it for now, but we may have more questions. Please keep yourselves available."

Mary nodded. Her husband frowned.

Barnes pocketed her pad and followed me out of the office.

There was a small alcove, next to Mary's office, that I hadn't noticed yesterday. A partition and a few folding chairs scattered along the walls—a waiting area. A young woman occupied one of the chairs.

Hmm, might be interesting to see how the recipients of their services view Mary and her crew. Maybe I was just being a cynical cop, but do-gooders always left me wondering if their motives were totally altruistic.

"Barnes, make yourself scarce for a few minutes," I said quietly.

My assistant headed for the restrooms' sign nearby, and I slipped into the alcove and took a chair three down from the young woman.

I watched her out of the corner of my eye. Her tight, too-short black dress stood out against fair skin. She wore a lot of flashy costume jewelry

and too much makeup, her blonde hair swept back into an artfully careless knot. Around twenty-five years old, but they had been hard years.

I gave her a little wave of my hand. "Hi, I'm Judy."

She looked at me, suspicion in her eyes. "Misty," she finally said.

I rubbed my palms down the thighs of my slacks. "I guess I'm kinda
nervous."

"Yeah, me too." Her tone was slightly sarcastic, but at least she was
answering me.

I blinked hard, as if fighting tears, bit my lower lip.

"You don't exactly look like a 'ho," Misty said, with a mix of curiosity
and suspicion in her voice.

For a second, I considered selling myself as a high-priced call girl, but
decided I was too old to make that ring true. I shook my head. "Um, my
husband..."

"He beats on you?"

I gave a small nod, bit my lower lip again. "I tried to leave last year. He
came to my apartment..." I trailed off.

"Men are pigs," Misty said.

I let out a nervous laugh. "No argument from me."

Raised voices could now be heard behind the closed office door nearby.

"Uh, what Mary and her husband are doing," I said, raising my own
voice slightly, "it's really wonderful."

"What, fighting?" The sarcasm was full blown now.

"They do that a lot?" I asked, trying to fake a crestfallen expression, as
if the angels had all fallen to the earth.

Misty opened her mouth, but Nancy raced past us and flung Mary's
office door open.

"Josh just got back from checking on Caroline. There's nobody there
and police tape is everywhere."

Heart racing, I jumped up. *Sam's murder victim?* "Caroline Baumann?"

Mary had come to the doorway. She glared at me. "We don't use last
names here."

I glanced back over my shoulder at Misty.

Her eyes had gone wide and now sparked with anger. "You're a cop,
aren't you?" she spat out. Without waiting for an answer, she was up and

rounding the end of the partition, headed for the front door. My last glimpse of her was her red stiletto heel.

Guilt squeezed my chest. Had I scared her away from her chance to get off the streets?

I shook my head to clear it and turned back to Mary. "Who is Caroline to you?"

"She and I co-founded Magdalene's two and a half years ago."

CHAPTER TWELVE

We were all crowded into Mary's office again, including Nancy and Barnes, who had come out of the restroom when she'd heard the commotion. I had just informed Mary that her co-founder was deceased.

Head down, elbows on her desk, she supported her forehead with the heels of her hands. "How did she die?"

Not well, I thought. Out loud, I said, "Home invasion."

The heels of her hands were now in her eye sockets, rubbing hard, trying to stem the flow of tears. "We knew this could get dangerous, but..." She choked up.

"So you think her death was related to your organization?" I asked.

Her head jerked up. Her eyes were red and puffy. "Don't you?"

"Yes." Now that I knew Caroline Baumann was connected to this group. "How did you two come to start all this?" I waved a hand in the air.

She sniffed. Barnes pulled a small packet of tissues from her pocket and handed it to her.

Mary swiped at her eyes. "We met at a charity function, for the local battered women's shelter. We hit it off, got together for lunch soon after. We were sharing some about our lives, and out of that conversation, Magdalene's was born."

"Was she on the streets in the past?" I asked, in a gentle voice.

Mary shook her head. "No, but her daughter was. Her youngest girl had gotten into drugs in high school. After several failed rehab attempts, Caroline realized she needed to save herself, so she kicked Lisa out of her house. A local pimp got his hooks into the girl, and a year later, she was dead from an overdose."

After a brief pause, I said, "Was Caroline the keeper of the car list?"

Mary's eyes went wide again as she nodded. "You think her death is related to Tatiana's?"

"Possibly," I said out loud while thinking, *probably.*

Mary's face crumpled. She let out a moan. Her husband stepped over beside her and wrapped an arm around her shoulders. She turned in her chair and buried her face in his tee shirt, sobbing.

He stroked her hair. "Shh, shh."

His actions seemed authentic, but he'd been a bit slow to offer comfort.

I rose, dropped a card on her desk. "Call me if you think of anything else. I'm very sorry for your loss."

Nancy followed me and Barnes out the office door and closed it softly behind us.

I turned to her. "How many people knew that Caroline had the car list?"

"Just me and Mary."

"How many women do you have in the pipeline at the moment?"

She blinked, then swallowed hard. "Two, plus the one who ran away." She grimaced. "She may or may not come back."

"Follow through with them," I said, "but don't take on anyone new. Not until you hear from me."

Nancy's eyes were full of anxiety and shiny with unshed tears. "Are you going to shut us down?"

I held her gaze for a moment. "I honestly don't know." But my gut was saying it wasn't safe for them to be operating until we knew what was going on. Was someone targeting their staff and clients?

"And be careful," I added.

⸺◆⸺

I had Barnes drive again, so I could make calls. The first was to Bert Deming.

"Send a copy of that partial print from Tatiana's driver's door to Sheriff Pierson."

"Will do, Chief. Um, we narrowed down those tracks to a certain brand of tires. I asked Sarge if a uniform could call tire stores, but he said he couldn't spare anyone. We're still processing evidence from the

sheriff's crime scene and Derek's going over his victim's laptop. Should
we put that aside to track down the tires?"

"No." I looked over at Barnes. "Who's the watch commander today?"

The question was meant for her but Bert answered, "Sergeant Lewis."

Figures! I ground my teeth. Lewis and I had locked horns before, when
he'd failed to follow up on a missing person, and she'd ended up dead.
"I'll take care of it. You all stay with the Baumann case. It's looking like
it's related to ours."

Discovering that connection—that Caroline was involved with the
Magdalene group—had thrown my system into overdrive. I decided I
wasn't in a good place to duke it out with Lewis, so I texted rather than
calling. *If Officer Dulles is on duty today, assign him to help Bert re: tires.
If not, assign someone else.*

Very little delay before his reply. *Already down one patrol officer because
of protection detail for that kid.*

I am aware of that. Do it. I paused, debating if I should add, *That's an
order.* Those were words I shouldn't have to say out loud, or in this case,
in a text. I was the damn police chief!

I did not add them. I hit send.

No response. Seconds ticked by. I ground my teeth again. At this rate,
they'd be down to nubs by the time this case was solved.

Acknowledge, I texted.

Dulles will be reassigned.

I took a deep breath and called Sam. "Sheriff, I'm in my car with
Barnes." That should keep him from whispering embarrassing sweet
nothings...although a few sweet nothings would go a long way to im-
proving my mood right now.

"Looks like our cases may be linked," I said. "A fingerprint is on its way
to you. See if it matches any of the unidentified ones from your crime
scene." I filled him in on the Magdalene Repurposing Center—he now
had need-to-know status regarding their secrets. Then I told him about
Caroline Baumann's connection to them.

Sam whistled softly when I'd finished. "The plot thickens."

Like congealed blood, I thought but didn't say, my mind flashing to the
grim crime scene at Caroline's house. And to the red sticky clumps in
Pipsqueak's fur as she'd rubbed against my ankles. A chill ran through
me.

"I'll let you know if there are any more developments on my end," I said.

"Same here. See you later?"

"Maybe."

"Yeah, same here," he said with a sigh. The cases would take precedence over our social life for the foreseeable future.

I'd no sooner disconnected then the phone rang. *Bradley* flashed up on my dashboard screen.

I punched the button to accept the call. "Chief Anderson."

"Some interesting developments, Chief, regarding the fella you collared last night, Pedro Juarez. That may or may not be his real name. Turns out he's a person of interest in eight suspicious deaths over the last few years, mostly in the Southwest, but a couple on the Gulf Coast as well, in Louisiana and Mississippi. And in some of those cases, he was using an alias."

"Suspicious deaths, not homicides?"

"Ruled inconclusive by the medical examiners or coroners involved. All the same MO. Cause of death was blunt force trauma to the head, and they looked like accidents—like the person fell and hit their head on something hard. But the detectives on the cases reported the scenes seemed staged. And in each case, someone matching Juarez's description was seen hanging around the victim a day or two earlier, looking somewhat out of place."

"How so?"

"A swarthy Mexican in a crowd of mostly lily-white businessmen at a conference, or in one case he was remembered by the wait staff of a swanky restaurant because of his heavy accent. Also, in each of these cases, there was someone who would benefit in a big way from the victim's demise. Full ownership of a lucrative business or a big estate. In one case, the victim was about to divorce his wife on grounds of adultery, which violated the terms of their pre-nup. She wouldn't have gotten a penny of his substantial wealth."

"This guy, Juarez, is a hit man?" I said, slightly incredulous.

"Could be," Bradley said. "And I'm afraid I've got some bad news. The ASA asked for remand without bail because the guy's a flight risk, but the judge at his arraignment decided a higher bail would suffice. He set bail at $50,000."

"But he had a gun and shot at police officers," I half yelled.

"He told the judge he was just having an argument with an acquaintance when some woman rushed in waving a gun. He didn't know she was police."

"What about his gun? I'll bet it isn't registered."

"There is no gun registration in Florida, remember?"

I shook my head. Damn, he was right.

"Bail was posted an hour later," Bradley continued. "He's back on the street."

I swore under my breath. "This is the same guy who said he didn't have money for a lawyer?"

"Yup. You want to offer Pirolnik protection?"

"I did last night and he refused, but contact him again. See if he changes his mind when he knows the guy is out."

"Will do."

We signed off, and Barnes said, "What's a hit man from the southwest doing in Florida?"

"Good question."

Sheriff Sam showed up at twelve-thirty, carrying a thick file folder and a bag from my favorite deli. Barnes brought him to me in the smaller conference room, where I was staring at the autopsy photos on the murder board.

He plopped the bag down on the table and walked over next to me. "I see you're old-fashioned like me, wanna see the photos printed out, not on a computer screen."

"I like to see them side by side." I touched one of the photos, a closeup of Tatiana's left thigh.

Sam leaned in close, squinting. "Railroad-track bruises."

"The ME's report says, quote, 'the parallel contusions were most likely caused by a smooth, hard object that pushed blood into the surrounding tissues at the point of contact.' But see that odd bruising along one edge?"

"Yeah, and I've seen it before." Sam stepped over to the table and opened his file, pulled out two photos, laid them out on top of my notes. He pointed to one of them. "Caroline's abdomen."

I leaned over. The scalloped pattern along one edge of the bruising was even more pronounced.

Sam gestured toward the other photo. "And her right thigh." It had a similar set of railroad track bruises. "That's why I came visiting. Wanted to compare the cases with you, 'cause the print you sent did match some from Caroline's house."

I nodded. "The ME speculates that the bruising on Tatiana's thigh was caused when it hit the railing as she was going over it into the water. But I think it was caused by the same weapon that was used on her head. Only there it broke the skin, so minimal bruising since the blood had somewhere to go."

I touched another photo, of the bridge's metal railing. "Also, Bert and Ernie found a print in–"

Sam snickered.

I gave him a small smile. "I'm guessing you were raised on Sesame Street as well."

"My mother's favorite babysitter."

"Anyway, this print in the blood smear on the railing, it's Tatiana's middle finger of her left hand. And…" I tapped yet another photo from the autopsy. It showed a distinct pattern of bruises from a big hand grasping Tatiana's right upper arm. "There's a spiral fracture in this arm."

"But only one hand print," Sam said. "They usually occur when someone holds a limb with two hands and twists in opposite directions."

"The fracture may have occurred as she twisted to try to get away, if he was holding her really tight."

"And she was desperate to get loose from him." Sam's voice was grim. "Her head is now turned away from her assailant, and he hits her on the back of it, hard enough to fracture her skull."

"Her free left hand automatically goes to the wound, comes away with blood on it."

"He pushes her toward the railing." Sam mimicked a shove. "And she grabs it with that hand. He wrestles her up and over it."

I nodded again, pointed to Ernie's diagrams of the layers of tire tracks and shared his theory of the order in which vehicles arrived.

"So two cars pin her in," Sam said. "Most likely, someone from one of those cars attacked her, and at least knocked her out. If they had left her functional, she wouldn't have stuck around. They both take off, then someone else comes along later–"

"We're assuming later," I said, "but how much later? He or she probably searched inside the car and was the one who wiped everything they thought they'd touched."

"The earlier people could've been the searchers and fingerprint wipers."

"True," I said. "I need to ask the ME's office how long it would've taken her to die from the head wound if she hadn't drowned first. Maybe the first pair hit her on the head, she lay unconscious or semi-conscious, and someone else came along and threw her into the river. There was water in her lungs so she was still alive when she went in."

I shook my head slightly. "When did she have time to carefully hide her shoe? She didn't just toss it under the seat. It was up against the side, in the shadows where it wouldn't be easily spotted. Her assailant wasn't likely to politely wait for her to hide it before hauling her out of the car."

Sam ran a hand through his sandy hair. "Maybe she recognized the people in those first two cars and quickly hid the shoe before they got to her."

"Quite possible. But here's another question. She obviously didn't tell her assailant where the boy was, or he would've been gone by the time we got to the storage unit the next day."

"And Juarez wouldn't have still been looking for him."

"Correct. So why kill her if he needs info from her?"

"Maybe he lost control," Sam said.

"Could be."

"Juarez's prints didn't match any from Caroline's house, by the way." Sam heaved a sigh. "So, you're thinking the killer is the boy's father?"

I nodded. "Or someone he hired, and maybe they screwed up, hit her too hard. It could be Butler, but he made a good point that he'd be unlikely to kill a, quote, 'valuable asset.' And what reason would he have to go after Caroline?"

Sam tilted his head to one side. "So how is Caroline connected? I mean she obviously is, since she worked for that group that was helping Tatiana, and she was attacked by the same weapon. But–"

"Oh, I forgot to tell you one other thing. Caroline was the keeper of the list of cars the group had given to some of the women." I repeated what Mary Striker had told me. "I've got Derek looking for the list on her laptop. Lemme call him and see what he has."

Derek did indeed have some things to report. "Come to the small conference room," I told him.

While we waited, we dug into the sandwiches Sam had brought. They were thick with tuna salad, lettuce and tomato, mayo dripping around the edges. Messy but delicious.

I'd just picked up the second half when there was a knock on the door.

"Come." I dropped the sandwich back on its wrapper, unwilling to have tomato juice and mayo on my chin while talking to a subordinate.

Derek entered, a laptop under his arm. "Chief, no luck with that gamers' chat room Mr. Pirolnik told you about. I got into the chat room, of course, but there's a really good fire wall protecting the admin information. Even if I got past it, I doubt there's any record of the real names of the users online. They'd most likely have that offline or on a separate server. And the escort service's phone number, no record of it with the phone company or any cell provider. It's a burner. No answer now, when I tried it."

I nodded, worried that they might have shut down operations after Butler was arrested. If so, what would happen to the women? Hopefully, they just changed the number.

Derek set the laptop on the table. "But I did hit pay dirt here." He opened the computer, tapped keys. "Ms. Baumann had the list hidden in a folder labeled *groceries,* which was inside another folder labeled *household.* And it was password protected, with a strong password."

My eyes skimmed the document. It gave detailed descriptions of make, model, and color of various vehicles, including dents and scratches. Next to each were initials. I scanned down and located a Taurus that matched Tatiana's. Sure enough, it had T.G. next to it.

"I found ten attempts to guess the password," Derek said, "around nine p.m. Saturday night. Then the list was accessed with the proper password a few minutes after ten."

I recalled that the TOD window was from five p.m., when a neighbor had seen her watering her flowers, and midnight. How long had Caroline endured being beaten before she told him where to find the list? But still she'd withheld the password for another hour. I struggled to hide a shudder.

I glanced at Sam. His face was grim, his mouth a tight line. His imagination must've gone to the same scenario as mine had.

He shoved himself to a stand so quickly that Derek jumped a little. "I'm gonna go to Caroline's house again, now that I know all this."

Sam's voice was strangled, like it was all he could do to keep from yelling. He swallowed hard. "Thanks, Derek." He headed for the conference room door.

I jumped up and followed, looking longingly over my shoulder. One of these days, I'd actually get to finish a lunch around here.

But the expression on Sam's face... My stomach roiled at the thought of leaving him alone with his emotions.

Plus, I wanted to examine Caroline's house more closely myself, now that we knew what we knew.

CHAPTER THIRTEEN

Sam and I stood in Caroline Baumann's kitchen. He pointed to the battered back door. A shiny new hasp and padlock secured it. "The perp came in there, kicked the door in."

He gestured toward the counter, where two yellow evidence markers rested. "There was a set of knives in a wooden block there, and a butcher knife lying in front of it. I think she pulled it out of the knife block, but..." He trailed off, leafing through the file he'd brought with him. He pulled out a photo and laid it on the counter. A close up of a bruised forearm.

"He broke her arm," Sam said, anger seething under the surface. He pulled another photo out and left the room.

I followed him to a bedroom. He dropped the photo on the bed. "Rope burns and cuts on her left wrist." He gestured toward a bedpost. It had fresh scratches down near the mattress—which had been stripped, the linens taken to the lab.

"She struggled to get loose." Sam's voice had shifted toward sad now.

"The door to a second bedroom had been locked." He turned and walked down the hall, stopped at another open doorway. The wooden jamb was splintered.

"The laptop was in there," I said softly, more statement than question.

He nodded, turned and nudged past me, headed for an informal sitting area around a TV, in the room next to the kitchen. Some of the furniture had been shoved around. A small table laid on its side. "She ended up here."

"She got loose?" I said, barely above a whisper. "Was trying to get out."

His eyes still on the floor where her body had been, he said, "The death blow was to the back of the head."

"Like Tatiana," I said under my breath.

Another slow nod. "One of the fingerprints that matches your print from the car handle was on a laptop key. All the other keys were too smudged."

"It's hard to type with gloves on."

Sam sucked in air. "He may have smudged the keys on purpose, knowing that it would look suspicious if they were wiped clean. But he missed one."

"Why didn't he just take the laptop?"

"Maybe he didn't want to draw attention to the fact that it, or something on it, was what he was after. Her jewelry box was searched, some valuable pieces missing, according to her son. And her wallet—credit cards were still there, but no cash. There was another partial on the wallet that matched yours."

"Also hard to take money out of a wallet with gloves on." I paused, thinking. "He was avoiding taking anything that could easily be traced back to her. The jewelry's likely at the bottom of the river by now."

"Yeah. Took just enough to make it look like a home invasion and robbery." Sam heaved a sigh.

I stepped over to him, wanting to touch him, maybe put a hand on his arm. But something stopped me.

He turned away, cleared his throat. "Caroline and I dated a few times," he said, his back still toward me, "when she first came down here. We were both northern transplants, had that in common. But I let it slide after a while. She never wanted to talk about herself."

He turned back, his face close to mine. "Now I know why she was so secretive."

My hand, of its own volition, reached up and touched his cheek.

And then he was kissing me.

We'd kissed before, but never like this. He tightened his arms around me.

I thought about nudging him away. But my hands cupped his shoulders rather than pushing against them. They were rock hard under his uniform shirt.

My fingers dug into them as the kiss deepened. Electricity shot through me, a tingling sensation lingering in its path.

I wiggled a little, and he let me go. We both took a half step back. I turned slightly away, shame heating my face as I scanned the room where Caroline had died.

A sideways glance. His face was pink as well.

"Maybe not the right time and place," he said, "but no regrets here." He took my hand and squeezed it without looking at me.

I found myself squeezing back.

———◆———

Sam drove me back to 3MB. At one point, he took my hand.

Something fluttered in my chest. It wasn't attraction this time. More like panic setting in. I gently pulled loose to push a nonexistent strand of hair out of my face.

Sam didn't say anything, nor did he try to take my hand back.

I wasn't sure how I felt about that.

I took out my phone and called Bradley.

"Hey, Chief."

"You at 3MB?" I asked.

"Sitting in my office."

"Good. I want a full briefing on everything we know about prostitution in Starling."

"Sure. By when?"

I glanced at my watch. "I'll be there in fifteen minutes."

A pregnant pause.

I wasn't usually so abrupt with Bradley. He's a good guy, easy to deal with, and he'd been an excellent second in command so far.

"Uh, Patterson's been working on something," he finally said, somewhat hesitantly. "Checking out that organization that's helping women get out of the life. The info on them is sketchy. There are actually a half dozen independent groups, in various cities around the state. They stay in touch with each other, though. Kind of a loose network."

"Good," I said, my tone still more clipped than I'd intended. "I'll get his briefing first, then yours."

"Sure, Chief." His voice had reverted to its normal good-natured tone. "See you soon."

I disconnected and sat silently, trying to figure out why I was suddenly in such a foul mood. Was it revisiting Caroline Baumann's crime scene, reconstructing her last hours on earth? Or knowing now that her death was more personal for Sam, that the woman had once meant something to him?

After a moment, I decided it was both, and neither—it had more to do with me not knowing about a major human trafficking ring operating in my city. Not until the JSO and the FDLE pointed it out. And they were still keeping me out of the loop, dammit to hell!

I should've asked for that briefing yesterday. Hell, I should've asked for it weeks ago, when I'd first started as chief. Had I been assuming that a small Southern city couldn't harbor such evil? Its crime statistics—much lower than Baltimore's—had fed into that assumption.

When you assume, you make an ass out of you and me. My cousin Paulie's favorite saying.

The evil might exist on a smaller scale, but it was still there.

I was mentally beating myself up for my naivete, when Sam looked over at me. "I like your watch."

Startled, I blinked, then stared down at the man-sized silvertone watch—big face, big numbers, analog, not digital. I'd had to have several links removed from the wristband. "Thanks. I like to be able to read the time at a glance."

He shifted his gaze my way again, his eyes warm, one end of his mouth quirked up. "It suits you."

"You don't think it's too manly?" I blurted out.

"Nah." His left hand on the steering wheel, he tugged the cuff of his shirt back from that wrist. "This is a manly watch." He wore a black sports watch. "Yours is attractive, but practical, no nonsense. Just like you."

Heat flushed my cheeks and I found myself smiling. I eyed him out of the corner of my eye.

His gaze was back on the road, but he was smiling too.

His right hand was now back in his favorite position while driving—on the knob of the gear shift in front of the console between us. His elbow rested on the top of that console.

Not giving myself time to lose my nerve, I took that hand in mine, gave it a squeeze, and let it go again.

His smile expanded into a grin.

A few minutes later, Sam dropped me in front of the municipal building. "I'll call you later."

"Yeah, good." I suddenly felt like I was fifteen.

This is why I don't date. Most men weren't worth the stress. But maybe Sheriff Sam was.

I gave him a small smile.

He smiled back and drove off.

On the third floor, Patterson was waiting outside my office door, and Bradley was hoofing it across the bullpen to get there before I did.

A subtle warmth spread through me, a sense of...what? But I didn't have time to analyze it now.

"I wish I could've found more on these people," Patterson was saying, as I unlocked my door.

I gestured with my head for Barnes to join us.

"Well," Bradley said, trailing in behind his sister, "they're intentionally hiding what they're trying to do."

Patterson eyed the comfortable visitor's chair but took one of the others. Smart move.

Bradley scooted past Barnes to grab the comfy one. She gave him the evil eye, and he chuckled under his breath. Barnes leaned her butt against the closed door, pad in hand.

I ignored their antics as I settled behind my desk.

"Most of the groups don't even have official names," Patterson continued, perched on the front edge of his chair. "They're referred to as Mary's group or Linda's group. No websites or other online presence. Email accounts are gmail or yahoo or such. And the few phone numbers I could find, none were registered with any phone companies."

"So they're burners," Bradley said.

I nodded. All that made sense. They were keeping as low a profile as possible.

"Starling's group, the Magdalene Repurposing Center, is an LLC," Patterson said.

I sat up straighter in my desk chair. "Not a nonprofit?"

Patterson shook his head. "Sole proprietorship, in Mary Striker's name. Only employees are her husband and a Nancy Owen. It makes a small profit each year, but no indication where its income is coming from. Mary Striker does not draw a salary, but her husband does, a small one, thirty-thousand a year."

"Cruthers had said she's got money from her first husband," Bradley reminded me. "And nonprofits are regulated, have to file paperwork with the government, meet certain requirements."

"She doesn't want that paper trail," Barnes said.

"Nor the oversight." I turned back to Patterson. "How else do the women find them, besides phone numbers on soap in ladies' rooms?"

"Best I can tell, they're not affiliated with the national human trafficking hotline," he said. "But I remembered seeing a flyer on a community bulletin board at a convenience store last week. It piqued my interest because of its vagueness. It just said 'In Trouble? Need Help? Call Us.' And it had the little slips across the bottom to pull off with phone numbers on them.

"So I went back there and pulled one off. It was a different number than the one on the soap. I called it and told the woman who answered that I'd been arrested for a DWI and needed a lawyer. She gave me the number for Legal Aid but she was rather brusque about it."

He leaned even farther forward. "Then I got Officer Peters to call and pretend to be a teenage runaway who'd been approached at the bus station by some creepy guy offering her work. This time the person who answered was very patient and gentle."

"They keep the offer of help generic," I said, "so the pimps are less likely to catch on, and people asking for other kinds of help are referred elsewhere. Nice initiative, Patterson."

Indeed, it was the *only* initiative I'd seen him take since I'd been chief. He nodded but didn't smile.

"Speaking of creepy men at the bus station," Bradley said, "there are three suspected prostitution operations in Starling, run by these guys." He stood and laid out three photos along the edge of my desk. "No record of this Butler fella being associated with any of them."

I scanned the photos. One was a mug shot. The others were a little fuzzy. Head shots blown up from other photos, perhaps.

"This one." Bradley tapped the mug shot. "He's your traditional pimp. Drives around town in a white caddie, wears expensive clothes. All of his girls are streetwalkers. They have their own rooms in dive motels or cheap apartment buildings. He pays their rent and basic expenses, keeps them supplied with drugs, and he keeps most of what they make. His girls get arrested on a fairly regular basis, and we've nabbed him a couple of times, but he's got a good lawyer."

Bradley gestured toward the other two photos. "These guys, we think they're running escort services but they're much more discreet. They've been seen escorting young women to hotels or houses around town. But when one of our people approaches them, the guy says they're on a date and the woman backs him up, although the women usually look nervous. I couldn't find any records of where these guys or the women live."

"Our department's never run an operation on them?" I asked, incredulous. "A sting maybe?"

Bradley shook his head. "Not since I've been here, and I did a quick check of our records. Nothing has ever really been done about them, best I can tell."

I glanced at Patterson, raised my eyebrows. He'd been with the department a few years longer than Bradley. But he shook his head as well, then quickly looked away.

I resisted the urge to roll my eyes. My predecessor had been a lazy s.o.b., but this was a pretty severe dereliction of duty, even for him.

Yeah, prostitution was the oldest profession and would probably always be with us, but cops were supposed to at least *try* to combat it.

Barnes stepped over beside her brother and tapped one of the fuzzy photos. "This guy looks familiar."

"Yes, he does," I said, but I couldn't place him.

She took out her phone and scrolled for a few seconds, then held it up. It was the computer drawing that Donna Glaser had made, with Derek's help, of the man she'd seen watching Tatiana's comings and goings. It looked like the same guy.

"Take a photo array to Glaser's place," I said to Patterson. "See if she can pick him out."

He rose from his chair.

As he exited my office, I said to Bradley, "Not sure when will be the best timing, but we're gonna do a sting and round up these guys."

He nodded and left, Barnes trailing out after him.

Not sure when will be the best timing... Why was I unsure about that? It wasn't like me to be wishy-washy.

My inclination was to start setting it up right now. I should coordinate it with Jacksonville's Sheriff's Office, though. I reached for my phone, and my hand stopped midway.

That was the problem. JSO and the FDLE were in the middle of this big operation to bring down the statewide trafficking network. If we did a sting right now, we could unwittingly screw that up.

My mind flashed to the FDLE agent, Grant, who'd practically accosted me in front of my own building. I did not want to be in a one-down position in an argument with him.

But why wasn't I in the loop regarding their investigation?

They sure as hell wouldn't have left the chief of police of, say, Starke, out in the cold. The *male* CoP of Starke! Or even Sheriff Sam if the operation affected his small rural county.

How was I supposed to run my department without knowing what's going down in the neighboring jurisdictions that might affect us?

Ah, that was the crux of it. I thought I was in control now. The top of the heap, queen of the mountain. *Ha!* Not if I'm going to be shoved aside and ignored by the *men*.

"Damn it!" I slapped the desktop. Enough whining that the boys won't let me play in their sandbox. Time to pull up my big girl pants and find out what the hell's going on.

Barnes appeared in my office doorway. "You said something, Chief?"

"No...Yes, get me a face-to-face asap with the head of the Jacksonville FDLE regional office."

"On it." She disappeared from the doorway.

CHAPTER
FOURTEEN

I turned to the computer on my desk that I'd inherited from my predecessor, John Black, and opened the folder that contained his old document files. I was hoping to find some explanation for why he'd essentially ignored the trafficking operations right under his nose.

Once again I cursed the man for the lack of any true orientation to the job. He'd spent less than a day with me, supposedly showing me the ropes, but mostly he'd bragged about all his alleged accomplishments.

His records were not very organized, and he had a tendency to give folders cute two-word labels. At least, *he* probably thought they were cute.

I skimmed through the folder names, trying to guess what might be in them. My gaze landed on *Big Cojones.* I clicked on it, expecting to find password-protected files.

But the folder was empty.

Hmmm...

I clicked on a few other folders. Some had mundane documents in them, about budgets and personnel matters. But several were empty.

Black created folders that he never used?

Yeah, no. I was pretty sure he had used them, but had deleted the files before his retirement.

I called Derek the Geek.

"Hey, Chief," he answered cheerfully.

"Hi, Derek. Can you retrieve files that have been deleted from my computer?"

"Sure. What'd you accidentally erase?"

"Nothing. I think there are some older files that got deleted before I arrived. I'm curious to see what's in them."

"If the hard drive wasn't reformatted, they should still be retrievable. You want me to come look at it now?"

"Yes, if you're not in the middle of anything important."

He chuckled. "Very little is more important than keeping the chief happy."

"What's going on with the tire tracks?"

"FDLE impounded Butler's car and towed it from that restaurant's parking lot. I called over there and they checked. His tires are not new. Officer Dulles is calling tire stores in town, gathering a list of people who have bought the brand we're looking for in the past two months." He paused for a beat. "But it's gonna be a long list."

I sighed. "Are you needed to help with that?"

"Not at the moment."

"Okay, then, come on over."

I walked out to Barnes's desk to tell her that Derek was on his way and she should let him into my office.

"You have a meeting in half an hour with Dorothy Wilder, acting Special Agent in Charge at the FDLE's Jacksonville Regional Operations Center."

"Great. I'm afraid I'm going to have to leave you out of this pow-wow."

Barnes smiled. "I expected that. I've got some paperwork to clean up." Her eyes darted away from my face. "And I was going to drop by your place and check on the kitten."

I blew out air. "I wish you'd put that energy into finding her a permanent home."

"Uh, I'm working on it, Chief."

Sure you are. She still wasn't quite making eye contact. She was such a lousy liar.

But I let it slide.

———————◆———————

As her assistant ushered me into her office, acting Special Agent in Charge Dorothy Wilder stepped around her desk, hand extended. She was tall and thin, blue-eyed and blonde, about my age, and dressed in a well-tailored skirted suit. "Chief Anderson, it's a pleasure to meet you. I apologize for not reaching out sooner to welcome you to Florida."

I shook her hand. "No problem. I'm sure you've had your hands full with your own transition."

I'd read up on Wilder briefly, before heading for Jacksonville and this meeting. She'd become the acting director of the regional center about the same time I'd started in Starling, also after the retirement of her predecessor—although I suspected he had not set her up for failure as mine had.

"Call me Dot." She gestured toward a well-padded visitor's chair.

"And I'm Judith." I took my seat as she returned to behind her desk. "I wish this was just a social call, but I'm here about the trafficking case."

"Yes, how is that going on your end?"

"Well now, I wish I knew. Someone seemed to forget to read me in."

Her face registered shock. It looked genuine. But she could be a good actor. "What are you saying?"

"First I heard about it was when the FDLE blocked a routine fingerprint search in our homicide case."

"What?" Her tone was sharp. I wasn't sure if that sharpness was directed at me or the situation.

"We managed," I continued, my own tone a little acidic, "to identify the fingerprint another way. But then I was warned off from attempting to interrogate the suspect again."

Something flashed in her eyes. "Warned off by whom?"

"One of your men." I'd intentionally said *men*, not *people*. I'd give her that much of a hint to help her narrow it down.

Another flash in her eyes. Her mouth flattened into a grim line. "I can make an educated guess, but I'd appreciate it if you would tell me who it was."

Pretty sure now that the anger wasn't aimed at me, I leaned forward. "Special Agent Grant. He drove all the way over to Starling to deliver the message in person."

"That son of a–" She caught herself, and I decided in that moment that I liked her.

"Hang on a sec." She grabbed her desk phone and punched in a number. "Agent Wellbourne, are you in the building?...Good. Are you alone?"

A pause. "It seems you and your partner neglected to inform the chief of Starling's PD about your operation."

A long pause, faint screeching noises leaking from the phone receiver against her ear. Dot Wilder winced. "Well, she's in my office now. Why don't you come up and fill her in?"

She hung up the receiver. "She'll be right up." Then she shot me a bright smile that lit up her somewhat plain face.

I flashed to Rose Hernandez, an acquaintance in Maryland...well, maybe a friend. She had that kind of smile, one that could stop traffic, especially if the traffic was male.

Dot and I chit-chatted for a few minutes. Not usually an activity I'm fond of, but in this case I was enjoying getting to know this woman.

"So you go by Judith?" she said.

"Yes, ever since second grade. Tommy Sanderson called me Punch and Judy and punched my arm."

"What did you do?" she asked, a half-smile forming.

"I bloodied his nose. Had to sit in the corner for a week, but nobody called me Judy again."

Dot threw back her head and laughed.

The door flew open and a young, light-skinned African-American woman rushed in. Her hair was reddish brown, hanging in thin corkscrew curls to just below her ears.

Dot and I had both turned toward her, smiles lingering on our faces.

That seemed to stop her onward rush. She screeched to a halt, anxiety morphing into confusion on her freckled face. "I'm not in trouble?" she blurted out.

"That depends. Close the door, Wellbourne." Dot gestured toward me. "This is Chief of Police Anderson, from Starling."

I held out a hand. "Pleased to meet you."

Wellbourne took the hand by its fingertips and gave it one quick up and down, then let go. I decided not to hold the wimpy handshake against her. It was obvious she was a green agent, and young.

Dot stood. "I never had lunch. I'm going to get something now. You two use my office so you have some privacy." She pointed at Wellbourne. "Tell her everything."

As she headed for the door, she said over her shoulder, "A real pleasure meeting you, Judith. We should get together soon, maybe over lunch."

I smiled. "I'd like that." And I was surprised to realize that was true.

I turned back to Wellbourne as the door closed. "Sit and fill me in." I gestured toward the other visitor's chair.

She tentatively perched on the edge of the seat.

<hr>

I was seething inside as I drove back to Starling. I'd kept my feelings under wraps in front of Wellbourne. It wasn't her fault.

But the operation to bring down the trafficking network had been in the works for months, long before I'd started as chief in Starling. I wasn't surprised that Black hadn't filled me in. But why hadn't anyone else, like Foster?

Had Bradley known about it? Probably not. He was not high on Black's good buddy list.

Wellbourne had implied it was an oversight, caused by the changes in leadership at both the FDLE office and in Starling. Informing me of the operation had somehow fallen through the cracks, she'd claimed.

But Special Agent Grant confronting me in front of my own building, telling me to butt out—*that* was no oversight.

My phone rang. *Derek* popped up on my dashboard screen.

I accepted the call.

"Uh, Chief, are you still in Jacksonville?" His tone was distinctly nervous.

"No, I'm on my way back. What's up?"

My phone beeped, indicating another call coming in. I ignored it.

I, um," Derek stammered, "I'd rather not say over the phone, but I...uh, did what you asked. And I have some stuff to report on...when you get back."

In my current mood, I was sorely tempted to snap at him to spit it out, but I didn't. No need to take my anger out on an innocent party, even if he was being annoyingly vague. "I'll be there in fifteen minutes."

"Good, uh, I'll be waiting in your office."

I disconnected, wondering what he'd found that had him so spooked.

New message came up on my Bluetooth screen, followed by *Detective Foster–JSO.*

"Play message," I instructed, while thinking, *You've got a lot of 'splainin' to do, Detective.*

"Chief, it's Foster. I just got off the phone with Wellbourne." His voice was tense. "*Please* call me, *before* you talk to anyone else."

I took the next right turn off of Route 301 and pulled into a convenience store's parking area. I threw the car into park and punched the *return call* button.

He picked up on the first ring. "Chief, thank God–"

"This better be good, Foster."

"Wilder's predecessor intentionally left Chief Black in the dark," his words rushed out, "because we suspected he was taking bribes from Butler to look the other way."

I fell back in the driver's seat, the angry pressure in my chest deflating.

"There's more," Foster said, slower and grimmer. "There are indications that others in your department might have been involved."

I shook my head. Now I had a pretty good hunch regarding what Derek had found on my computer, and why it was making him so nervous.

Back at 3MB, I strode across the bullpen. "Requisition a new desktop computer for me, asap," I said to Barnes as I passed her desk.

Her eyes went wide. "Right away, Chief."

My office door was slightly ajar. Derek sat behind my desk, beads of sweat on his forehead. He'd closed all the blinds.

After closing the door behind me, I shooed him out of my chair. He started around the desk.

"No. Stand right here." I pointed to the floor next to my chair.

I unlocked the desk drawer that held my laptop, hauled it out. "I need you to witness which files I'm transferring."

I connected the two computers, called up my own files on the desktop, pointed to one. He took out his phone. "Okay if I take a video?"

"Good idea." I copied and pasted that file to the laptop, then continued the process for the rest of my files.

I pointed to two folders on the list, labeled *Personnel* and *Budget and Expenses.* "These two are confidential." After I copied and pasted, I deleted them from the desktop.

"Okay, how do I make those two files go away completely from this computer?"

Derek gestured toward my chair. "May I?"

I traded places with him.

He hit a dozen keys. "They're gone completely from the desktop now."

"Good." I pulled a large evidence bag out of my bottom desk drawer, then buzzed Barnes to bring me the biggest plastic bag, opaque, that she could find. I didn't particularly want to announce to the bullpen that my computer was being taken into evidence.

To Derek, I said, "Show me what you found. Then take this computer down to your office and make sure you've found *every* one of his deleted files. *Then* take it to the evidence room."

He gave me a forlorn look and pointed to a pile of papers on the corner of my desk. "I printed out what I found."

He helped me slide the desktop's hard drive into the evidence envelope, and then into the large PetSmart bag Barnes brought in.

My stomach growled.

Barnes smiled. "I'd put the rest of your sandwich in the break room's fridge. I'll get it for you."

Awkwardly cradling the bulky package in his arms, Derek said, "You want an update on the tire search, Chief?"

"Of course."

"Officer Dulles has a list of 218 people who have bought those tires in the last two months in Starling. He's checking them for criminal records."

"Thanks," I said, while thinking we were looking for a needle in a haystack. If we didn't find it in Starling, should we expand the search to include Jax? That would be one hell of a big haystack.

Derek left, and I slid into my desk chair, picked up the pile of paper.

My stomach turned queasy as I read. The half sandwich Barnes brought in remained untouched.

There were copies of saved emails, sent to and received from an aol address for a C.B. Nothing too specific, but they implied that bribes had been paid out to Black, some of which were passed on to others.

There were also copies of random incident reports. Some noise complaints that were marked resolved, and several arrests for suspected solicitation where charges had been dropped. But the names of the respond-ing officers had been blacked out.

Why had he kept all these at all? As insurance maybe, in case C.B.—no doubt, Conrad Butler—turned on him. But what would he do with them? Claim he'd been building a case against Butler, maybe?

I flipped to the next page.

Cruthers suddenly filled my doorway. My already unhappy stomach heaved at the ashen tone of his face.

"Donna Glaser and an unidentified man were brought into the ER." His voice was rushed, anxious. "Both unconscious, no ID on the man. They were found in her apartment after a neighbor called in about suspicious noises. When they'd cleaned up the man's face some, an ER doc recognized him..."

Guilt squeezed my chest. I knew what he was about to say, and I'd sent the detective to Glaser, with a photo lineup.

Cruthers had paused to suck in air. "It's Patterson."

CHAPTER FIFTEEN

The young and harried ER doc's report was succinct, straightforward, and not without sympathy. "Your detective suffered blunt force trauma to the side of his head. He's still pretty groggy. We're doing a CT-scan and we'll know more after we have those results."

The doc paused. "He's lucky though. If the blow had been half an inch over, it would've hit his temple and could've killed him."

"When's he likely to be coherent?" I asked.

"Not sure, but we're keeping him at least overnight, and he needs *total rest*." He came down hard on the last two words. That and the glint in his eye said we weren't getting in to question Patterson anytime soon.

I clenched my teeth to keep the swear words in my brain from leaking out.

"And Ms. Glaser?" Cruthers asked.

The young doc's expression shifted to anxious. "I'm not sure if I can tell you about her condition. You know, HIPPA rules and all that."

I clenched my teeth again, counted to five—no time to make it to ten. "She's the victim of a violent crime. You're gonna make me get a *court order* for her records?" My tone was a carefully calculated blend of incredulous and pissed as hell.

The doc sighed. "Even though she was beat up worse than the detective, she didn't have as much head trauma. She's awake now. But..."

"But what?"

"She has a broken jaw. She can't talk."

"We'll take awake," I said. "We need to see her."

The doc hesitated, then nodded. "But just for a few minutes. She also needs rest."

A nurse showed us the way to Glaser's room. She looked like hell, but her eyes brightened when we entered. She had the head of her bed raised and was propped up farther with pillows.

A nurse had thoughtfully provided her with a pad and pen, so she could communicate. But her right arm was in a sling, the left side of her face one big swollen bruise. A large gauze bandage was taped over her jaw.

Cruthers hung back as I stepped forward. "Hope they've got you on some good painkillers," I said.

She scribbled on the pad. I leaned over and read, *Better living through chemistry. Fortunately, I'm left-handed.*

My chest warmed. This woman had spunk.

"Did you recognize your attacker?" I asked.

She started to shake her head, winced. *No,* she wrote.

"Not the guy you saw watching Tatiana then?"

No. Taller.

Cruthers had walked around the bed to see the pad from the other side. "How tall?" he asked.

At least 6 foot. Wore a ski mask.

Damn! "Race?"

Not sure. Brown eyes. Skin around them whitish. Gloves, but saw his wrist. More a beige color.

I scrolled through pics on my phone, found the mug shot of the possible hit man, whom the judge had so graciously allowed back on the street. He was far swarthier than *beige*, but to be thorough I held it out for her to see. "This guy?"

She started to shake her head, caught herself. *No,* she wrote on the pad.

Great! I thought. *We have yet another evil dude out there, wreaking havoc.*

Is Alejandro okay? Donna wrote. *The guy was trying to find out where he is.* She looked up at me, fear in her eyes.

"You didn't tell him anything?" I tried to keep my tone neutral, but the words came out slightly rushed.

Of course not, she wrote.

I gently patted her left shoulder. "We have Alejandro and his foster family under police protection."

Although I was no longer sure that one cruiser sitting in front of their house would be enough. We probably needed to get them into a safe house.

"What happened, ma'am?" Cruthers asked.

I was watching TV. Door burst open. I jumped up but then froze for a sec. He locked the door. I took off for the fire escape but he caught me, told me he wouldn't hurt me if I told him where Alejandro was.

Her handwriting was deteriorating as she scribbled.

"It's okay," I said. "Take your time."

She took a deep breath, shuddered, then winced. *He hit me several times,* she wrote, a little clearer. *I was struggling to get away. Then the other man kicked the door in. Ski-mask guy hit him. And I passed out.*

Donna drew something on her pad and scribbled some words above it. She held it up for me to see.

He was hitting us with this.

The line drawing resembled a canoe paddle, an oval that was thinner on one end than the other.

Cruthers squinted at the pad. "Some kind of club?"

Donna closed her eyes, her face tense. She took in a long, slow breath. Then her eyes opened and she wrote, *No. Maybe a foot long. Black leather. Something hard inside.*

"A blackjack?" Cruthers said, at the same time as I said, "A sap!"

I flashed to the *parallel contusions* in the autopsy reports on Tatiana and Caroline. A sap, leather tightly wrapped around packed sand or metal pellets to make an incredibly painful weapon—it would definitely leave railroad-track bruises like that. And some were stitched along the sides, which could be what caused the scalloped edge on the bruises.

Also called blackjacks, saps had once been standard equipment on a police officer's duty belt. Now they were banned in most departments, because they could easily do more damage than intended. They'd been replaced by extendable metal batons.

A sap might be the weapon of choice of our alleged hit man. The injuries it caused could easily be mistaken for those incurred in a fall.

I turned my attention back to Donna, intending to ask her if she could tell us more about her assailant. But her head was drooping to one side, eyelids fluttering at half-mast.

A nurse bustled in.

"Don't worry," I whispered. "We're leaving." I gently lifted the pad from Donna's lap and tore off the top page, with the picture of the weapon.

<hr />

Once back in Cruthers's car, I called the watch desk.

"Sergeant Lewis." His tone was clipped. The other sergeants immediately acknowledged me with *Chief* since my name appeared on their caller ID. But not Lewis. I suspected he wasn't too happy that I *was* the Chief. Well, I wasn't too happy with him either.

"Sarge, I need two more people on Ada Johns's house. One in front, one in back, one inside."

"I don't have that kind of personnel to spare," he said, then belatedly added, "Chief."

I counted to five. "Pull them off patrol for now, then contact the off-duty officers. Pull three in and identify any others who are willing to work overtime today."

My inner accountant winced, but the overtime budget would just have to be stretched to cover this. I wasn't letting anyone else get hurt, or worse.

"That's still—"

I cut him off. "If need be, call up the auxiliary folks for minor calls."

"What do you consider minor?" again the slight delay before, "Chief."

I ground my teeth. "Cats in trees, loud music, minor car accidents...And I'll need one other officer. Have him or her report to my office in half an hour."

I disconnected before Lewis could object again.

Cruthers's phone rang and *Collins* flashed on his dashboard screen. "He's working the case now," Cruthers said. "He skipped the second day of that training to help out."

I groaned inside. I would be hearing about that from the brass. Collins had recently been promoted to detective and was in the middle of a two-day mandatory training that covered all things cops weren't supposed to be doing these days, such as sexual harassment and racial profiling.

While I understood and agreed that the training was necessary, I also secretly sympathized with the cops who tried to get out of it. Collins was no doubt ecstatic that we had a big case, requiring all hands on deck.

Wait a minute! Who's going to get on me about him skipping the workshop? I'm *"the brass"* now.

It was a state requirement, but somehow I didn't see Dot Wilder bawling me out over half a workshop. I'd get him into the thing again, next time it was offered. And as punishment for skipping out on it without my permission, I'd make him take the first day over again.

I chuckled softly to myself.

Cruthers had accepted the call and he and Collins had exchanged greetings. "The chief is with me," Cruthers said.

"Hey, Chief," Collins's cheerful voice rang out from the speaker. "I'm making headway on locating the boy's dad. There are three villages near the place where Tatiana most likely crossed the Rio Grande. Well, there are more than three, but you said the victim had implied her husband was an important man. These three towns have some rich people living in or near them."

"We're not sure it's her husband she was running from," I pointed out. "It could've been her employer, or boyfriend. See if any of the rich people are missing any members of their households, including employees. And good work, Collins."

"Thanks, Chief." He disconnected.

Back at 3MB, I stopped to check in with my second in command. "Did Pirolnik agree to protection?"

Bradley pushed back from his desk and looked up at me, standing in his doorway. He sighed. "He did, but Sergeant Lewis informed me he couldn't spare anyone else for protection duty."

Oh he did, did he?

"I wasn't sure how to respond to that," Bradley continued, "since he and I are technically the same rank."

"Let it slide, *this* time. I already have a solution." More like a work-around, but I shouldn't have to "work around" my own watch commanders. I gestured toward the paperwork on Bradley's desk. "When you come to a good stopping point in whatever you're doing, come over to my office."

Cruthers had wandered off to talk to Collins, who was at his desk in the bullpen, squinting at his computer screen.

Barnes followed me into my office. She plopped down in the comfy visitor's chair.

I filled her in on Patterson's condition and the interview with Donna Glaser, then told her we were adding protection for Ada Johns's family and for Gabe Pirolnik.

"I'm going to need you to help out with him." I paused. "Where'd you get such a big bag from PetSmart?"

She blinked, caught off guard by the abrupt topic change. Which had been my intention.

"Um, I bought some things for the cat."

"What *things*?"

"Some toys."

My eyebrows shot up. "Toys for a two-pound kitten required a bag that big?"

"Well, I got her a scratching post too."

I sat back in my chair. I had to admit, that was a good idea. Once I was sure she would only scratch the post, not my furniture, I could let her out in the rest of the apartment.

"Why does a cat need toys?" I asked.

"Because she's a baby cat," Barnes said, with exaggerated patience. "A child, and children need toys."

"Uh, huh." I watched her for a beat. Something was off. But what? "Well, thanks for getting those things. How much do I owe you?"

"Nothing. You're, um, doing me a favor to keep her."

"Temporarily," I reminded her.

"Sure, Chief."

A high school student in an SPD uniform appeared in my doorway, stood at attention. "You, uh, wanted to see me, Chief?" His voice cracked a little. He cleared his throat.

It took me a moment to realize this was the officer that Sergeant Lewis had sent me. "How long have you been with us, Officer...?"

"Thompson, sir, I mean ma'am, I mean..."

"Just call me Chief."

"Right, uh, Chief. I've been on the force two months." He proudly threw his shoulders back even farther than they had been.

"At ease, Thompson, before you dislocate something."

He shifted into parade-rest position, which wasn't exactly at ease.

"I have a protection assignment for you. Are you available 24/7 for the next few days? You'll get overtime pay, of course."

"Yes, ma'am. Uh, I mean Chief." The shoulders went back again.

"Officer Barnes here is going to take you to the assignment, introduce you to the person you will be protecting. You are not to allow anyone but me, Barnes, or Detective Bradley into his apartment, no matter what they tell you. And you are not to tell anyone, not even the watch commander, what your assignment is or the address of said assignment. Is that clear?"

"Yes, ma'am, Chief."

"Good. Dismissed."

Barnes started to follow him out.

I said, "Hang on a sec, Gloria."

Her shoulders tensed and she turned slowly, a touch of apprehension on her face.

"Are you okay with doing night duty at Pirolnik's place? You and the rookie take turns sleeping for a few hours each." I figured if I was shelling out overtime pay, Barnes should get some of it.

The relief on her face was unmistakable. "Sure, no problem." She turned and hustled after Officer Thompson.

What the hell is she up to?

I shook my head, then using my private line, I called Dot Wilder's office. Her assistant informed me she was gone for the day. "Can I help?"

"Maybe. Does FDLE have safe houses in this area?" I asked.

"Yes, ma'am."

"Could I borrow one?"

"Is this related to the trafficking case? Because Special Agent Wilder said we were to give you full cooperation with that."

"Well, maybe. We're not sure yet if the cases are related."

"Good enough for me. Hang on." Keyboard keys clicking. "The nearest one available is in Clover County. Sheriff Pierson has a key to it. Have you met him yet?"

I swallowed a chuckle. "Yes, I have."

"I've assigned it to you for a week. Is that long enough?"

"Should be. Thanks." I disconnected and called Sam's cell number, explained my need for the safe house.

"Stop by the department and get the keys from the front desk...Hey, I was about to call you."

"Oh yeah," I said in a softer voice.

"Yeah, but it's business, not pleasure, sadly. You familiar with the Clover Sinkhole?"

"No, afraid not."

"It's in the northern part of the county. Fenced off, but kids still get in there and like to poke around. Two of them found a body, at the bottom of a dropoff. Guess who?"

Several flip answers came to mind. I didn't say any of them.

After a beat, he said, "It's Pedro Juarez, that guy we caught beating up your video game genius."

A gasp escaped before I could catch it. "What the hell is he doing way out there? He didn't strike me as the hiker type."

"Me neither, and most people don't take hikes in a business suit."

CHAPTER SIXTEEN

I was torn.

I really wanted to get Alejandro and Ada Johns's family into that safe house. But I also really wanted to get to Sam's crime scene and see the body *in situ* before the ME's people moved it. And before it got dark.

Cruthers was on his way to check out Donna Glaser's apartment and reconstruct what went down there.

We've got a few too many crime scenes at the moment.

Hell. We've got a few too many crimes *at the moment!* And it was looking more and more like they were all related, to some degree.

Well, I needed to get the key to the safe house anyway, so might as well head for Clover County. I'd call Jenny Coleman at DCF on the way and get things rolling on her end.

I retrieved Derek's printouts, which I'd locked in my desk earlier, and stuffed them in my laptop case. They were going with me.

Bradley was coming into the bullpen as I was going out. "You busy at the moment?" I asked.

"Nothing that can't wait."

"Come with me then, and can you drive? I need to make some calls."

We swung by my car so I could retrieve the sneakers I keep in my trunk—much better for climbing around sinkholes than my low-heeled pumps.

Once in Bradley's car, I called Jenny Coleman. After explaining the situation, I asked, "Can you convince Ada to go into the safe house?"

"Maybe. She's hypersensitive about anything that disrupts the kids' routines."

"As she should be, but they are in real danger."

"My guess is she'll want to leave the other kids with her husband and go with Alejandro to the safe house."

I stifled a groan. "Jenny, I would still have to have protection on the rest of the family then. And my department is getting stretched thin. I need some of my cops left to actually solve the case so everybody can get back to normal."

"You think the threat is that great?"

I sighed. "Keep all this to yourself please, but the guy who's looking for Alejandro beat up Mr. Pirolnik last night. We now have protection on him as well."

Jenny sucked in air. "Is he okay?"

"Yeah, he held his own, and we caught that guy. Unfortunately, a judge granted him bail." I left out the part that he was now dead. "And this afternoon, someone else beat up a sixty-four-year-old retired teacher and attacked my detective when he came to the rescue."

Why is it that our people are showing up just after these guys get there? I asked myself.

Because they're one step ahead of us, that's why!

"Are they okay?" Jenny was saying.

"Not okay, but they'll both recover."

"I'll talk to Ada right away. I may even go over there and help her pack."

"To convince her the whole family has to go, you might point out that whoever's looking for the boy will be more than willing to harm her husband and the other kids to get answers."

I signed off and turned to Bradley to tackle the real reason I'd asked him along. "We've got a new development regarding the former chief." I had decided that I needed to trust him. He'd never been in Black's inner circle, and I needed at least one ally inside the department.

I filled him in on what I'd found in Derek's printouts so far, finishing with, "I've got another ten pages to go, but there's definitely enough there to show he was corrupt. And several places that imply there were others in the department in on it."

"Want me to make some educated guesses about who was in on it in our house?"

"Nope, 'cause I'm probably thinking the same people, but let's not jump to conclusions." I pulled the papers out of my laptop case. "I'm going to sit here quietly and read while you drive. Then on the way back, if you're okay with me driving your car, you can read these for yourself."

"Sounds like a plan," Bradley said, his voice and face grim as he stared out the windshield.

It was a great place to dump a body.

Juarez was on his back, and even from the top of the cliff, I could tell that his eyes were open, staring unseeing at the sky. If not for two inquisitive boys—standing nearby with a woman, most likely the mom of one or both of them—the critters in the surrounding woods would have made short work of the corpse within days, leaving little behind but remnants of clothing and a few bones.

Sam's solo crime scene tech and a couple of deputies were in the ravine created by the sinkhole. The former was taking pictures, the other two carefully crisscrossing the ground, heads down, scanning for evidence.

A portable ladder, made of chains and metal steps, dangled over the side of the drop-off. It was anchored to a nearby live oak's three-foot wide trunk and was certainly sturdy enough. Still, my stomach tensed at the idea of climbing down it.

"Only other alternative," Sam said from beside me, "is a one-mile hike along the ridge to where the ground slopes up. There's a trail there. That's how the boys got in and out."

In office clothes, the idea of a two-mile hike, round trip, was even less appealing than repelling down the cliff on a swaying ladder. And dusk was moving toward dark faster than I wanted it to.

The mom cleared her throat.

Sam glanced her way. "Let me talk to the boys again, so they can go."

Bradley eyed me up and down, frowning. I had remembered to change into my sneakers, so what was he looking at?

"I can go down," he said.

I intentionally returned the up and down scrutiny. Bradley's partner was an accountant, made good money, and they had no kids, so Bradley could afford to spend a good chunk of his own salary on clothing. His gray suit probably cost more than my entire work wardrobe.

Of course, that wasn't saying much. I had a half dozen pantsuits, all black, and a dozen white shirts. Kept decision-making in the morning down to a minimum.

Apparently Bradley had interpreted my silence as agreement. He was taking off his suit jacket. "Should've left this in the car anyway."

"You're not going down." I shed my own jacket and laid it carefully over a tree branch. "I am. Hold onto the top of the ladder to steady it."

He had an odd expression on his face, frowning, with what looked like worry in his eyes.

He and I'd fought off a serial killer together, but I'd never seen that expression before. It pissed me off but now was not the time to analyze it.

Checking that my Glock was secure in its holster at the small of my back, I walked to the spot where the ladder went over the edge. Turning, I knelt, grabbed the chains with my hands, and backed onto the ladder.

Halfway down, the whole thing dropped a couple of inches and sand showered onto my hair. Stomach hollow, heart in my throat, I shook my head and carefully looked up.

Sam's face appeared above me. "Forgot to mention that the edge is unstable," he called down, a slight chuckle in his voice.

I really wanted to give him a middle-finger salute but resisted the urge—one, because there were other people around, and two, because my fingers were currently frozen around the chains of the ladder. I edged downward again.

My right foot hit the ground and I blew out air. Kicking loose of the last rung of the ladder, I turned and surveyed the scene before taking a step toward it.

The tech was now photographing bits of evidence the deputies had flagged, then bagging the items. So far, she had collected a half-dozen cigarette butts and a condom, all of which probably had nothing to do with our corpse.

I was always reluctant to jump to conclusions, but I seriously doubted this guy had come out here for a romantic tryst. He seemed more the cheap-motel-room type.

I took two careful steps, to get a better look. The guy's clothes were twisted some around him and covered in sand and twigs. But his dress shoes were mostly shiny, with no dirt on the soles.

He did not walk here from the road on his own steam.

Rustling in the underbrush to my right. My hand flew to my gun butt.

I recognized the figure emerging along a narrow trail—one of the pathologists from the ME's office. A petite, blue-eyed blonde, she lugged a large medical bag in one hand, and a body bag was folded and tucked under the other arm. A bright pink blouse collar stuck up a little at the neck of her navy coveralls.

She stopped several feet from the body, taking it all in.

"Dr. Krone, right?" I said.

She nodded, her eyes still on the corpse. "Call me Sandy." Her voice was soft.

I let her soak up the scene. After a few moments, I said, "I doubt he's been out here long or the animals would've gotten to him."

"Yeah, but rigor has set in. Lying in the sun would speed that up, though."

Today wasn't particularly hot, but even in November, the Florida sun was intense.

"I'm not seeing any blood," I said.

"There might not be from a fall. All the bleeding could be internal."

I was pretty sure he didn't die from the fall, but I kept my own counsel. She needed to come to her own conclusions.

I said, "He was arraigned in Starling this morning, for assault, and let out on bail."

She glanced at her watch—man-sized like mine—made some notes on a pad. Then she looked up and met my gaze for the first time. "Thus your interest in the case."

I gave her a small smile. "Exactly. I can check the time of his release for you."

"Thanks." She stepped over and crouched next to the body, checked his pockets. "No ID," she said without looking up. "Actually, nothing." She began her in-field examination.

Sandy couldn't be more than mid-thirties but her actions were quick and precise. I trusted that she knew her stuff. Otherwise the elderly doc who oversaw the District Four Medical Examiner's Office in Jacksonville wouldn't have let her come to a crime scene on her own.

By the time she was ready to turn the body over Sam had joined us. He stood beside me, his Stetson wannabe cocked back on his head.

Damn, he looks good. Even with sweat stains on his khaki uniform shirt.

Glancing down at my own clothes, I self-consciously brushed dirt off the front of my blouse.

A soft grunt from Sandy. My head shot up.

About to apologize for fouling even the edge of a crime scene, I stopped, my mouth hanging open.

Dried blood crusted around a wound on the back of the guy's head, a deep rounded impression in his skull that widened out on one end.

Sandy rocked back on her heels. "I doubt he died here and probably not from the fall."

***

Sam was still tied up at the crime scene. Bradley and I swung by his department to pick up the safe house key.

Then, while Bradley drove, I called Barnes to check on Gabriel Pirolnik. "All's quiet here," she reported.

"Ask him something for me," I said. "Did the guy who attacked him use any kind of weapon, other than the gun? If he says no, follow up by specifically asking about a sap or blackjack. People call it different things so make sure he understands what you mean."

"Hang on." Voices in the background. "He says no. No sap, no weapon except the gun, and his fists."

"Thanks." I filled her in on the crime scene we had just left.

"What do you think this means?" she asked.

"Still sorting that out. I'll check in with you later."

I disconnected, and Bradley said, "So, if the guy at the bottom of that sinkhole was our hit man, who killed him, most likely with his own weapon?"

"Good question, and why didn't he use his sap with a big guy like Pirolnik? And then later this afternoon, we've got a different guy, taller and lighter skinned, going after Donna Glaser, with a sap."

"It's pretty confusing," Bradley said. "Maybe Juarez ended up dead because he went after the wrong person, and they got the sap away from him."

My mind flashed to Mary Striker's husband. Could this guy have gone after him? Striker was slender but muscular. Or maybe Juarez went after

Mary, trying to locate Alejandro, and her husband defended her? That was more likely.

"But why would they dump the body instead of calling the police?" I muttered under my breath.

"Pardon?"

"Oh, talking to myself." I shared my shaky theory with him. "I was with Mary and her husband at about the time Juarez was being bailed out. Striker could've ended up in an altercation with him at some point after that, but why dump the body?"

Bradley shook his head. "I can't think of a good reason for that, unless he panicked. The average person, if they accidentally kill someone, even in self-defense, they aren't always thinking straight afterwards."

"Maybe," I said.

"Or," Bradley said, "a completely different scenario. Maybe whoever hired the hit man to take out Tatiana, and find the boy, was unhappy with Juarez's lack of success with the latter. And he showed his ire in a permanent way."

"Then he sends someone else to Donna Glaser's place," I said.

"That fits better."

"But why sic a hit man from the southwest on a Florida call girl?" I paused, scrubbed a hand over my face. We had way too many questions, and not enough answers.

"Who did you talk to out west?" I asked. "We should let them know Juarez is dead and that his weapon of choice was a sap."

"The sap explains the suspicious looking wounds on his victims, that *could* have been caused by a bad fall or a car crash, but..." He pulled up in front of the Clover County Sheriff's Department. "The LEO who was most helpful was the sheriff of Cochise County in Arizona, a Joanna Brady. One of the homicides was in her county. I'll call her and let her fill in the others."

He made the call while I went in to get the safe house key.

I drove on the way back to Starling. Bradley sat in his own passenger seat, speed-reading Derek's twenty-five sheets of retrieved documents. When he'd finished, he grunted softly. "Black doesn't name names but there's definitely references to at least two other members of the department receiving bribes, besides himself."

I said, "The question is who's the second one." We both knew that one of them would have been the lieutenant that Bradley had replaced as second in command. He and Black had been thick as thieves—literally, apparently.

"It's probably easier to eliminate who it isn't," Bradley said. "Most of the uniforms wouldn't have enough clout to make them worth bribing."

"Those who patrolled in an area where a criminal operated might be."

"True. Or maybe a watch commander and/or a detective." Bradley shook his head slowly. "I can't see Cruthers taking bribes."

"Me neither, but I've been a cop long enough to know that people can fool you."

"Yeah." He fell silent, his face sagging as he stared sightlessly out the windshield.

I drove, leaving him to his thoughts. After a moment, I said, "You gave me a funny look as I was about to go down that ladder. What was that about?"

"Oh." He shrugged. "I guess I was a little worried you'd get hurt."

"It was certainly a risk, but I'm not fragile."

He glanced over, one side of his mouth quirked up in a half smile. "Oh, I know that. I watched you take down a killer, while tied up, no less."

"So why the sudden protectiveness?"

"I wasn't being protective," he said, too quickly.

I arched an eyebrow in his direction. "You weren't?"

He was quiet for a couple of beats. Then he ran a hand through his hair. "Speaking of protecting, you will protect those who *aren't* corrupt, won't you?"

Those words surprised me—so much so that I wasn't sure I'd heard him right. "Come again?"

"You've got the backs of the honest cops on the force, right?"

"Of course I do."

Why would you even need to ask that? I kept that offended thought to myself.

"I know that you would. I um..." He looked away, stared out his side window.

I wished I wasn't driving so I could watch his face more closely.

"I think it flashed into my mind," he finally said, "that if something happened to you, I might end up somebody's scapegoat."

"Why?" A niggling worry entered my mind. *Could* he be in on the corruption?

He gave me a surprised look. "Because I'm gay, and not everyone in the department likes me."

"And some resent your rapid climb, even though you've more than earned it."

He smiled at the compliment and fell silent again.

Ten minutes later, as I turned into the municipal parking lot, he said, "Have you told Gloria what's going on?"

"Not yet. I'm not sure if I should. She's pretty good at hiding her thoughts, but she's still a rookie. If she gave something away to the wrong person, even with just a facial expression..." I trailed off.

I did not want my assistant in danger, at least, no more so than a cop normally is. She'd been in jeopardy during the serial killer case, and that had forced me to realize how fond I'd grown of her. "I don't want her getting caught in the middle of something and getting hurt."

"Neither do I," her brother said vehemently.

But then again, would her not knowing make her more vulnerable? I shook my head in frustration as I pulled Bradley's car into a parking space.

CHAPTER SEVENTEEN

It was almost eight by the time I'd gotten Ada Johns and her family, including Alejandro, settled in the safe house in northern Clover County.

Even though I would practically be driving past Sam's house on the way home, I called and begged off from our tentative plan to meet for dinner. "I'm beyond exhausted," I said.

Which was true, but mostly I was kind of spooked by that earlier kiss, not sure where that was going to lead. Wherever that might be, I wanted to be a lot sharper than I was tonight to deal with it appropriately.

We chatted for a few moments, then signed off just as I was passing the turnoff for his place.

What does it say about us that I feel the need to be "sharp" in order to deal with him?

After a moment, a little voice in my head answered me. *It has nothing to do with him. What does it say about you?*

I snorted softly, acknowledging the truth of that.

I was longing for a hot shower, a chilled glass of wine and my soft pillow, but when I got to my apartment a loud, annoyed meow greeted me.

I opened the door of my study, and the kitten bolted out. She raced around the living room twice before scrambling up my pants leg. I reached down to stop her ascent and save my slacks. She bit my thumb.

"Ow!" I yanked my hand back, examined the thumb. She hadn't broken the skin, but still.

I grabbed her, disconnected her gently from the fabric of my pants, and held her up at eye level. "That's a helluva way to greet the person who's going to feed you tonight."

I carried her into the mostly unfurnished study and discovered I would not be feeding her after all. The room was now half full of cat paraphernalia, including a large scratching post, a cat bed, and a black plastic contraption that apparently dispensed both dry food and water as needed. Several cat toys were scattered about.

"Barnes." I shook my head slowly. Then I spotted something on top of the bookcase. A book lay open, with a note resting on top. I sucked in air at the sight of the book's pages. They had been shredded into confetti, no doubt by tiny razor-sharp claws.

"You!" I scowled at the kitten still in my hand and plopped her down on the carpet before I gave into the temptation to strangle her.

She shook herself and strolled over to the feeder. A dainty pink tongue flicked out and lapped up water.

I lifted the book and examined the cover. It was not one of my more treasured ones—the first editions or the books from my childhood—but a hardcover by one of my favorite authors. I'd intended to reread it eventually.

"Grrrr," I said to the kitten, but found myself not as angry as I should be.

She pranced over and rubbed against my pants leg, purring softly.

I sat down cross-legged on the floor and put her on my lap. "What am I going to do with you?"

She looked up at me, with those blue eyes that were way too big for her face, and meowed.

I picked up the note that had fluttered to the floor. Barnes's handwriting.

So sorry, Chief. I'm sure now that she has a scratching post, she won't bother your books again. And I'll pay to replace this one. Please don't be mad at her, she's just a baby. Gloria

Ah, thus Barnes's weird behavior today. I shook my head again and rose, carrying the cat with me to my bedroom.

She watched me from the bed as I shed my clothes and put on my ratty white terrycloth robe. Then we went to the kitchen for my wine.

At bedtime, I wasn't quite sure what to do. If I locked Pipsqueak in the other bedroom, she'd probably howl off and on all night, waking me and the neighbors. In the living room, who knew what she'd get into.

I moved her litter box into my room and closed her in with me, praying I wouldn't regret that decision.

The woman lay on the kitchen floor.

My heart pounded in my chest. Would she get up this time?

She did, rising slowly, her back to me. My throat closed.

But when she turned, it wasn't my mother's face. My stepmother, her expression hurt, whined, "Why did you go behind our backs, Judith?"

A seventeen-year-old me stood frozen, no words coming into my head or out of my mouth. I knew she was referring to my petition for emancipation.

I looked down. Somehow, there was another woman on the floor. She didn't move.

My stepmother stared down at her and cried, "How could you do this to us?"

Hot pressure surged in my chest. This time, words formed. How could she do this to you? Look at what you all did to her!

But when I opened my mouth to yell those words, something else came out instead. A howling sound.

I jolted partway upright. Painful pinpricks punctured my chest, through the oversized tee shirt I sleep in. The kitten hung on, yowled again in my face.

I flopped back onto my pillow. "It's okay, baby." I stroked the soft fur of her back.

She slumped down, the pinpricks subsiding, and purred quietly. After a moment, she belly-crawled forward until she could reach my face with her tongue. It was slightly raspy as she licked my cheeks.

With a jolt, I realized she was licking away tears. She purred louder.

I should put her back on her bed. That was my last thought until morning.

While dressing the next morning, I placed a call, putting my phone on speaker. I was impressed when she answered on the first ring, at seven a.m.

"Special Agent Wellbourne." Her voice sounded so young.

After identifying myself, I said, "I want to come over there to re-interview Butler. Any problem with that?"

"No, ma'am. Special Agent in Charge Wilder said that you should have full access to the investigation's records, witnesses and suspects." She dropped her voice. "By the way, Grant is on leave at the moment."

I smiled at the phone, suspecting it was unpaid leave, as in a suspension. While it was a bad thing to have made an enemy of Grant—although that status was more his doing than mine—it was good to know that Wilder wasn't going to tolerate her agents pushing around the local LEOs.

"I'll be there about eight," I told Wellbourne.

I disconnected and called Barnes. "I'm heading over to Jax to talk to Butler again. Wanna come?"

"Yeah, sure...uh..."

"I found the book, and the note," I said. "And the cat is still alive. Meet me out front at seven-thirty."

As it turned out, the interview was a good training opportunity for Barnes, as she watched from the observation room, but it produced little else, except some clarification of minor details.

Butler still denied that he'd sent anyone to hurt Tatiana or her son. He was a little more forthcoming though, since he'd struck a deal with the State's Attorney's office. Now he was willing to admit that he was her "handler." He rejected the *pimp* label.

"Why would I destroy a valuable asset?" he said again. "If I'd known she was about to run, I would've stopped her, but I wouldn't kill her. That's just plain bad business."

"But you did search her car. How did you know about it?"

For the first time, his eyes darted away briefly. Then they came back to my face, and a slow smile spread across his. "I'm not giving away all my secrets. Let's just say, I got word that night from a member of my staff that a car was on the bridge and it might be hers."

"So you searched it why? To make sure there was nothing in it that would lead back to you?"

"Exactly."

"And to see if you could figure out where the boy was." I made it a statement, not a question, but he shook his head.

"For all I knew, she'd taken the boy with her, had drowned him too." He shrugged. "Besides, he's got no value to me. He was only leverage to keep her under control."

"You took her ID from the car." Again, a statement.

"Nope. Wasn't any in there." His eyes did not flicker at all this time. Either he was telling the truth, or he was being more careful now about what his body language revealed. "My associate and I dumped the glove box, searched the trunk, then wiped down everything we'd touched."

No doubt they'd arrived in the associate's car and said car had brand new tires on it.

"You didn't take anything at all?"

The slightest flicker of his eyes. "Nope."

Pirolnik had said he'd given Tatiana money that night. My guess was Butler had found it in the car and helped himself.

But I doubted I could prove it, and it wasn't all that important now, except maybe to Pirolnik. My mind flashed to his grief-stricken face. No, the money wasn't important to him either.

"You didn't see anything under the driver's seat?" I asked.

"A shoe, but it didn't connect her to me so I left it there."

"What time were you there, at the car?"

"Around five, a little before dawn."

I slid the mug shot of Juarez across the table. "You sure you don't know this guy?"

He glanced at it, shook his head. "Who is he?"

"He's been running around beating on people, trying to find the boy. He went after Gabriël Pirolnik, for one."

Butler's eyes widened some. "Now, *that* I would never order. Mr. Pirolnik is a valued client."

I resisted the urge to point out that he wasn't likely to get any repeat business from Gabe, now that Tatiana was gone.

"I don't suppose you ordered a hit on this guy," I tapped the photo, "to keep him from beating up any more of your *clients*?"

"He's dead?" Now the wide eyes were feigned. But that didn't mean Butler was behind the guy's death.

"Yeah, he's dead. You have anybody on your staff whose weapon of choice is a sap?"

Butler frowned. "A blackjack? Don't know anybody who uses them these days. You have to get too up close and personal with them."

I nodded. Yet another reason cops stopped using them. The new batons were extendable. You could knock a perp's knees out from under him from far enough away he likely wouldn't be able to slug you.

"So, where have you stashed your women in Starling?" I asked, now willing to get confrontive if necessary.

"Not part of the deal. I'm giving up those above me, but I must remain loyal to my staff."

I snorted. "More like you're thinking you can pick up where you left off when you get out of prison."

"Oh no, Chief." He gave me a mock serious look. "I've learned the error of my ways."

Sure you have.

"You said the boy has no value to you. You weren't renting him out to the highest bidder?"

Butler's eyes flashed and he came partway out of his chair.

"Down!" I said.

He sank back again, still glaring at me. "I don't exploit children."

"Except as leverage." I rose. "Thanks for your time, Mr. Butler."

He visibly pulled himself together. "Always a pleasure, Chief Anderson." He gave me a smarmy smile.

I responded with a curt nod and left the room, wishing I had time to stop home for a shower to wash his slime away.

Once outside, Barnes said, "You really think he'll try to revive his operation when he gets out? How long is he going to be in prison?"

"Not long enough, thanks to his plea deal. And he probably has plans to continue to operate everything from the inside."

Her eyebrows shot up. "You think he could pull that off?"

"Hell no," I said as we reached my car, "because we're not going to let him."

─────◆─────

Back at 3MB, Cruthers had good news. "Collins definitely has a lead on Alejandro's dad. One of the rich guys that lives in the state of Nuevo Léon in Mexico—he used to have a wife and son. But no one has seen them in two years."

"And I take it Nuevo Léon is near where we think Tatiana crossed the Rio Grande," I said.

Cruthers nodded. "There are a couple of favorite spots to cross in that state, where the river is normally shallow anyway. And two years ago, that area had a drought so the river was really low. I know a guy on the force there. I was gonna call him, ask what he knows and see if he can make some discreet inquiries."

I raised a skeptical eyebrow. "What if he's on this rich guy's payroll?"

Cruthers frowned. "Not all Mexican police are crooked. I think he's one of the good guys. Met him through a training conference on Zoom, during the pandemic lockdown. Chief Black was willing to spring for it because there were no travel expenses."

He grunted. "They did that dumb break-us-up-into-groups thing. Someone else in our group implied that he must be corrupt if he was in Mexico. He got pretty offended. Good thing we were online or they might've come to blows. He and I lingered in the chat room afterwards and exchanged contact info. We've stayed in touch."

"Okay," I said, "by all means, see what he can find out, but ask him to be discreet. I don't want to show our hand yet."

"You got it, Chief."

As Cruthers left my office, I spotted Bill Walker entering the bullpen. I stepped out of my office and greeted the janitor. "You're here a bit early, aren't you?" His shift didn't start until ten p.m.

He gave me a shy smile. "I just got done with my morning classes, figured I'd stop by and check in before I go home and get some sleep. Make sure you're happy with everything." Walker was an ex-con and reformed wife beater, now studying to be a social worker and divorce mediator, specializing in domestic violence cases.

"You got a minute?" I asked. "I'd like to pick your brain about something. Oh, and yes, I am quite happy with your work." The premises were always spotless when I came in each morning, even though they rarely stayed that way, especially around the coffee station.

"Sure." He followed me into my office.

"Close the door and have a seat." I gestured toward the comfy visitor's chair. "How's school going?"

"It's going great. I graduate this coming spring."

"Excellent. I want an invite to the graduation."

He grinned, flashing straight, white teeth that must've cost his parents a fortune.

"Tell me something," I said. "How likely is it that the wife of a rich man would risk everything, including her son's safety, to get away from a batterer?"

He gave me a wry look. "As you know from my own history, domestic violence cuts across all socio-economic strata."

"Oh, I know that from my own life," I said. "My father was a college professor, but he still beat my mother." I didn't usually reveal that history to people, but I wanted to shift the dynamics of our relationship some, from head honcho and lowly janitor to professional colleagues. I was hoping I'd be able to continue to pick his brain in the future.

I had Kate Huntington, my therapist friend up in Maryland, but it never hurt to have two psychological consultants.

"Sorry to hear that, Chief." And I suspected he meant it.

I gave him a nod. "Getting back to my question..."

"A lot of factors play into whether the woman stays or leaves," he said. "How long were they together?"

"At least three years. They had a son who was two at the time she left."

"Does this guy have power as well as wealth?"

"Probably." I paused. "Keep all this to yourself, please. It's about a current case."

"The woman on the bridge?"

"Yes. She's from Mexico. I suspect in that country, rich pretty much equals powerful."

Walker nodded. "And she may have been from a poorer background, might've married him more to get out of poverty than because she loved him."

"Even if he's abusive?"

He shrugged. "Maybe. But she likely didn't know that about him beforehand. Abusers are usually quite charming at first. They sweep the woman off her feet, lavish her with gifts and attention, tell her what she wants to hear. It's only after she's fallen for him—the hook is set, so to speak—that she starts to get an inkling of how controlling and abusive he is."

"It's mostly about control, isn't it?"

"For many batterers, yes. They almost always come from abusive backgrounds themselves, as I did. They felt out of control as kids so now they have to have complete control over their families. They're trying to recapture the sense of power they lost when they were helpless kids who couldn't stop the abuse."

"Even if they themselves weren't abused, just saw their mothers being beaten?'

"Yes. They were powerless to protect her. All those things come together, plus they are full of frustrated rage that they couldn't express as a kid. Bad role model, suppressed anger, control and power issues, and often a buried sense of insecurity as well, maybe even a poor opinion of women because his mother never fought back. He takes all that out on his woman, who's too lovestruck and/or afraid to leave him."

"Buried insecurities?"

"Growing up in that kind of environment doesn't exactly promote self-assurance and a sense of well-being."

My chest and stomach tightened. I was pretty sure I covered up my reaction, but that had hit a little too close to home. I tucked those thoughts away for later contemplation.

"These guys may accumulate power and money," Walker was saying, "and learn to look self-confident on the surface. But underneath, they're still a needy little boy."

I nodded. "So, getting back to this case. Why would our victim put herself and the child at risk by crossing the Rio Grande, to trade in the life of a rich woman for that of an illegal immigrant?"

"I'd say she was pretty terrified," Walker said. "Either the abuse had gotten so bad she was sure he would kill her one day, or he'd started beating the child..." He trailed off, dropped his gaze to his hands in his lap. "Although that doesn't always make women leave, even then."

I knew that it hadn't in his case. His father had abused both him and his mother.

He shook his head, then jerked it up, his gaze meeting mine. "Or another scenario, the batterer wants a divorce and threatens to use his wealth and power to take the kid away from her."

"Aha," I said. "That's a good possibility in this case."

CHAPTER EIGHTEEN

Bradley came into my office, looking pleased with himself. He closed the door. "Checking out those tire tracks has paid off."

"Good," I said. "I was afraid that would turn out to be a wild goose chase."

He sat down in front of my desk and leaned forward. "Twenty-six of the new tire owners have criminal records beyond traffic tickets and such. Dulles and Collins dug deeper into their backgrounds, and the tenth person they checked out turns out to be... Drumroll, please." He used his index fingers like drumsticks on the edge of my desk. "Butler's son. Name's Jerome Porter."

My heart rate kicked up. "Oh, yeah?"

Bradley grinned. "Yeah. He's twenty-two, so a product of Butler's misspent youth. Butler is listed as the father on the kid's birth certificate and the mother, one Tessie Porter, apparently doesn't exist, at least not in the State of Florida."

"An alias, for a prostitute maybe?"

"That's what I'm thinking, especially since...wait, I'm getting ahead of myself. The address on Jerome's driver's license is an abandoned building. But he gave a different address to the company that issued the credit card he used to buy the tires. It's a somewhat rundown house in not the best neighborhood, but it's owned by a company located in the Cayman Islands."

"Doesn't sound like the kind of property investors would buy."

"They might, to renovate and flip it, but the company's owned the house for thirty-four years. And they've owned another house a few blocks away for twenty-seven years."

I stared at him, my entire body clenching as the implications sank in. "These bastards have been doing this for decades!"

"Yup. My guess is that if we could dig far enough into the Cayman company, we'd find that it originally belonged to Butler's father. He inherited the family business."

"Have we got enough for warrants?" I asked.

"Not yet, but Cruthers and Collins are discreetly canvassing the neighborhoods, seeing what they can find out about the comings and goings of those houses' residents. We should have enough to take to a judge soon."

"Good." I picked up my phone and hit the button for my private line.

After Dot Wilder's assistant put me through, we exchanged greetings. Then I asked, "You have any reason why we shouldn't raid our local houses of ill repute tonight?"

A beat of silence. "Um, yes," Dot said. "We have one more player we haven't tracked down yet. Someone who apparently keeps in the shadows. He wasn't at that breakfast meeting."

"You know who it is?"

"No, but my team is working on it. We're afraid if we don't get him, he may take over the whole operation, move the women to new locations and we'll be close to back to where we started."

"Why would our raiding these houses matter?" I asked.

A pause, the sound of air being blown out. "We think this person operates out of Starling. Your raid might spook them, and they'll disappear."

"Only to pop back up later." I paused. "Waiting presents a problem. My people are already spread thin. Now I'll need to keep surveillance on these locations, to make sure they don't try to move the women elsewhere."

"I can lend you a couple of people," Dot said.

"Who?" My tone was a bit sharper than I'd intended. Wellbourne had said Grant was on leave, but...

Wilder chuckled softly. "Not Grant. Wellbourne and another agent."

"Okay. How long do you need? I'd rather not wait more than another day."

"We might be able to nail this person down by then. Look, I'd like to tell you more, but not over the phone. I'm tied up the rest of today, but can you meet me for lunch tomorrow?"

We arranged to meet for an early lunch at a diner halfway between our offices.

"I take it we're waiting," Bradley said, as I disconnected.

I frowned, not happy about it. "Yeah."

I filled him in. "Keep all that under your hat, by the way."

"You thinking this in-the-shadows person could be a cop?" Bradley asked. "Maybe one of ours?"

I nodded, my stomach churning at the thought.

His mouth flattened into a grim line. "This not being able to trust our own people really sucks."

I blew out a sigh. "Yes, it does."

Who *could* I trust to surveil the houses where we thought Butler's women were being held? That was a very good question indeed.

I trusted Cruthers almost as much as I did Bradley. And since Collins had helped locate the houses... I assigned the two of them to one house for the three-to-eleven shift.

For the night shift, I split up the FDLE agents and partnered each with a uniform.

And Bradley and I took the three-to-eleven stint at the other house.

Bradley had the back. He'd changed out of his sartorial splendor into baggy sweats and a hoodie. Dirt rubbed into his face and on his hands completed his transformation into homeless dude. Currently, he was rooting through trash cans in the back alley, with an earbud and a tiny microphone tucked inside the hood.

Barnes had been pissed that she wasn't in on the action. I'd pointed out that surveillance was more about inaction—boring as grass growing most of the time. Grumbling, she'd followed orders and gone home to catch some sleep before her own graveyard stint as Pirolnik's bodyguard.

"I'll stop by your place and check on Pipsqueak," she'd said.

I'd forgotten all about the cat, again. I chose to ignore the slight warmth in my chest at the memory of the kitten waking me up from my nightmare last night.

Once I'd positioned my car partway down the block but still within sight of the two-story clapboard house, I called Sam. I had mixed emotions about having to cancel on him. Ever since that kiss...

After I'd delivered the bad news, Sam sighed dramatically. "Relationships when one is in law enforcement are hard enough, but with two LEO schedules...Don't know how this is gonna work, Chief Anderson."

My throat tightened. *Is he breaking up with me?* I hadn't yet admitted to myself that there was anything to break up.

"What do you mean?"

A low chuckle. "Relax, Judith. I'm teasing."

"Not funny."

"Sorry. So maybe lunch tomorrow?"

"I've got a meeting then."

"Oh." A pregnant pause. "I'll try my luck later tomorrow. Take care, Judith." His tone was neutral.

He disconnected before I could say anything else.

My chest felt like a vise had closed around it. *I blew it.* I wanted to feel relieved but my eyes stung. *Get a grip, Anderson.*

I tried to focus on the surveillance, but I was finding it hard to breathe. Finally, I worked up the nerve to text Sam.

I really am sorry. I'll make it up to you after this case is over.

A response came right back. *I'll hold you to that.*

My chest relaxed. I took in a slow, deep breath.

Two hours later, I was getting drifty, despite the audio book I was playing on my phone. Thanks to my nightmare, I'd not gotten quite enough sleep last night. And now that my body was relaxed, sitting still, it was demanding a nap.

I lowered my window a little for fresh air, but the Florida humidity made even November evenings muggy sometimes. This was one of those evenings. I cranked up my air conditioning instead. But despite those efforts, after another twenty minutes, my eyelids were drooping again.

The sharp rap of knuckles on glass. I jumped and hit my head on the ceiling of the car, then jerked around toward the noise.

Sam's grinning face, framed in the passenger-side window. He held up two brown paper bags. The grease stains on one indicated it held food.

Great detective work there, Anderson. My stomach growled.

I clicked the locks open and moved my hand-held radio from the passenger seat to the center console.

He climbed in and shoved the seat back to accommodate his long legs. "Thought you might like some company. These surveillance gigs are deadly tedious."

"Yes, they are. Thanks for the grub."

He opened the bag and pulled out burgers and fries. "No onions on yours, right?"

I smiled. "Right."

"Can't understand why you don't like onions."

"I like them," I said, glancing at the front of the house to make sure all was still quiet there. "They don't like me. Give me heartburn."

My eyes on the house still, I slowly exhaled. I normally hated small talk, but it was getting us back to the easy way we usually interacted. *Whatever happens, I don't want to lose his friendship.* I felt the urge to say that out loud, but didn't. *Coward!*

We ate in silence for a few minutes. He reached into the other bag and produced two bottles of iced tea. "Figured some caffeine would be welcome as well."

"You figured right. I brought a thermos of coffee, but it's almost gone already."

I chewed and swallowed my last bite of burger. Then sucked in air. "Whatever happens, Sam, I hope we'll still be friends."

"Oh, that sounds ominous. Is this the official brush-off?"

"No, no," I quickly said. "Anything but. I'm only saying that if...other things don't work out..." I felt heat creeping up my face. "Well, I really don't want to lose your friendship. It means a lot to me."

One end of his mouth hiked up in a lopsided grin, as he chewed on a French fry. He swallowed and said, "Same here."

He gathered up our trash and stuffed it back into one of the bags. Then he took my hand. Looking straight ahead through the windshield, he said, "This isn't the right time for a serious discussion, but sometime soon I'd like us to consider taking things to the next level."

I swallowed a nervous snicker at his formal tone. "I agree this isn't the best time, but yes we should discuss, um, that...soon." I resisted the urge to pull my captured hand loose from his.

We sat in awkward silence, while I worked up the nerve to ask the crucial question. "What do you consider the next–"

Crackling from my radio. Bradley's low voice. "A van just pulled up in back of the house."

"Shit!" I pulled my hand loose, grabbed up the radio and jumped out of the car. "I'm on my way." I ducked my head back in. "Call our dispatcher. Tell her half the force needs to go to the other location, and half here. Lights, no sirens."

"Got it. I'll cover the front." He jumped out of the passenger side, his phone already to his ear.

I raced down along the side yard of the house next door, checking my Glock in its holster as I ran. Just before the back of the house, I vaulted the low chain-link fence between the yards and plastered myself against the house's wall.

Gun now in hand, I eased to the corner and looked around it.

Bradley was working his way up the backyard, pretending he was searching for something in the scraggly bushes along one side.

The van was parked in the alley, its side door open. I saw no signs of anyone inside it.

"I disabled the driver," Bradley's voice, low, from the radio.

"Got it. I'm at the corner of the house," I whispered back. "We wait for back-up."

"No time." Bradley bent down, poked at the ground under the bushes and side-stepped closer to the house. "If they take off with these women, we may never find them again."

"Hey, old man." A voice yelling from the house. "Get outta here!"

Bradley waved a dirty hand in the air without looking up, and took a small step closer still.

"I said, get out of here." The guy was now on the back porch. Gray paint flaked from its wooden railing.

"Where's my bottle?" Bradley said in a mumbling voice. "Left it around here somewhere."

"Not in our yard you didn't." The guy—white, wiry, average height, dark hair—moved forward, to the edge of the steps. "Now get the hell out of here before I beat the shit outta ya."

I eased around the corner, Glock in both hands, aimed at the guy's back. Sliding quietly along the wall of the house, I reached the edge of the porch. The backs of the man's shoes were now at my eye level.

"Okay, okay," Bradley put his hands in the air, but took another step closer. "You wouldn't have a little nip for a man in need, would ya?" He let one hand drop, scratched his side as if he had fleas.

He's not a bad actor.

Wiry Guy reached toward his pants pocket.

"Don't move!" I yelled. "Police!"

The guy froze, hand hovering near his pocket. He turned slowly. "You a cop? Arrest this guy for trespassing."

"I don't think so. Keep your hands where I can see them." I glanced at Bradley. He now held his pistol in his hand and was rapidly closing the last few steps to the porch.

The guy looked from me to him and raised his hands. His face sagged.

"Anybody else inside, besides the women?" I said.

He shook his head, but I didn't believe him. "Come down the steps slow, hands up, and lay down flat on your stomach."

I kept an eye on the back of the house as the guy followed my orders and Bradley used a plastic zip tie to restrain his hands. He frisked him, pulled a pistol from the pants pocket. Then he lifted him to his feet and walked him to the side fence. Using another plastic tie, he secured the guy to the chain-link.

He moved back toward the porch again. The back door was hanging partway open.

"Just in case," I called out in a low voice, "climb up the side of the porch, out of sight of the doorway." The railing was out of my reach, but Bradley had several inches on me.

He shifted course, grabbed the side railing, and clambered up onto the edge of the porch. Ducking under the flaking rail, he put his back against the house wall and eased toward the doorway.

He looked down at me, crouched at the foot of the steps.

I nodded. He shoved the door hard, yelled, "Police! Don't move," and was swallowed by the darkness inside the house.

I took the steps two at a time and paused by the doorjamb, scanning the interior. A kitchen, all shadows, but I made out a group of people huddled on the floor to one side. No one hiding on either side of the door.

I stepped inside, my Glock on the group.

"Clear," Bradley's voice from the front of the house.

"Wait!" I called back. I was debating. If I left the women unattended, they might take off. We needed their witness statements to make charges stick against their captors. And I wanted to help them—if they fled on their own, with no resources...

But I knew Bradley's next move would be to clear the upstairs. We couldn't let down our guard until we knew no one was up there. Not by himself though, too dangerous. *Where the hell is our back-up?*

My eyes had adjusted enough to be sure there were no men lurking in the group. I lowered my Glock but didn't holster it. "Relax, ladies. We're not going to arrest you. Anybody else in the house?"

They were all silent, staring at me wide-eyed. I counted five black women, four white and six Latinas, ranging in age from mid-teens to early thirties.

"Just one other guy," one of the black women finally said. "I think he went out the front." Her arms encircled a young teen who looked enough like her to be her daughter.

Movement out of the corner of my eye. I turned my head.

A white woman had stood up—tall and lean, about thirty. She was glaring at the mom who'd spoken.

Another woman cleared her throat. I glanced her way, then quickly brought my gaze back to Ms. Tall and Lean. There was something off about her.

Belatedly, I realized I knew the woman who'd cleared her throat. "Hey, Misty," I said without looking her way again.

"Uh, she's one of th–"

Tall and Lean lunged, shoved me aside, and took off out the still open door.

My back banged against the edge of the sink. Pain shot up my spine, but I managed to hang onto my gun. "Stay here!" I yelled at the other women and bolted after Tall and Lean.

I'd almost caught up when we reached the van. She darted around it and jumped into the driver's seat. The engine roared.

I dove into the open side door, landed hard on my side on a rubber mat. I rolled up onto my knees and brought my gun arm up. But she had turned in the driver's seat, a pistol in her own hand, pointed at my chest. "Drop it!"

"Shooting the chief of police is a bad idea."

"Drop it and get out!"

I laid the gun down slowly on the mat, stalling for time, and eased back out of the van.

I was barely clear when she took off, roaring down the alley. I prayed no kids were playing nearby.

And suddenly Sam was beside me. We ran after the van. "She's armed," I huffed out.

He had his weapon in his hand. "I blocked the other end of the alley with your car, after I caught the guy who came out the front."

I barked out a laugh. "You've been a busy boy!"

Then the van screeched to a halt, red and blue lights flashing beyond it.

Bradley hauled past us, running all out. He was ten years younger than both of us.

The woman jumped out of the van and frantically looked around.

Slowing, I swooped down to grab my backup piece from its ankle holster.

But Tall and Lean apparently got it that she was boxed in and outnumbered. She lowered her pistol to the cement and raised her hands in the air.

"Lock your fingers behind your head," Bradley yelled. She complied.

He reached her, grabbed her wrists and twisted her around against the van's fender. Out came another plastic tie.

"We got 'em all?" Sam asked from beside me.

"Yup, we did." We exchanged a grin.

CHAPTER NINETEEN

I was pissed, but having it out with Special Agent in Charge Dorothy Wilder—about how her requested delay meant we'd conducted a raid we weren't prepared for—would have to wait.

Probably for the best. I needed to calm down considerably, before that conversation.

Tonight, we had a lot to do. Thirty women to interview and four perps to interrogate. One of the keepers at the other house had gotten away. But we had netted the man in Donna Glaser's drawing, Tatiana's watcher. He was the wiry white guy from the porch.

Cruthers had asserted his rights as lead on the case and was interrogating him first.

I planned to interview some of the women, starting with Misty. But Sergeant Armstrong informed me she'd been taken to the ER.

"She was hurt in the raid?" I didn't recall anything happening to her.

"No, not in the raid," Armstrong said, his rugged face a little pale under his tan. "Her hand was wrapped in gauze, blood seeping through. When I asked what happened to it, she said they'd chopped off her little finger, in retribution because a friend of hers had escaped."

My stomach heaved, threatening to give back the burger and fries from earlier. I let out a string of expletives, ending with "ruthless bastards."

Armstrong's eyes went wide, I suspected due to my extensive vocabulary. "Yeah, ruthless for sure. Apparently that was one of the ways they kept the women in line."

I shook my head. "Okay, I'll start with the black woman with the teenage daughter. The girl can come in with her."

We walked to the conference room area. Cruthers had covered the murder board in the smaller room so interviews could be held in there. It was currently occupied by Collins and one of the women from the other house.

The larger conference room—most often used for press conferences—was crammed full of women.

Armstrong spoke to Officer Peters, a young black woman who was guarding the larger room's door. The women weren't under arrest but they were material witnesses. We weren't letting them leave until we had their statements.

But I was going beyond that. I'd dragged Jenny Coleman away from a pleasant evening with her husband, and she now had case workers researching temporary housing for the women.

Peters went inside the room and came back with the teen and her mother, the woman who'd dared to speak up at the house.

I gave them both a warm smile. "Peters, come with us, please. Armstrong, you okay with taking her place?"

He nodded.

"Where we goin'?" the woman said, now wary.

"Only to my office, where we won't be overheard." I'd already closed the blinds.

Once there, I told Peters to wait outside and gestured for the mom to take the comfy visitor's chair. She sighed when she sank into it. The girl had settled on one of the other chairs.

"Afraid that one isn't as comfortable," I said to her. "That's on purpose. I have people sit there when I don't want them to linger." I pointed to my own chair behind the desk. "Why don't you sit there? I'll take one of these."

The girl's eyes went wide, and she snickered. "You really choose where people sit depending on..."

"Whether or not I like them. Yup." I chuckled.

She grinned and her mother, whom I was watching out of the corner of my eye, relaxed even more.

I pulled a small recorder out of my desk drawer, clicked it on, and sat on the edge of the visitor's chair next to the mom. "I'm Judith Anderson, the police chief, and you are?"

"Charlotte," she said, then added after half a beat, "Tate. This is Sherrell."

"Are you okay with telling me how you all ended up with these guys?"

Her expression showed surprise. Maybe it was the question itself, but I suspected it was the way I'd phrased it. Taking a page from Mary Striker's book, I was going to give these women as much autonomy as possible.

She took a deep breath and let it out. "I brought us down here from Tennessee after the factory where I worked shut down. Ran through my savings right quick after that, and we were gonna be evicted. Down here, we stayed in a homeless shelter, and I'd go out during the day to try to find work. But I had to take Sherrell with me, didn't dare leave her alone at the shelter."

I nodded. "When was this?"

"We came to Florida in fall of 2018. Sherrell had just turned eight."

I glanced at the girl, who had been quietly swinging my swivel chair back and forth. She was well developed for eleven. I had guessed her to be about thirteen or fourteen.

The mom followed my line of vision. "Pete had started lookin' at her lately," she said in a low voice. "I knew it wouldn't be long 'fore they broke their promise. They'd sworn they wouldn't let no one touch my girl, as long as I cooperated."

The girl's stomach rumbled. "Sorry," she said timidly. "They never gave us supper tonight."

"Hang on." I stood and dug my wallet out of my pocket, took out several five-dollar bills. "Afraid all we have is vending machines, but the food's at least edible, most of the time. Sherrell, how about you go with Officer Peters and pick out something to eat for yourself and your mom."

She looked at her mother, who nodded. The girl jumped up and grabbed the bills. "I can get anything?"

I glanced at the mom. She had an indulgent expression on her face.

"Yes, anything," I said. Charlotte and I exchanged a smile as the girl whooped and danced out of the office.

I got up and closed the door, then sat again. "How did they get you?" I asked a bit more bluntly. I wanted to get the goriest of the details out of the way before Sherrell returned.

"I was working the mall one day, going in each shop, askin' if they needed help, when this woman approached me. She said she could get me a good job, good pay. I remember thinkin' at the time that she was an angel sent by God." Charlotte snorted. "More like the devil's minion."

"I take it that was the woman Misty fingered."

"Lorraine." Charlotte spit out the name. "She and Pete are in charge, when L'Hombre isn't around. Jerome's just muscle."

I tensed at the name *Jerome*. But first things first. "Pete—the wiry, white guy?"

Charlotte nodded.

"And Jerome," I made sure to keep my tone light, "he's the light-skinned black guy who went out the front?"

"Yeah. Not the brightest knife in the drawer, as my mama would say."

He *had* seemed rather out of it when we'd retrieved his trussed-up self from the sidewalk where Sam had tackled him. I'd thought he was just dazed at the time.

"Does Jerome have a last name?" I asked.

Charlotte shrugged. "Most likely he does, but nobody used last names around us."

I let that go, since I had other ways of confirming that he was Butler's son.

"Who's L'Hombre?" It was the same name Tatiana had used, when talking about the guy in charge with Pirolnik. He'd thought she'd made it up, as a derisive nickname.

"Never knew his actual name. That's what we were told to call him. *The Man*." She curled her upper lip.

"Did he live at either of the houses?" Butler owned a lavish property in a much pricier section of town—FDLE had searched it and had found nothing useful—but I was curious as to how hands-on he was.

"Not ours. He just stopped by, maybe once a week or so."

About what I'd suspected. "How else did they control the women? We heard about the amputations."

Charlotte shuddered. "We knew if we ran, one of the other women would suffer for it. They'd tie her down and gag her so she couldn't scream very loud, and cut off a finger or a toe."

I swallowed hard, willing my rebellious stomach to behave. "No wonder Tatiana, and you, were reluctant to leave."

"They threatened to hurt Sherrell too, if I tried to get away."

I ground my teeth, then willed my face to relax as the girl came back. Her arms were full of goodies—wrapped sandwiches, packages of cakes—one chocolate and one with yellow icing, and two canned sodas.

Charlotte and I both smiled at her. I gestured. "Put them on my desk."

"Got ya tuna salad, Mama," the girl said. She handed over a sandwich, the yellow cakes—probably meant to be butterscotch—and a soda.

"Good girl. You remembered."

The girl's eyes clouded some, but she nodded. "I remember how grandma used to make it, with celery and onions and hard-boiled eggs." Her voice was wistful.

I looked over at Charlotte. Her eyes were shiny. "We need to call your grandma, let her know we're okay."

My chest ached at the thought of her mother not hearing from them for years, assuming the worst had befallen her daughter and granddaughter. Well, it wasn't quite the worst that had happened, but damn close to it.

"A couple more questions," I said, and heard the choked sound in my voice. I cleared my throat. "Tatiana Gomez was allowed to have her own place. Why was that?"

"The kids caused problems," Charlotte said. "L'Hombre gave strict orders the men couldn't touch the kids, not even to discipline them, and they weren't supposed to cuss in front of them. But some of the women still used pretty rough language, and the mamas would get upset. Both Daniella and Tatiana were real docile round L'Hombre, though. And they're gorgeous, brought top dollar. He let Daniella have her own place first—she's got a little girl—so's she wouldn't fight with the other women over their language no more. But he kept a close eye on her, used threats against her kid to keep her in line.

"Then he got the bright idea to set up a demerit system. He told the other women they could get their own places too, if they behaved. But the rules were real strict. Any little thing—it could be yawnin' while one of the handlers was talkin'—and you got a black mark on this board. You had to have three months of no marks to be considered for an apartment. Nobody ever made it that long, except Tatiana."

Charlotte sighed. "I guess I wasn't docile enough, or classy enough. So I didn't make a fuss about the women cussin'. Just told Sherrell that grownups said bad words sometimes, but they weren't words for a young girl to use."

My chest ached again and my throat closed. This woman still tried to guide and raise her child right, even under horrific circumstances.

I faked a smile for them. "Thanks for all your help. Officer Peters will take you back to the conference room for now. But the Department of Children and Families will be finding you temporary shelter."

Charlotte jumped up from her chair, her face and body tense. "They ain't takin' my baby away from me, are they?"

I stood as well. "Not as long as I'm chief of police, they won't."

"Miss Judith…"

I turned toward Sherrell, still sitting in my chair, a streak of chocolate icing on one cheek. Her eyes were shiny.

"Girl, that's Chief Anderson to you," her mother said.

"No, Miss Judith is fine."

Sherrell ducked her head. "Thank you for the food, and everything."

"You're welcome." I turned back to the mom, handed her one of my cards. "We're gonna make sure you all get settled okay, but you call me personally if you ever need anything. It was an honor to meet you." I held out my hand.

Misty, back from the ER with a more substantial bandage on her hand, told me essentially the same thing as Charlotte had. Only in Misty's case, she'd been approached at the bus station.

"If a man had come up to me like that, I would've told him to go pound sand," she said. "But a woman, I assumed she was on the up and up and really was looking for workers.

"She asked me if I could sew, and when I said I could, she said she worked for a small clothing company. They needed more seamstresses right away, to fill a big order."

Misty sighed. "I was thrilled to find work so quick like that, even if it sounded kinda temporary." She made a scoffing sound. "Little did I know it would be quite permanent."

I was quiet for a moment, then said, "Another of the women told me about the punishment." I nodded toward her bandaged hand. "Who got away?"

"My best friend, Allie Franks. One of her regulars was getting really rough with her. She was scared for her life, but L'Hombre wouldn't do anything. This guy was paying extra—enough extra that the bastard was willing to let the guy kill one of his girls.

"He was always quick to remind us we were expendable. He could send out Lorraine and pick up a new girl whenever he wanted. I think he was actually planning on expanding. I'd overheard some talk about a third house and a 'fresh batch of girls,'" she made air quotes, "coming from the border."

A chill ran down my spine.

"That was another way they got women, buying them from guys who kidnapped immigrants sneaking over the border." Misty's expression was sad, but then she straightened her shoulders. "Anywho, Allie and I pretended to have a big fight. I told her that would keep them from taking her leaving out on me, but I knew it wouldn't work. Allie seemed to believe me, though."

"Why were you at Mary Striker's office the other day? I assumed you were there to get away yourself."

"I wanted to, but I knew if I disappeared too, somebody else would get it." She held up her bandaged hand again. "Double, for Allie and for me. I was there to check on her, make sure she was truly on her way to New York State. She's got family there. This really sweet client of mine, Joey, he drove me to the center and waited outside."

"So, how did it work, when the women went to the...clients?"

"We were escorted there by one of the handlers. That's what L'Hombre called Lorraine and the men, our handlers. The client paid for a certain amount of time. The handler came back when the time was up. Sweet Joey, he gave up some of his time to take me to the center, and then I never did get to talk to Mary."

"I'm sorry about that. I'll see if I can locate your friend in New York. I know a few cops in the Albany department. Where did you meet the clients?"

"It varied. Sometimes at their homes, sometimes hotel rooms. You gonna try to round them up? 'Cause if you are, I'm not giving you Joey's full name."

"I haven't decided yet." I hadn't even thought about the johns yet. We had our hands full for now with the traffickers and the women.

"Another question," I said. "None of the women seem to be drug users..."

"No, drugs were strictly forbidden. We could smoke marijuana or drink alcohol with the clients. But nothing addictive. L'Hombre kept reminding us that we were call girls, not street whores. We were supposed to be classy, although a lot of the clients, they didn't care if we were classy or not," her voice became derisive, "as long as we had a place where they could poke us."

I gave a sympathetic nod. "I'm surprised none of the women ever tried to report what was going on to the police."

She shook her head. "We were told that they had cops who were on the take, both here and in Jacksonville. That if we tried to report anything to the police, they'd know right away and would kill us." She shook her head again, more vehemently. "And they didn't mean just kill the one who squealed on them. They would kill all the women in the house and start over."

Pressure built in my chest at the thought of cops in my department who were taking money to let this evil thrive in Starling.

I slowly breathed in and out. Then I gave Misty the same spiel as I'd given Charlotte, that we would get her settled somewhere. I also repeated, "It was an honor to meet you." I'd meant it both times.

I closed my office door behind her and leaned against it, feeling humbled by these strong women who'd endured and survived...

"Every woman's worst nightmare," I whispered out loud.

CHAPTER TWENTY

It was almost ten p.m. by the time I got home. I kicked off my shoes in the middle of the living room and headed for the kitchen and a glass of wine. I was exhausted, and yet restless, for reasons I could not pinpoint.

I veered back to my laptop case that I'd dropped on the sofa and pulled out my personal phone. Once I had wineglass in one hand and phone in the other, I plopped onto my black leather sofa. I set the wine on the packing box I use as a coffee table and texted Kate Huntington, my psychological consultant and—I had only acknowledged recently—a friend.

Is it too late for me to call?

Nope, I'm still up.

I placed the call and Kate answered on the first ring, just as an unholy howling emanated from the second bedroom. I sprang up again. I'd forgotten the damn cat!

"What's that noise?" Kate said.

I opened the room's door. "My kitten," I answered, as I extracted the cat's tiny claws from my pants leg.

"You've got a kitten," she said, her tone way too gleeful.

"Yes, but it's temporary. Barnes is supposed to be finding her a permanent home."

"Does she have a name?"

"Um, Pipsqueak," I admitted, then rushed on, "but I didn't name her. Sam did."

"Ah, Sam. So that's still happening?"

I shook my head. *When did I lose control of this conversation? And why do I even think I ever had control?*

If I were in a better mood, I would have laughed at myself.

"Yes, that's still happening." I returned to my seat on the sofa. "Look, I'm sorry to call so late, but I need a consult." The cat jumped up and settled on my lap.

"No problem," Kate was saying. "I've got teenagers now, who like to stay up late. I try to wait to go to bed until they are at least semi-settled in their rooms. What's up?"

I paused, gathering my thoughts. Then I gave her the background on Tatiana's case, told her about tonight's raid and summarized my interviews with Charlotte, Misty and several of the other women. I shuddered when I got to the part about Misty's amputated finger, as retribution for another woman's escape.

Kate was quiet for a beat when I'd finished. "They used the women's tendency to affiliate and put others over self against them." Her voice was low and angry.

I blew out air. "If that's psychobabble for they took advantage of the fact that the women grew to care about each other, then yes. And it worked a lot of the time, until the stakes got too high. In the case of M's friend," I'd used only first initials to identify the women, "her life was in danger from an abusive john."

And that gave me a possible answer to the question about the men who'd used the escort service. We would round up the ones that the women identified as exploitative and/or abusive. Maybe not the ones like Pirolnik and Misty's Joey.

"Or in the case of your murder victim," Kate was saying, "there was a second enemy she feared even more than this L'Hombre. Maybe feared for her son's sake, more than for herself."

I sighed. "Yeah, and unfortunately, all this info has not yet netted us her killer."

"Probably not Butler," Kate said, "as he has a good point. She was a valuable asset."

"Unless he decided to make an example of her, to keep the other women in line...Hey, I have another question. Would you view all men who go to prostitutes as exploitative?"

She was quiet again, for several beats this time. "Well, assuming a more normal arrangement, where the prostitute is not enslaved like these women were, there are some men whom I wouldn't say were exploiting the women *per se*. Some are too shy to make normal connections with the opposite sex. They might even fancy themselves in love with a prostitute that they went to regularly."

That certainly described Pirolnik.

"I had a client once," Kate continued, "who had been a prostitute in her youth. She'd run away from an abusive situation and ended up on the streets for a while. She said there were some men who were more interested in conversation than sex. They mostly wanted some woman's attention, somebody they could talk to without worrying about whether or not the woman really liked him. She was paid to pretend that she liked him."

I ran my idea about the johns past her.

"I like it! It gives the women some autonomy. They're playing a direct role in punishing the men who deserve it, but can choose not to mention the ones they feel some sympathy for."

"Thanks," I said, my mood definitely improved. "As usual, you've been quite helpful. Send me a bill."

"Nah, this one's on the house. I like hearing from you, Judith. Are you coming this way to visit any time soon?"

"Um..." My aunt—the only family member besides her son whom I still kept in touch with—lived in Maryland. I sometimes spent Christmas with her and Paulie, but I hadn't really thought about what I was doing this year. "Maybe at Christmas," I finally said.

"Well, if you do, let me know as soon as you can, so I can clear my schedule to get together."

Warmth spread through my chest. Then I heard myself saying, "Hey, don't you come down sometimes to visit your folks in St. Augustine? I'm only about an hour from there."

"Great. I didn't realize Starling was that close to them. I'll let you know next time I'm coming down."

We said our goodbyes and disconnected. I looked down at the ball of fluff sleeping in my lap. A strange sensation began in my chest and stomach and flowed outward.

It took me a few moments to realize it was my body relaxing, maybe even experiencing something like contentment.

———◆◇◆———

At lunchtime the next day, I was very glad I had not called Dot Wilder while I was still angry—for two reasons.

One, she immediately apologized as she took the seat across the table from me at the diner. "I'm so sorry, Judith, that the delay I requested meant you went into those houses less than ideally prepared."

I shrugged. "Only one perp got away and no injuries among my people, except the bruised ego of the uniform who wasn't able to catch him. Based on what we learned from the women, that guy wasn't a major player anyway."

Besides, I had known they might try to move the women. That's why I had the houses under surveillance. I should've had a contingency plan in place.

Hindsight, and all that jazz. But my attempt to blow it off internally was only partially successful. As CoP I needed to think ahead, anticipate things better.

So you learn from your mistakes and move on, the voice of my former partner and mentor, Dolph Randolph, echoing in my head.

I know, Dolph. But I was finding it disconcerting to be back in that insecure newbie position, after years of taking competence in my job for granted.

Dot was chuckling. "Glad the ad-libbing went well." She picked up her menu.

"So, you think there's someone else still out there who could take over?" I said, pretending to peruse my own menu. The second reason I was glad I hadn't made that angry phone call—I wanted to know what this woman knew.

"Yes...Their poached salmon lunch plate is pretty good here, by the way."

I put my menu down. Salmon wasn't my favorite but I was happy not to be distracted by having to choose what to eat. "What makes you think there's another major player?"

Dot let out a small sigh and closed her own menu. "There are signs that there's some kind of enforcer in the organization. Did you know that there's a group, based in Starling actually, that tries to help these women get out of the life?"

"Yes. Our victim, Tatiana Gomez, led us to them. She had a bar of soap with their phone number on it. I've met with Mary Striker a couple of times."

"Well, several of the women that Mary's group helped, that they thought had gotten away clean—we now know they ended up right back in the life, in some other part of the state."

The waitress appeared with glasses of water. "Are you ready to order, ladies?"

"Two salmon plates," I said, anxious to get back to our discussion.

"Actually," Dot said, "I'll have a chicken salad sandwich, with extra mayo."

I considered getting pissed, until she smiled at me. "It's really good too, if you're willing to do the extra calories."

I smiled back. "Two chicken salad sandwiches, extra mayo." I handed the waitress my menu.

Once she was out of earshot, I leaned forward. "Back in the life as in prostituting willingly? Or taken captive again?"

"At first," Dot said, "we thought it was the former, that they just couldn't break drug habits maybe, or they didn't know how else to make a living. But when some of the sex slave rings in South Florida were raided, we found a few of the women from this area. They were kept on a very short leash, never let out of the sight of one of the handlers."

She dropped her gaze to her silverware, still bundled in a paper napkin. "I can't even begin to imagine how horrible that had to be, to think you've gotten away and then..." She trailed off.

"So someone had the job of tracking down the women who escaped," I said.

"Yeah, and that person wasn't housed with any of the women, or the other men who worked for the traffickers." She shook her head. "We're kind of at a loss where to begin looking for him."

"The women who were recaptured, they couldn't give you a description?"

"The descriptions of the men who kidnapped them were all different. Apparently, someone in the network locates the women and informs the local group, who recaptures them. We think this guy is based in the Jacksonville area, maybe in Starling, but that's about all we have on him."

I opened my mouth, but closed it again when the waitress arrived with our sandwiches.

We each took a couple of bites. The chicken salad was delicious.

"Are you sure it's a him?" I told Dot about the woman, Lorraine, who'd been working with Butler.

"Hmm, good point. A woman could get closer to these gals, gain their confidence, maybe get them talking to confirm they are the run-aways she's looking for. Then she walks away from that conversation, calls her boss, who sics the local traffickers on the poor woman."

Dot took another bite of her sandwich, chewed and swallowed. "Our greatest concern is that this enforcer probably knows all of the local groups, where they're based, who was running them. If he or she gets away, they may be able to rebuild the network, and our work will be for naught."

"Not to mention the women who end up trapped in their web again."

"Exactly."

"Do you want to do line-ups with any of the women we liberated, to confirm that Butler is L'Hombre?"

She thought about that while taking another bite of sandwich. Nodding, she said, "Maybe with a few of them, those who are least likely to be retraumatized by doing so. It wouldn't hurt to have a few more pieces of evidence, in case he reneges on his plea deal."

"I have a question about Butler," I said, "that you might not be able to answer. He's pretty slick, but when I asked him about selling the kids to the highest bidder, he immediately lost his cool, came up out of his chair even. And the women I interviewed last night said their handlers weren't allowed to touch the kids, not even swear around them."

Dot was chewing and nodding. She quickly swallowed. "We have a forensic psychologist on staff. She interviewed him. He came from an abusive home."

"No surprise there."

"Right. Everybody was beaten, except his little sister, but the father sexually abused her. Butler's sure his mother knew what was going on and let it continue."

"Maybe, maybe not." I made a mental note to ask Kate about those dynamics. "But that makes sense about Butler, that he has little respect for women, a lot of anger toward them even, but he's protective of children."

"Another tidbit," Dot said, "that came out of the discussion with our shrink. The mother of Butler's son was one of his father's women. The old man was a more traditional pimp who kept the women subdued and dependent on him by hooking them on drugs. Young Butler fell in love with one of them and got her pregnant. His father let her get clean until after the kid was born, but then he started feeding her drugs again. She died of an overdose a couple of months later."

"And that explains his no-drugs rule. But the ways he used to control the women were maybe worse." I told her about Misty's finger.

Looking a little pale, Dot put the remains of her sandwich down on her plate. She cleared her throat. "There's something else I wanted to talk to you about, away from either of our offices."

"You think I've got a rotten cop in my department."

Her eyes went wide. "You'd already figured that out, hunh?"

I blew out air, set my own sandwich down. "That there is one, yes. Who it is, no real clue yet."

"We think your predecessor was taking bribes from Butler."

"I'm pretty sure he was." I was tempted to tell her about the secret computer files that Derek the Geek had found, but I held those cards in my hand for now. I liked this woman, but I didn't trust her completely, yet.

"No ideas at all who else might be on the take in your department?" Dot asked, her voice a little too innocent.

"Do *you* have any ideas?"

"Um, maybe, but it's more somebody's hunch than anything else. If you don't mind, I'd like to keep Wellbourne on loan to you, let her get friendly with your people and maybe catch some of the gossip. I mean, you are short-handed right now, so it wouldn't look all that weird."

"No, it wouldn't." I wasn't sure how I felt about an FDLE agent nosing around my department, but I didn't want to alienate Wilder by saying no. "We could use her help. We still have a murder to solve."

Three murders, counting Sam's cases, Caroline Baumann and Juarez. But I didn't want to mention them. I wasn't sure how the FDLE worked.

If there were related cases in more than one jurisdiction in the state, did they take over? I'd have to ask Sam about that.

"How sure are you of your detectives?" Dot asked.

"I'd trust Sergeant Bradley with my life." Indeed, I had already done so, when we'd faced down a serial killer together.

She nodded, her face blank, but was that a touch of relief in her eyes? He wasn't who she suspected of being bent. "He's your second in command, isn't he?"

"Yes. He's going to sit for the lieutenant's exam after the first of the year."

"And the other detectives?" Dot asked.

The waitress appeared at my elbow. "Anything wrong?" she asked, looking concerned as she glanced at our abandoned sandwiches.

"No." Dot gave her a smile. "Could you wrap up the rest for us?"

"Sure." She swept our plates away.

I waited until she was well out of earshot. "I've worked more closely with Cruthers. I doubt he's bent. I don't know Collins or Patterson all that well yet." And I left it at that, unwilling to speculate about the latter two's honesty without any evidence, one way or the other.

<hr/>

Collins jumped up from his desk when I entered the bullpen. In his mid-thirties, medium height and build, brown hair and eyes, his main distinguishing features these days were the glint in his eye and the enthusiastic grin on his boyish face.

We'll see how long that lasts. I kept the cynical thought to myself.

He intercepted me halfway across the room and fell into step. "Cruthers heard back from his contact in Mexico. We're pretty sure this guy is Alejandro's father."

Cruthers had also risen from his desk. He met us at my office door.

I gestured for them to come in. Barnes followed, closing the door behind her.

Cruthers pointed to the comfy visitor's chair. "You deserve it, son."

An eerie moment of *déjà vu*—a flashback to twenty years ago, when, as a rookie detective, I'd come up with the lead that broke a major homicide case. My partner Dolph, in response to a commendation from our chief, had said, "You deserve it, girl."

From anybody else, I would have taken offense at the "girl," but from Dolph...

Cruthers, still standing, said, "His name is Manuel Felipe Gutiérrez. He has a *hacienda*, which was once a working cattle ranch, in Nuevo Léon. My contact says the rumor mill is ripe where this guy's concerned. He's a recluse, rarely leaves the *hacienda*, and another rumor says he's a direct descendant of the Emperor Montezuma."

Collins jumped in, his voice excited. "His wife disappeared two years ago, along with their two-year-old son. Some of the locals are his servants, and they say the wife ran away and took the boy with her. The official word was that she went to take care of a sickly family member in southern Mexico, and..." He paused for breath.

"The boy is supposedly at boarding school," Cruthers said.

"At age four?" Barnes exclaimed, from where she leaned against the doorframe.

"Yeah, I don't think anybody believes that," Cruthers continued. "The scuttlebutt is that he beat his wife, before her disappearance. He's the jealous type, saw her and the boy as his possessions."

"Any reports of him abusing the boy?" I asked.

Collins and Cruthers shook their heads in unison.

Collins, who had been a watch sergeant, technically outranked Cruthers, but the older and more experienced detective was his *de facto* trainer. I'd come to think of them as the double Cs, although I'd never call them that to their faces.

"So where do we go from here?" Collins asked, his eyes a bit wide. This was his first homicide case since becoming a detective.

"Good question," I said. "Assuming Tatiana was his wife, we actually have two questions. Is Gutiérrez her killer? And if not, what about his paternal rights?"

Barnes bolted upright from her slouch against the doorframe. "You're not gonna turn Alejandro over to him, are you?"

I sighed. "If we clear him of his wife's murder, we may have to do just that. He's the boy's father."

Barnes opened her mouth.

I gave a slight shake of my head.

She clamped her lips shut, but her face turned an unbecoming shade of red.

"Thanks, gentlemen," I said. "Please send the details about the village and the *hacienda* to my phone."

The double Cs took the hint and trooped out of my office, closing the door behind them.

Barnes opened her mouth. "Chief–"

I held up my hand. "I will do everything in my power to keep that boy out of the hands of a batterer, but I may not succeed."

Again, she clamped her mouth shut.

I picked up my desk phone and punched the button for my private line, calling Jenny Coleman at DCF to fill her in.

"Do you think Mr. Gutiérrez would be willing to come here to be interviewed?" she asked when I'd finished.

"I don't know. He's rumored to be a recluse. But first and foremost, I need to determine if he put a hit out on his wife. If he did, his paternal rights become a moot issue. We'll be arresting him for murder."

"Except that he's in Mexico," Jenny said. "And it sounds like he has some clout down there."

"Yeah." I thought for a moment. "Do you have the means to go to Mexico to interview him?"

She laughed. "Half the time, I don't even turn in my mileage for home visits within Starling or Clover County, when I know that'll throw us over our travel budget for the month."

I leaned forward in my desk chair. "Here's what I'm thinking. He might come here if we tell him about Alejandro, but I'd prefer to *see* his reactions, in person, to the news that we have the boy and to our questions—without giving him time to prepare himself. Let me check on some things on my end. If I can come up with the funds to get us both to Mexico, are you willing to go with me and interview him there?"

A brief pause. "I agree that it might be best to take him off guard. And a home visit is normally part of the process. I certainly don't want to turn that child over to an unfit father." Another pause. "Yes, I'll go with you."

I thanked her again for her help last night, with finding the women temporary housing. Then we signed off.

I turned to Barnes, still looking grumpy in her chair. "Any ideas on how to find out how flexible our budget is, without setting off alarm bells in the mayor's office?"

Her expression softened slightly. "I've got a friend in accounting."

Of course you do.

CHAPTER TWENTY-ONE

I was wading through reports when Bradley stuck his head in my office door. "Patterson was discharged an hour ago."

"Let's go pay him a visit." Anything to get away from the reports for a while, and he might be able to add to Donna Glaser's description of their assailant.

Plus I was feeling a little guilty that I'd never made it back to the hospital yesterday. It was part of the chief's job, in my opinion, to visit injured officers, offer support to families, etc. It was a part of the job I was lousy at, but I needed to do it nonetheless. It was important that my people knew I cared. And I did, it just made me damned uncomfortable trying to convey it.

Patterson's house was a modest white bungalow on a side street in an okay-but-not-great part of town.

A forty-something woman answered the front door. His ex-wife, maybe? Maybe she'd brought him home from the hospital.

I spotted Patterson in the living room behind her, propped up in one corner of the sofa, wearing jeans and a tee shirt and a white gauze turban wrapped around his head.

His seventeen-year-old daughter sat in a kitchen chair nearby.

The woman stepped back to let us in, as Patterson and the girl burst out laughing at some shared joke.

A flash to my father and me, laughing together over something silly…I was maybe thirteen. I shook my head to clear it.

The woman pursed her lips, as if she'd tasted a lemon. *Yup, ex-wife*.

"Hey, Chief, Sarge," Patterson greeted us. "Good of you to come by."

Bradley strode over and held out a hand. Patterson shook it.

I followed suit, feeling a little off-kilter.

I nodded at the girl, who gave us a shy "Hi."

"Glad to see you're doing so well," I said to her dad.

He shrugged. "I've got a hard head."

A snort from the ex, who'd taken up residence in an armchair across the room. She was flipping through a magazine.

"How's Ms. Glaser doing?" Patterson asked.

"Not bad," Bradley said. "She was pretty banged up, but the perp wasn't trying to kil–" He stopped abruptly, glanced at the girl. "Anyway, she's recovering well."

"Can you give us a description of the guy?" I asked.

Patterson hesitated, then turned to his daughter. "Sweetheart, would you make me a cup of tea?"

"Sure, Dad." She jumped up and went through a doorway leading to a small kitchen.

"I don't remember the actual fight with him," Patterson said in a lowered voice. "The docs said it's normal, with a bad concussion, to have some amnesia.

"But I remember hearing Ms. Glaser yelling. I kicked the door in and saw him beating on her. He was all covered in black, including a ski mask. About six-one. Biggish guy, but muscle, not fat. He was strong." He paused, gazing off into space. "His eyes were dark, and angry. He was spewing out Spanish so fast I couldn't translate it."

Bradley perked up. The Spanish was new info.

"Did you catch any of it?" I asked.

"Something along the lines of having to find the *puta*'s brat." He paused for a moment. "He might have had a mustache. I think I remember a fringe of black hair above his mouth. Oh, and the bastard took my wallet."

"You think he was trying to make it look like a robbery?" Bradley said, more to me than to Patterson.

The daughter came back, carefully balancing a cup of tea on a saucer.

I gave Bradley a shrug.

The tip of the girl's tongue stuck out of one corner of her mouth. She set the cup on a small tray table next to the sofa. "One sugar and a lemon slice."

"Just the way I like it," her dad said, giving her one of his rare smiles. She grinned back and returned to her seat.

"Keep taking good care of him." I patted her shoulder, hoping the gesture didn't seem as awkward to her as it did to me.

"Glad to see you're on the mend." Bradley shook Patterson's hand again.

The ex started to rise from her chair. I waved her down. "We can see ourselves out."

———◦———

Barnes had gotten myself and Jenny on a direct flight the next morning, leaving Jacksonville airport at six-ten EST. Via the magic of time zones, after a five-hour flight, it was only four hours later when we landed in Monterrey, Mexico.

We were greeted by a man in a dark business suit. He introduced himself as First Sergeant Emiliano Herrara, of the Nuevo León state police, and explained that the rank of first sergeant was closer to that of a lieutenant in a U.S. police department.

"Thank you for picking us up," I said. "But you didn't have to come to the airport. We could've taken a cab to your station."

"It is an honor to assist Detective Cruthers's chief of police," he said in a rich baritone, a smile flashing across a tan face that couldn't be much more than forty. Slight crow's feet bracketed dark, intense eyes.

His face sobered as he ushered us through the crowded airport toward the baggage claim area. "I think it best that we not involve my station, if possible. I have taken a day of leave to help you." He paused for a beat. "Also, it is not safe for two women to travel alone in that part of Mexico. I am thinking you need backup."

Jenny Coleman opened her mouth—maybe to protest, maybe to ask why it wasn't safe—but I held up my hand. "I agree. I debated bringing one of my male detectives, but honestly, my department couldn't afford it."

We'd barely been able to cover the airfare for myself and Jenny, diverting funds from the detective's billet we hadn't yet filled. I'd also been tempted to ask Sam along, until I told him about the trip over the phone last night.

And he'd insisted on coming. "This macho guy isn't going to be honest with two women," he'd said, "and he's dangerous. At the very least, he's a wife batterer."

"Alleged," I'd said, only to irritate him—because he was irritating me. "And I'm counting on him being uncomfortable when confronted by two professional women, questioning his fitness to get his son back, no less."

I'd started to chuckle at the thought of this guy realizing he had to be nice to us if he hoped to see Alejandro again.

But Sam didn't recognize the landmine he'd barely avoided, one that had the potential to blow apart our relationship, or whatever the hell this was that we had.

Had, not *have*. Probably past tense now. Because he'd gone on to play macho man himself, insisting that he go. "Judith, this scares me. You'll be on your own in a strange city, a strange country. You don't even speak very good Spanish."

I'd longed to say that it scared me some too, to confide in him things I usually didn't admit to a living soul, sometimes not even to myself. But I wasn't about to say any such thing to this guy, whoever he was. Where had my sweet and supportive Sam gone?

Instead, I'd said, "Jenny Coleman has the Spanish covered."

The arrival of my bag on the luggage carousel brought me out of my reverie. Jenny had brought a carry-on only.

I declined politely when Emil—as he'd instructed us to call him—offered to carry the small suitcase, which I'd had to check because of its contents.

We made our way to the curb in front of the airport building. Emil gestured toward a white car parked off to our left, under a sign that read *Policía*. The car, however, was unmarked. "One of the few perks for an honest cop," he said. "Convenient parking."

Jenny and I exchanged a look. *Doth he protest too much?* If this guy was in Gutiérrez's pocket, we could be walking into a trap.

But surely even in Mexico, I argued with myself, *there's a certain amount of respect for American law enforcement.* Or at least fear of the pressure and scrutiny the U.S. government would bring down on them, should something happen to an American LEO on Mexican soil.

Great! Could we be setting off an international incident? I shook my head slightly to clear it of paranoid thoughts and climbed into the passenger seat.

"Get comfortable, ladies." Emil glanced up in the rearview mirror and smiled at Jenny in the backseat. "It is almost a three-hour drive to Señor Gutiérrez's *hacienda*."

I sighed. I'd looked it up on Google Maps. We would be backtracking through the same countryside we had just flown over. But Monterrey was the closest commercial airport to Gutiérrez's place.

Jenny leaned forward and whispered in my ear, "Is this guy going into the *hacienda* with us?"

I turned some in my seat. "We need to go in alone," I said to Emil. "Having you along would change the dynamics."

He nodded. "I understand." He glanced my way, then back to the busy road exiting the airport. "Or at least, I think I do."

"I want him off balance, having to deal with American professional women who control whether or not he gets his son back."

One end of his mouth quirked up. "That's what I thought. I'd use that word *control* carefully, though. From what I've heard about this guy, it could set him off."

"Thanks. Good to know." I gave him a genuine smile. "What are you going to do with yourself while we're in there?"

Emil looked in the rearview mirror. "Ms. Coleman, do you see a hat on the seat next to you?"

A second later, her hand snaked between us, holding a chauffeur's cap. "Call me Jenny," she said.

"Thanks." Emil took the hat and put it on his lap. "When we get closer, I'll put it on. And you should move to the backseat then." A quick glance my way again. "You have my cell number in your contacts?"

"Yes." I patted the pants pocket that held my phone.

The car coming to a stop woke me.

"Glad to see I'm such stimulating company," Emil said in a teasing tone.

I prayed I hadn't been snoring. "Sorry. We had to get up pretty early to catch our plane."

"No apologies required." He chuckled. "I'm happy you were able to have a *siesta* during the long drive."

I gave him another smile. This guy was growing on me. "I take it that it's time to get in the backseat."

"*Sí*. We're a mile from the *hacienda*." He put on the chauffeur's cap, pulling it low over his eyes.

"I need to get something from my bag," I said.

I got out and jogged around to the back of the car. Emil had popped the trunk. I inserted a key in the lock of my small suitcase and extracted a metal box. I unlocked it with a different key as I walked to the driver's side back door.

Emil already had the door open. Before getting in, I lifted the lid on the box and showed him my snub-nose revolver, in its ankle holster, and my Glock. His eyebrows went up but he said nothing.

"Another perk for being law enforcement," I said. "One is allowed to fly with these." I removed the revolver, usually my backup piece. The Glock, however, would be too easy to find if we were searched. I put the box on the ground for a moment and strapped the holster to my ankle.

When I straightened, Emil's expression was now blank. He clicked his heels and gestured to the inside of the car. "*Por favor, Señora.*"

Then he beamed, his dark eyes dancing. "Just getting into character."

"*Gracias.*" I gave him a mock aristocratic nod and ducked into the backseat.

He chuckled, as he leaned his head in. "Slide the box under my seat."

I did as he suggested, glancing over at Jenny. She was watching us intently, but she didn't ask what was in the box.

At the turnoff for the *hacienda*, an armed guard stood in front of a high wrought-iron gate. He was a big dude, in dark slacks and a white short-sleeved dress shirt that stretched tight across his broad chest. The buttons were threatening to pop and sweat darkened the armpits.

He casually cradled a rifle in his arms.

Emil lowered his window. I caught only Jenny's and my names from the rapid-fire Spanish.

The guard seemed unimpressed. He grunted and asked something.

"He wants to know if the Señoras have an appointment," Emil said over his shoulder, his accent much heavier than earlier. I suspected that was intentional.

We didn't, because we'd wanted the element of surprise. We'd taken a risk, but if he wasn't the recluse he was rumored to be and happened not to be at home, we were prepared to stay over and come back tomorrow.

I lowered my window and held out a photo to the guard, of Alejandro playing in Ada Johns's backyard. "No appointment, but show him this. I think he will be willing to see us."

CHAPTER
TWENTY-TWO

The guard did not take the picture. Instead, he pulled out a phone and walked away from the car, still keeping himself between it and the gate.

In less than thirty seconds, he was back. The phone had been replaced with a small black box, the remote for the gate. It opened slowly. "You may go in," he said, his accent thick.

It took three full minutes to reach the house. I timed it. The smooth driveway was in sharp contrast to the pothole-riddled road we'd just left.

Finally, we passed through a line of trees and rumbled onto a large cobblestone area in front of a sprawling ranch-style house. The walls were a pale-yellow stucco, the roof terracotta tiles. It could have been a Hollywood movie set for a Mexican *hacienda*.

Except the landscaping was more British countryside. Boxwood bushes lined up neatly across the front of the house, with a border of summer flowers in front. English ivy grew up the walls.

My mind flashed to the bio Collins had prepared on this guy. Manuel Gutiérrez had gone to boarding school in the UK. Recalling my conversation with Bill Walker, I wondered if Gutierrez had been abused as a child. Maybe England had been a happy reprieve from an unhappy home in Mexico.

Emil opened the door for me, and I stepped out of the car. An alarming hiss came from the boxwoods. My body on full alert, eyes scanning in search of its source, I leaned sideways to grab my gun from its ankle holster. And spotted a sprinkler head nestled in the bushes.

I almost fainted from relief. No doubt, misting the greenery was the only way to keep it from withering in the hot sun. Willing my galloping heart to simmer down, I covered my odd movements by pretending to shake an imaginary stone from my shoe.

A massive wooden front door opened, and a young woman in a maid's uniform stepped out onto a low fieldstone porch. She spoke more slowly than the guard.

I caught most of it, but Jenny and I still looked expectantly at Emil, not wanting to let on that we understood Spanish.

"She is asking that you follow her, *por favor*," Emil said.

I noted that he already had his cell phone in his hand. As we walked toward the porch, I glanced over my shoulder. He was casually leaning his butt against the front fender of the car, scrolling on said phone.

My heart rate slowed, closer to a normal pace. He had our backs.

The maid led us through large, cool rooms with low lighting and out into the bright sunlight again. We were in a courtyard, again populated by British flora rather than the tropical plants one would expect in Mexico.

Tall trees provided ample shade and large fans stood on poles in each corner, creating a pleasant breeze. It was a delightful oasis, or would have been had we not been about to beard a potential killer in his own den.

Under one tree, a fortyish man stood next to a table, the remnants of lunch on it.

My stomach rumbled. I hoped he couldn't hear it. I hadn't given food any thought so far today.

The man could easily be the one who attacked Donna Glaser and Patterson. Right height and build, beige skin tone. He too wore dark slacks and a white dress shirt, open at the collar. But his were much better tailored than his guard's. Muscles rippled under the shirt. It registered that he was clenching his fists, down at his sides.

Jenny glanced my way, waiting for my cue.

Striding forward, my hand outstretched, I said, "*Buenos días, Señor Gutiérrez.*" I intentionally mispronounced the words slightly. "Our apologies for arriving unannounced."

He brushed a cloth napkin across a black mustache and smoothed a hand over neatly trimmed dark hair. "*Buenos días, Señoras.* I'm afraid you have me at a disadvantage. I do not know your names."

I used my unclaimed hand to gesture toward Jenny. "This is Jennifer Coleman, director of the Department of Children and Families in northern Florida." I was giving her a bit of a promotion but I didn't want to waste time on jurisdictions. And I demoted myself. "I'm Lieutenant Anderson, of the Starling, Florida police department."

A flicker in his eye, then Gutiérrez nodded. "Pleased to meet you, ladies. Can I offer some refreshments? I was about to have dessert."

"No, thank you," I said.

"But I insist. Some chilled tea perhaps?" He gestured toward two of the four empty chairs around the table.

"Thank you," Jenny said. "That would be great." She stepped forward and took the chair in the middle, leaving an empty one on either side of hers. She pulled a pad, a pen and a business card from her purse and laid the card on the table in front of Gutiérrez's seat.

I started to take the chair between her and Gutiérrez.

"Surely you are too warm in that coat, Detective," he said. "Please make yourself comfortable."

I took off my black jacket and hung it on the back of the chair. I sat and pulled the chair in, glad that I'd thought to put gun and phone somewhere other than my jacket pockets.

Gutiérrez had resumed his seat. He nodded at the maid.

Her face taut, eyes anxious, she quickly cleared away the dishes.

Damn! I'd hoped to snag a piece of cutlery. Then I wouldn't have to play games later.

"You seemed to recognize the name of our fair city," I said. "You've been to Starling?"

He hesitated. "I have had some business dealings in Jacksonville recently, so yes, I have heard of Starling."

Hmm, interesting. A good number of the *residents* of Jacksonville didn't know Starling existed. I was itching to ask more about his "business dealings" but that might seem suspicious. Apparently he wasn't a total recluse, though.

Alejandro's photo was in my jacket pocket. When I leaned to one side to extract it, Gutiérrez tensed. I pulled the picture out slowly and laid it next to Jenny's card. "Sir, we have reason to believe that this is your son."

He examined the photo by leaning forward. He did not touch it.

Double damn!

"That could be Alejandro," he said, his voice cautious.

I pulled out another photo. Thank heavens, Tatiana had not been in the water long—her face wasn't bloated. I'd cropped the edges of the photo. She looked like she was sleeping, rather than lying naked on an autopsy table.

I laid her beside her son. "Is this your wife?"

I didn't look directly at him but watched his face carefully in my peripheral vision.

Something flashed across it, making his eyes squint and his mouth tighten into a long firm line. But I couldn't read the emotion accurately. It could've been anger, or pain.

He didn't say anything, just nodded.

After a beat, I added, "I'm afraid she was captured by human traffickers. But she somehow managed to keep the boy with her, and keep him safe."

His face was blank, no reaction at all. "Suppose that this is my boy, how do I get him back?" His voice was tight, betraying more emotion than his expression.

Interesting... No questions about the wife, not even if she was alive or not. I suspected he already knew she was dead. But was that because he'd killed her, or had he learned her fate some other way?

"First, we need to ascertain two things," I said. "Is this child your son, and if so, is it appropriate to return him to you? Do you believe this is your son?"

"He quite possibly could be, but I would want proof also."

"Of course." I nodded, as a couple of puzzle pieces clicked into place. He thought we might be here to scam him with fake pictures of a child that could be his. And he couldn't tell for sure that the boy in the photo *was* his. No doubt, Alejandro had changed a lot from age two, when he would've been a pudgy toddler.

I gestured toward Jenny. "Ms. Coleman has some questions for you."

Her expression was sympathetic. "First, let me say how sorry I am for the pain you must've gone through, not knowing where your wife and son were."

His face pinched again, and he gave a curt nod. "Thank you."

She asked a few standard questions about his age and physical health, jotting his answers on her pad.

The maid arrived with a tray of glasses and a pitcher of iced tea. We fell quiet as she placed the things on the table and deftly poured the tea, not making eye contact with any of us.

I'd been afraid that Jenny had forgotten my instructions to not eat or drink anything, but she left the sweating glass untouched. Pen poised over her pad, she asked, "What is your annual income?"

He let out a low laugh, spreading his arms wide to include the entire *hacienda*. "As you can see, I am quite wealthy."

Jenny gave him a warm, and no doubt well-practiced, smile. "Your property is beautiful, sir." She waved a hand vaguely in the air, also indicating our surroundings. "But you could be in debt up to your ears. I need to confirm that you have the income to sustain a good home."

He frowned, then heaved a sigh. He pulled out a cell phone and scrolled, showed us the screen, a contact's name and number. Jenny jotted them down.

"Mine is old family money," Gutiérrez said. "Honestly, I do not know my exact worth from day to day, but that is my accountant's number. I will instruct him to give you the information you need." He gave her a fake smile.

Jenny asked more questions.

Gutiérrez sipped his tea, grimaced and picked up a long-handled iced tea spoon. He added sugar to his glass and set the spoon back on the table.

I eyed it, trying to think of a way to pilfer it without being obvious. Just in case the trick I was about to pull didn't work.

"Who would take care of the boy on a day-to-day basis?" Jenny asked.

Again, Gutiérrez made the expansive gesture. "Of course, I will hire a nanny, and tutors as well."

"Forgive me, sir," Jenny said, "but you have a reputation as a recluse. Would you keep the boy always at home here? He needs the company of other children, and adults for that matter, to learn good social skills."

Gutiérrez was frowning again. "What is *recluse*?"

"A hermit," I interjected, my tone slightly derisive. "Someone who never leaves their house."

Something flashed in his eyes. I was pretty sure it was anger this time. *Good!* I wanted him off kilter.

"It is true that I rarely leave my property, but I would not say I am a hermit. And I will see that the boy is appropriately socialized." His tone was stiffer than before.

I leaned forward. "Rumor also has it that you beat your wife."

His head jerked around toward me. His mouth was a firm line again. Red crept up his cheeks. "Who has said that about me?" he demanded.

I shrugged nonchalantly. "No one in particular. It's only the scuttle-butt."

Was that the sound of his teeth grinding together? I resisted the urge to smile.

"By *scut-tle-butt*," he said slowly and firmly, "I assume you mean un-founded gossip."

I shrugged again. "That, and other sources."

"What other sources?"

A third shrug. "Your wife..."

His hands now clutched the edge of the table. For a second, I feared he'd up-end it in our laps.

"What has that *puta* said about me? She always was a liar!"

"If she's a *puta*," I said, my tone almost casual, "I guess that's part of why you're not sure the boy is yours, huh?"

"That bloody ungrateful slut!" He let go of the edge of the table and banged on it instead.

Jenny jumped in her chair, but I'd anticipated something along these lines. This guy wasn't nearly as calm, cool, and collected as he liked to pretend he was.

"I gave her everything she could ever want or need," he growled, his face now a mask of rage. "But still her eye wandered. And I was a naive fool," he spat out. "I even sent her to that fancy clinic in Tucson, when she was having a difficult pregnancy."

"She had problems during her pregnancy?" Jenny asked in a soothing voice.

No Jenny, I don't want him soothed yet.

"The doctor said she might lose the baby, if she didn't stay in bed." His face was still furious, but his tone was somewhat calmer.

"She had–" Gutiérrez broke off, pink creeping up his cheeks again. I suspected it was from embarrassment this time.

"Break-through bleeding?" I said just to make him squirm.

Pink shifted to red. He looked away. "She could've stayed here, been waited on hand and foot. But no, she needed to go to that clinic. Cost me a fortune! But the doctor backed her, said she needed to reduce her stress level if she was to make it to term."

Pirolnik was right. Tatiana always had a plan. She'd managed to get away from her abusive husband, until her baby was safely born.

It's now or never. This was probably as off-kilter as I was going to get him.

"So," I said, "it's in everybody's interest here, that we find out for sure if this is your child." I reached down to my right and pulled one of two plastic zipper bags from my other jacket pocket. They each contained the contents of a home DNA kit, but I'd gotten rid of the boxes, not wanting Gutiérrez to realize they weren't official test kits. I wasn't all that interested in *officially* getting his DNA. I wanted his fingerprints!

And as a precaution, I'd brought two kits, just in case something went wrong with the first one.

"I'm sure you won't mind giving us a cheek swab so we can compare your DNA to his."

He paled slightly. "I assumed you had brought his DNA with you."

I looked at Jenny. "Dang," I said, "we should've thought of that. It would've moved things along faster. But since we didn't–"

"I do not want my DNA in your American database!"

"No worries, by federal law..." I removed a swab packet and the collection envelope it went into once the sample had been taken. "*U.S. federal law*, that is—DNA info is confidential. We'll only use this to compare to the boy's, then we'll destroy it."

"Here," I handed the collection envelope to him, "hold this for me."

He reluctantly took it, holding it gingerly between his thumb and fingers.

Good! Need to work fast now, not give him time to think.

I quickly broke open the swab packet and extracted one, stood and leaned over. "Open wide."

He hesitated, glanced sideways at Jenny. She was watching him intently, making it hard for him to refuse without it looking suspicious. He opened his mouth.

I swabbed his cheek and snatched the envelope away from him at the same time. I popped the swab into it, then dropped it into the baggie.

"All done," I chirped in a cheery voice. Holding the baggie firmly in one hand, I scooped up my jacket off the chair back with the other. "It's been a pleasure meeting you, Señor Gutiérrez. We'll be in touch."

I took off at a power-walk pace across the courtyard, Jenny hustling to catch up. I glanced over my shoulder.

Gutiérrez stood next to the table, a mix of emotions now naked on his face—the most prominent anger.

As soon as we were out of his line of sight, I pulled out my phone and called Emil. "Start the car. We need to get out of here fast."

He had both back doors hanging open when we got there.

CHAPTER TWENTY-THREE

Gutiérrez might try to stop us. He'd had some time to think now. Would the gate be closed?

I wasn't too worried about scaling it myself, but Jenny was so petite, and she wore a skirted suit and pumps. I had trouble visualizing her getting over that gate.

You're getting ahead of yourself, Anderson. I didn't know if he was going to come after us or not. But that expression on his face…

I was cursing myself for not anticipating the possibility. I'd prepared for what I thought would be the worst-case scenario—a violent confrontation—by bringing my guns. But I'd figured the more likely negative outcome would be Gutiérrez refusing to give us anything, neither DNA nor fingerprints, and throwing us off his property. Which would have told us something, in and of itself.

We rounded a curve, and the gate came into sight. My heart raced. It was sitting open.

Emil floored it. "He wants us off his property first," he yelled over the squeal of tires. The gate posts flew past our side windows.

First, before what?

I turned and looked out the back window, and got my answer. A dark sedan, surrounded by a cloud of dust, was moving toward us. "How good are you at evasive driving?"

The crack of a gunshot.

"*¡Ay, mierda!* I guess it's time to find out." Emil swerved to one side of the road and back again.

"Get down, Jenny!" I yelled over the screech of tires. I glanced over, discovered the command was unnecessary. She was down in the foot well between the front and back seats.

"My cell's on the front seat here," Emil yelled. "Grab it and hit one."

I had to undo my seatbelt to lean over the back of the seat. That did not make me happy, but the distant crack of another gunshot said Emil dared not slow down nor stop his zigzagging.

I grabbed the phone off the passenger seat, punched one and held it up to the side of his face.

He rattled away in Spanish for a good twenty seconds. "*Bueno.*" He nodded and I took the phone away.

"Leave the line open. My sergeant is bringing backup."

I leaned forward to drop the phone back on the passenger's seat. That's when I noticed he was grinning from ear to ear.

I acknowledged the zing of excitement shooting through my own system, as I sat back and awkwardly rebuckled my seatbelt, while trying to keep my head down behind the seat back.

Jenny's eyes were wide. "Who's shooting at us?"

"Gutiérrez's men would be my guess," I said.

"Why?" she asked, her tone incredulous.

"Again, just guessing, but I think he wasn't planning on giving us his fingerprints, along with his DNA."

He knows he got careless and left some fingerprints at Caroline Baumann's house.

Tires squealed again as Emil swerved back and forth.

"That's the main thing you wanted, wasn't it?" Jenny yelled over the noise. "His fingerprints."

I nodded.

We hit a big pothole and I bounced upward, got a quick look out the back window, then ducked down again. Two dark sedans were following us now, and gaining ground.

We went around a curve on two wheels. Emil swung the steering wheel and we were suddenly on another road. "I'm going to take the back roads. It's the only way to lose them," he yelled.

"I thought that *was* the back road." I pointed behind us with my thumb.

"Hang on!" Again, he spun the wheel, turning the car onto an even narrower track. This one was unpaved.

"At the very least," Emil said, still talking loud to be heard over the crunch of gravel, "they'll have to split up, not knowing which way we went."

I stared out the back window. "I don't see them. I think you can get up now, Jenny."

She wiggled up off the floor and sat on the seat, quickly buckling her seatbelt. "Why didn't they just stop us from leaving the *hacienda*'s grounds?" she asked.

"Gutiérrez didn't want us to be associated with him," Emil said. "They've probably been instructed to make it look like *banditos* got us."

"*Banditos*?" Jenny's voice squeaked.

Emil didn't seem to hear her. "There would be quite the scandal if two Americans, one a police chief no less, and a Nuevo Léon officer turned up dead. Gutiérrez wouldn't want that kind of negative attention."

He glanced in the rearview mirror, must've seen Jenny's stark-white face. "Don't worry. If *banditos* do find us, they'll hold us for ransom, not kill us."

I could hear Jenny gulp even over the crunching gravel. "Somehow I don't think that's all that reassuring, Emil," I said, "but thanks for trying."

The car lurched slightly to the right. "Uh, oh," Emil said. "I was afraid of that."

"Of what?" Jenny said, her hand clutching the front of her blouse.

I was beginning to worry that she'd have a heart attack.

"I think we have a flat tire." He slowed the car to a stop.

Jenny flopped back in her seat and blew out air. I wasn't so sure she should be relieved just yet. We would be sitting ducks if *banditos* came along while we were changing a tire.

Emil looked up in the mirror and caught my eye. "Could you help?"

"You bet." I reached under the driver's seat and pulled out the metal box holding my Glock.

When I lifted the gun out, Jenny's eyes went wide. "I didn't know you had a cannon in there. Why didn't you shoot back at them?"

Because this isn't the Wild West, I thought but didn't say. "You noticed that they didn't hit us. It's hard to hit a moving target, even one as big as a car. Especially when you're in a moving car yourself. Me shooting back would've been a waste of ammo, and I might have accidentally hit some farmer out in his fields."

Emil was nodding. "But I'm not sure they didn't hit us. My guess is they were aiming at our tires, because that's what *banditos* would do. Blow out the tires to stop us. Then they can sell the car, with-out bullet holes in it to diminish its value. And they have healthy hostages to demand ransom for."

During their interchange, I'd put both DNA kits—the used one and the extra—in the gun box. Now, my heart stuttered some at Emil's words, *healthy hostages*. If Gutiérrez's men caught up with us, were their instructions to take us back to him? Did he intend to torture us to find out Alejandro's location?

I shuddered, then locked the gun box and tucked it under my arm as I got out of the car.

I followed Emil to the trunk. He got out the jack and spare tire, while I retrieved my laptop case and put the gun box in it. The zipper wouldn't quite close all the way, but now I could keep the all-important DNA kit on my person, without risking it falling out of a pocket. I looped the laptop case's leather strap over my head.

We walked around to the right side of the car. The back tire was pretty close to pancake status.

Emil crouched down and ran a hand over the sidewall. "Yeah, they grazed it."

"I'll keep an eye out for them, and for *banditos*." I leaned a hip against the car fender and did a slow 180-scan behind us. I glanced over my shoulder to the road in front. I repeated the whole process, holding my Glock against my thigh, the finger resting on the side of the trigger guard.

"So," Emil began jacking up the car, "why did Gutiérrez suddenly object to whatever the hell you did in there?"

My eyes continuing to scan our surroundings, I said, "He was a little anxious when he realized we wanted his DNA, concerned it would go into the U.S. criminal databases. About what you'd expect from someone who doesn't have a criminal record."

"Which he doesn't." Emil grunted as he removed a stubborn lug nut. "I checked, as I'm sure you did also."

"Not in the name of Manuel Gutiérrez, at least. And probably not at all, if my hunch is right."

Emil glanced up at me. "Are you dragging out the suspense on purpose?"

I chuckled, my eyes still on the road behind us. "No, not intentionally. But I'm multitasking here." I looked over my shoulder again. Nothing but dirt road and bare fields stretching to the horizon.

"I took him by surprise, though, when I handed him part of the DNA kit to hold, and snatched it away again before he could think what to do about the fact that he'd just produced an excellent set of prints for me. Then I got us the hell out of there."

"You think his prints are going to be in the databases?" Emil was working fast. He now had the spare halfway on, two lug nuts to go.

"Unlikely if his DNA isn't in there. But we have unidentified prints from two different crime scenes. They match each other but weren't in the system. My hunch is that his are going to be a match."

"Two crime scenes?" He tightened a lug nut with a grunt and reached for the last one.

"Dust on the horizon behind us," I said, raising my gun.

Emil pocketed the lug nut and quickly lowered the jack. Leaving it and the deflated tire on the side of the road, we raced around the car. He jumped into the driver's seat.

It took me a few extra seconds to get myself and the cumbersome laptop case into the backseat. Emil floored it before I'd even gotten the door closed. It slammed shut on its own. Fortunately, all my fingers and toes were inside.

"Hang on, Jenny," I yelled, struggling to get my seatbelt on.

The car behind us never got all that close, though.

It caught up just enough for me to make out that it was a dark sedan, but I couldn't tell if it was the same one. However, in Mexico, like in Florida, the hot climate meant there were far more light-colored cars than dark. So odds were good this dark car held Gutiérrez's men.

Within minutes, we entered a village. Staring pedestrians forced Emil to slow down some. He veered off onto a side street that was barely wider than a sidewalk. Another turn onto an equally narrow street. I winced when his side mirror scraped a stucco wall.

Yelling from the main street behind us. My stomach clenched. Had our pursuers hit someone? I prayed that no one was hurt, except maybe the bad guys.

But we weren't likely to get that lucky.

Luck was with us, however, in another way, as Emil turned yet again, into an alley. Ahead was a warehouse, its overhead door hanging open, a wide empty space for trucks to pull in to unload.

Emil pulled in instead and screeched to a halt.

He and I were both out of the car in less than a second. He flashed his badge at the befuddled warehouse manager, then turned to the open door.

But I was already there. I jumped up to grab the dangling rope and yanked. The door came down with a crash, barely missing my foot.

I turned to Emil, adjusting my laptop bag's strap that was trying to strangle me. "Well, that got my heart pumping."

He was grinning. "Yes, it did. I haven't had that much fun since I got promoted and now sit behind a desk."

I grinned back. "Been there, done that."

Jenny stumbled out of the car on shaky legs. "What are you two grinning at? We could've gotten killed."

"Yes, but we didn't," we said in unison and grinned some more.

CHAPTER TWENTY-FOUR

Emil's sergeant called when our backup had reached the village.

The warehouse manager had been gracious about our invasion, once he'd gotten over his initial shock. He'd even offered us beer or bottled water. Jenny and I opted for water. Emil took a beer.

Well, that's a strike against him. I hated beer breath. It reminded me of my father. The only times he'd drank beer were when he was working himself into a rage and was about to beat my mother.

Wait a minute! Why was I thinking about strikes against this guy? Was I actually *attracted* to Emil?

I shook my head to clear it and took another sip of water, hoping the stuff really was purified as the label claimed. Emil took a swig of beer, giving me a good look at his left hand. No ring.

I shook my head again.

The sergeant reported in to Emil. Of course, there were now no signs of dark sedans in the village. And the stalwart citizens had nothing to tell the *policía* about the car chase. "'What car chase?' most of them say." The sergeant mimicked their shrugs.

Emil tagged a couple of uniforms to take us back to Monterrey Airport, where hopefully we could catch a late flight home. "Sorry I cannot be your escort, but I must attend to some things here."

I gave him a quizzical look.

"Señor Gutiérrez will expect the *policía* to come talk to him, since his guests were chased by *banditos* just outside his compound. But do not worry, I will not let on that he is suspected of murder. And he, of course, will deny any knowledge of what happened."

I nodded, and we transferred our luggage to the cruiser's trunk. But I held onto my laptop case and its precious cargo.

Emil shook Jenny's and my hands as we were about to climb into the cruiser. Was it my imagination or did he linger longer over my hand?

"I hope we can meet again, Chief," he said with yet another grin. "Perhaps under less intense circumstances. I'd love to show you around Monterrey. It is a very entertaining city."

"Oh, I thought you did a pretty good job of entertaining me this time," I said, gently tugging my hand loose.

What am I doing...flirting with this guy?

But even as I mentally chastised myself, "Call me Judith," came out of my mouth.

He nodded, gave me another charming smile. "Have a good flight, Judith, and Jenny." He leaned down to her open window, to include her in the conversation.

She gave him a curt nod. "Thank you for all your help, First Sergeant."

We lucked out at the airport and caught the last flight, connecting in Atlanta and then on to Jacksonville. Jenny was quiet during the first leg of the journey. I thought she was sleeping, but when I glanced over, her eyes were open. She was staring sightlessly at the back of the seat in front of her.

When we'd settled into our seats on the shorter second flight, she said, "It would've been nice if you'd warned me it would get..." She trailed off.

"I didn't know that it would get like that." I paused, considering. "But I do owe you an apology. I suspected it might get dicey at Gutiérrez's house. But I thought he'd just throw us out on our ears when we asked for DNA, and try again to find Alejandro's location by other means." I cleared my throat. "I didn't expect him to send his henchmen after us."

Which got me to thinking. Why does an innocent, supposedly reclusive rich guy need multiple henchmen? A guard or two on the gate, yes, but I'd seen two heads in the front seat of the lead car, and probably the other car had at least two occupants as well.

On a hunch, I opened my laptop and connected to the in-flight wifi. It took most of the rest of the flight, but eventually I found what I was looking for. A private airplane owned and registered to Manuel Gutiérrez.

So much for you being a recluse.

Records gave a name I didn't recognize as the pilot who had filed a flight plan to Jacksonville Airport—the date was a month prior to Tatiana's death.

"Closing in on you, you bastard," I muttered. That's why he'd admitted to having business in Jax—he knew we might find the flight plan.

Jenny glanced my way.

"Again," I said, "sorry about the harrowing car chase, but the case is coming together."

"Against Gut–"

I quickly held up a hand. "No names in public. But yeah, against him."

Jenny sighed. "No happy ending for our little boy, then."

"I'm not so sure about that. Why couldn't Señor P adopt him?" I figured I should take my own advice and avoid names.

She blew out another sigh, this one exaggerated. "Look, did I tell you how to do your job, even when you were scaring the pants off of me?"

"No…Okay, I get it. Sorry." I turned back to my laptop.

Another half-baked hunch was hovering in the back of my brain. I searched for flight schools in Nuevo Léon. There was only one, in Monterrey. I expanded the search to all of Mexico and found eleven more.

I made a list of them, Monterrey at the top, and emailed Cruthers with instructions to check their student rolls for Gutiérrez's name, going back twenty-five years.

The flight attendant instructed us to buckle our seatbelts. We were beginning our descent into Jacksonville Airport.

I imagined Cruthers reading that email. I could almost hear him groaning from thirty-thousand feet below us.

———◆———

In the airport, a man in a khaki uniform and a wannabe Stetson stood at the edge of the luggage claim area. He was hard to miss since he held a huge bouquet of flowers.

Not sure what to do or say, I walked past him. "Gotta get my guns."

I headed for one of the luggage carousels that was beginning to move, making its obnoxious noise, the light flashing.

"Ms. Coleman," Sam said behind me, "There's a deputy and a cruiser waiting out front. He can get you home in record time with lights and siren. That is..." he raised his voice, "if you'll let me ride back with you, Judith?"

Before I could answer him, Jenny said, "I'd rather he go at a normal speed, thank you very much. I've had enough of speeding cars to last me a lifetime." She gave me a curt nod and walked away.

Sam stepped up beside me, next to the carousel. He had both eyebrows in the air.

"Long story," I said. I let him dangle a few seconds longer. "Yes, you can go home with me." I immediately wished I'd phrased that differently, but I opted not to try to dig out of the hole.

He chuckled, knowing I hadn't meant it like it sounded. "I appreciate the ride."

Gawd! Even that sounded like a double entendre.

I stepped forward and grabbed the sturdy, hard-sided bag that held my small gun safe inside—the two pistols and ammo double-locked and checked, as required by TSA.

Sam was watching me, waiting. Waiting for what? Some cue that I'd forgiven him for being an overprotective jackass?

At least he had the good sense not to reach for the suitcase. I might have had to break his arm.

"Look, Judith, I was a jerk. I hope you can forgive me."

I turned toward him, the case now on its wheels, the handle extended.

"A total jerk," he added.

"You left out *overprotective* total jerk." I walked past him, dragging the case.

I'd left my car in short-term parking, so we didn't have far to walk. I kept up a brisk pace and he hung back a few steps. I glanced back once.

He looked kinda lame, all dressed up in his sheriff gear, but with that huge bouquet I'd yet to acknowledge. Some of my anger drained away.

We arrived at the car, and I stowed my carry-on and laptop case in the trunk. I was struggling to lasso the anger again, keep it going so I didn't have to...

Have to do what? Accept his apology? Or maybe acknowledge that I was now the one being a jerk?

Or admit that he had been right. The trip had been far more dangerous than I'd thought it would be.

"Look, all I want to do is talk," Sam said. "On neutral ground. I know this diner on the outskirts of Jax."

I blew out air and handed him my keys. "You drive. I'm exhausted."

At the diner, we took a booth and both ordered coffee.

"Decaf?" the waitress asked.

We shook our heads in unison. Whatever was coming, I figured I needed to be alert. And Sam never got decaf, no matter the hour. Said it was against his principles.

I half smiled at the memory of the first time he'd said that to a waitress—and I'd snorted my coffee out my nose. Not one of my finer moments.

And not the funniest joke ever, but Sam had good timing. His delivery was usually spot on.

But now he was stalling, playing with a sugar packet, even though he took his coffee black.

The waitress was back already, with a coffee pot. She poured dark liquid into thick white mugs and walked away. I took a sip and sighed.

Sam leaned forward. "Nothing I'm about to say is meant to be an excuse. It's only an explanation."

He paused. I swallowed more caffeine.

"I've only been truly in love once," he said.

"I know. You told me you were divorced." I was hoping to move things along. The coffee was waking me up, but it wasn't making me any less tired.

He shook his head. "I married my wife because she was sweet and funny and reliable, the kind of woman a man wants to come home to. And I did." He stopped, took a sip of coffee.

"Did what?"

"Want to come home to her...until I didn't. I met a woman who absolutely fascinated me, and I realized that what I'd thought was love with my wife was really just contentment."

The acid from the coffee made my stomach churn. I should probably try to eat something.

The waitress came by to check on us, and suddenly I didn't want to hear the rest of Sam's story. "Could I get a grilled cheese with tomato, to go, please?"

Maybe not the best thing for a queasy stomach, but it was my go-to comfort food.

Sam had a confused expression on his face. He cleared his throat as the waitress bustled off. "This woman was a detective in my precinct, in the special victims unit, only we still called it sex crimes back then. She was a few years older than me. I watched her in action for months. She was confident and yet compassionate. And she had more guts than three of our best male cops combined."

My stomach roiled. "So you had an affair." I tried to keep my voice nonjudgmental, but I was pretty sure I'd failed.

"Only in my fantasies," he said. "But after a while I realized I wasn't being fair to me or to Lil, my wife. Still, I didn't know what to do. I didn't want to hurt Lil, only to find out that this woman wasn't interested in me. And then I made detective and was working with her."

He sipped coffee. "Her name was Glenda. I was partnered with her, to learn the ropes." He waved a hand in the air. "Lemme make a long story short. I'd finally worked up the nerve to, um, feel her out, when we got this big case. A human trafficking ring. Sound familiar?"

I nodded.

"These were the really bad guys. Before I'd been dealing with perverts who couldn't keep it zipped around kids, and guys who got off attacking women weaker than themselves. They rarely fought back all that hard when we arrested them." He fell silent, stared off into space.

The waitress arrived with my sandwich, wrapped in deli-style paper and inside a paper bag. But through all those layers, I could still smell the grease and cheese, with a slight tang of tomato. My stomach growled, loudly.

Sam chuckled, even though his eyes seemed...what? Haunted, maybe.

"Lemme guess," he said. "You haven't eaten all day."

"Do airline pretzels and peanuts count?"

"Not really. Go ahead, eat it." He smiled indulgently as I unwrapped the sandwich and devoured half of it in three bites.

I groaned. My mouth and stomach were much happier.

Then I caught the expression on Sam's face. *Haunted* was the correct word alright. "Tell me the rest."

"There isn't a lot more to tell. We raided the building where they had the women, and things went south. I don't think I made any mistakes, but still it's always felt like it was my fault. That if I'd been a more experienced detective, she wouldn't have..." He trailed off.

"She was killed?"

He nodded. "I was a mess afterwards. Lil kept asking what was wrong, and I couldn't tell her." His words rushed out. "It would've broken her heart and what was the point now? I took a leave of absence, and told her we needed to separate, that I needed some space to think, to heal."

He shook his head. "But the healing was a long time coming—years, before I could put it in perspective. Or at least, I thought I had."

"Until our raid the other night on that house," I said.

"No, ironically that didn't set me off. At least, I don't think so. That was kinda therapeutic. You see, there was a woman in that raid too, who was posing as one of the girls, but who was really a member of the ring. She got the drop on Glenda and then got away."

"So catching Lorraine was some kind of coming-full-circle thing?"

He shrugged. "I guess."

He sat forward, took my hand. "What set me off was you going to Mexico, without me. Going into a situation that could go south really quick." He gave me a weak smile. "No pun intended."

What pun? I must've looked confused.

"You know, south, to Mexico."

I snorted softly. His timing was definitely off tonight.

He shook his head again. "Suddenly I was back there, that rookie detective, not sure what was going to happen, feeling out of control. I freaked out." He squeezed my hand. "Please forgive me for being an *overprotective* jerk."

I patted his hand on top of mine. "Apology accepted. Now let go so I can finish my sandwich."

He did so, and I chomped off another bite of gooey cheese and tangy tomato.

I chewed and swallowed, then set the remainder of the sandwich down. "I, um, have a confession to make. Things got a little dicey, more than I'd expected them to." I told him about the car chase.

I braced for an "I told you so."

But he didn't go there. "Why does this guy need so many armed men?" he said instead. "I mean, sure, he's rich and Mexico isn't the safest place, but..."

"I was wondering the same thing. Is there something else going on there, besides an abuser chasing down his escaped wife and child?"

"He could be a drug lord."

I nodded, then filled him in on the private plane and the flight plan filed for a month before Caroline and Tatiana had been killed.

"Hot damn," Sam chortled. "It's looking like he is our man!"

"Yeah." I picked up my sandwich. It was now cold. I nibbled along the edge. "I feel like an idiot for not planning better."

"Planning what?"

"The whole trip. I shouldn't have involved Jenny for one thing."

Sam took my hand again. "Hey, hindsight is twenty-twenty and all that. You had no reason to believe this guy had a small army."

I gave him a weak smile and extracted my hand, picked up the remnant of my sandwich and popped it into my mouth. Anything to delay my next admission.

After I'd chewed and swallowed, I said, "I keep making mistakes. I'm not sure–"

"Of course, you do," Sam cut me off. "You've only been head of your own force for two months. You expected to know how to do everything by magic."

I shook my head. "I'm just not used to feeling like a rookie."

He gave me a sympathetic smile. "I didn't like the feeling much either, when I was a newbie sheriff. The learning curve is pretty steep, but I have confidence in you."

I sighed. "Most days, I do too, but after *this* day..." I sat forward and picked up the strap of my laptop case from beside me on the booth's bench.

Sam cleared his throat. "Um, getting back to the subject of being over-protective. The other evening at Pirolnik's building, when we arrested Juarez..."

Apparently we weren't leaving yet. I settled again against the back of the bench. "What about it?"

"Do you remember screaming 'no' over the phone?"

"Vaguely, but I don't remember why."

"You'd asked me to get a good look at him when he came out of the fire stairs, and I said something like, 'I can do better than that'..." He trailed off again, looked at me expectantly.

I shrugged.

"I meant to bring this up the other night," he said, "over our romantic repast during your stakeout. But then all hell broke loose."

He paused, lowered his gaze to the table. "It seemed like you were trying to protect me that night at Pirolnik's place, from the guy who was running down the stairs. And you seemed angry with me because I'd tackled him."

I stared at Sam, trying to remember what he was talking about. I vaguely recalled snapping at him. We were standing next to that tree, the perp sitting beside it, his hands cuffed behind him.

Sam lifted his head, made eye contact. "It was kind of annoying, considering I'm a sworn law enforcement officer and all."

The memory came flooding back, not of the scene on the sidewalk, but of that moment on the stairs, when I'd realized I'd put Sam in harm's way. Every muscle in my body had clenched and I had indeed yelled *no* into the phone.

I took a sip of lukewarm coffee. I was stalling, trying to process now the feelings that I'd shoved aside then. "I think it was about..." I floundered for a moment. "I'd brought you into that situation. That somehow made you an innocent and me responsible for protecting you. It wasn't rational, just a gut reaction at the time." I shook my head. "I didn't give any thought to the fact that you're a trained and armed LEO yourself."

Sam nodded. "That makes sense. We both take the protect and serve to heart. But that doesn't mean we have to protect each other." He paused, rubbed his chin.

I noted it was free of stubble. He'd shaved a second time, before coming over to Jax to meet me. Somehow that warmed my chest more than the flowers had.

"I'm beginning to realize," he said, "that I'm only truly attracted to women who are my equal in that realm, who can take care of themselves, and then some." He grinned. "What's that say about me that I like my women tougher than I am?"

I held out my hand. "Let's make a pact."

He went to take my hand, but I snared his little finger with my own. "I pinky swear that I won't be an overprotective jerk if you don't go there either."

Sam threw back his head and laughed.

I slept like a rock, right through the alarm. I finally dragged myself out of bed and stumbled, groggy, out to the kitchen for caffeine. There was no time for exercising this morning, unfortunately.

The half glass of red wine and the opened bottle still sat on my break-fast bar. I'd poured it last night, drank half, then was so sleepy I couldn't even stay awake long enough to finish it.

Nor put it away, apparently. But first things first.

I got my coffee maker going. While it gurgled, I corked the bottle and dumped the wine from the glass down the drain.

Finally, caffeine in a mug firmly secured in my hand, I walked toward the bathroom for a quick shower.

Wait, where's the kitten?

A loud meow from the other bedroom's door answered my question. I opened it and Pipsqueak wound between my ankles. "How'd you get in there?" I'd closed her in my bedroom with me last night, or at least I'd thought I had.

I stuck my head inside the room to make sure she hadn't shredded something in frustration. Everything looked normal. I'd probably left both doors ajar last night, in my sleepy fog, and she came in here, rubbed against the door, and nudged it closed.

Ten minutes later, I was showered and dressed. I gathered my things, slipping my little revolver into its ankle holster and my Glock into the one at the small of my back. I headed for the living room, with the niggling feeling that I was forgetting something.

I stopped by my sofa and patted my pockets. I had my wallet and my cell phone. *Wait, my laptop case!*

I glanced at the sofa, where I'd plopped down the black leather case last night, the gun box sticking out of the top of it.

I froze. The sofa was empty, nothing on the leather cushions but cat hairs.

CHAPTER TWENTY-FIVE

By the time I was headed for 3MB, I was over an hour late, not that I answered to anyone regarding my time, but still.

I'd spent forty-five minutes searching my apartment. Nothing else seemed to be missing or disturbed. Even the small suitcase I'd transported my guns in was there, next to the sofa.

After sending a text to Barnes to let her know I was on my way, I called Sam.

"Good morning," he said cheerfully. "Thanks for the company and the chat last night."

Warmth spread through my chest. "You're welcome. Thanks for the coffee and the sandwich." I paused. "Afraid this is an official call, though. I think someone was in my apartment last night, and they took my laptop."

"What? Last night while we were at the diner?"

"No, last night while I was sleeping."

Sam let out a short stream of expletives.

"Yeah, my sentiments exactly."

"They had to be quite the stealthy cat burglar to not wake you up," Sam said. The words were light but his voice sounded shaky.

"Maybe, or..." My brain, now more fully awake, was putting together puzzle pieces. I had been tired but not all that sleepy when I'd gotten home. Thus the glass of wine to help me wind down, but still I shouldn't have gotten sleepy quite that fast.

"I might have been drugged."

"What?" Sam yelled.

"I had a bottle of red wine started, sitting corked on my counter. I had a glass of that before bed, and couldn't even finish it, I was suddenly so sleepy. And the cat was in the study this morning, door closed, when I could've sworn I took her in my bedroom with me last night."

"So someone did come in while you weren't home," his voice sounded calmer but more angry now, "drugged the wine, and watched for the lights to go out in your apartment after you got home."

My insides clenched and a cold shiver ran down my spine, as it sank in that someone had been creeping around the place while I was sleeping. I swallowed hard, shoved the emotions down.

"Anything crucial or super sensitive on the laptop?" Sam asked.

"Yes, but it's pretty secure. Derek rigged it so it needs my thumb print to unlock it. And there isn't much on there that isn't duplicated somewhere else." My stomach knotted as I remembered the sensitive files I'd transferred, then deleted from the desktop. I shook my head, nothing to do about that now. "My gun box is missing too. It was sitting on top of the laptop case." I was having trouble keeping my voice even. "I, uh…"

"Are you freaked out? Because I am. And I'm not being protective," he quickly added. "Just putting myself in your shoes."

My stomach and chest loosened some. I blew out air. "Yeah, freaked out would be a good way to describe it."

"Why would someone go to all that trouble to get your laptop?"

More pieces fell into place. "I don't think it was the laptop they were after, but what they thought was in the case. That DNA test kit. While I was in Mexico, I was carrying it around inside the gun box, which was crammed down into my laptop case, so I could keep it with me."

But last night, we'd stopped at the municipal building, where Sam had left his truck. I'd taken the gun safe out of my suitcase and holstered my guns on my person. Then we'd gone up to the third floor, where I'd put the used DNA kit into a proper evidence bag and logged it into the evidence room. The empty gun safe had gone back into my laptop case to take home.

But it wasn't entirely empty.

"I'd taken two DNA kits with me," I said, "just as a precaution. The unused one was still in the gun box."

"So they found it and thought it was the used one. In the dark, they might not have noticed that it hadn't been opened. And maybe they took the laptop too, to make it look like a robbery?"

The cold shiver was back. "That would be my guess."

"Good thing we dropped the used test kit off last night then."

"Yup." I swung my car into the municipal parking lot. "I'll call you back as soon as I have the techs' report on the fingerprints."

"Uh, Judith, would it fall into overprotective jerk territory if I asked you to watch your back today? I'm pretty convinced this guy's our killer, and he's a ruthless s.o.b."

I smiled at the dashboard screen. "No, I think that falls into concerned friend category, and I will watch my back, for sure. You too."

"For sure. Talk soon."

<hr />

I found Cruthers, Collins and Bradley in the conference room, staring at the murder board. Agent Wellbourne was also there, standing back a bit, as if waiting for an invite into the club.

Might need to give her some tips for negotiating the male world of law enforcement.

"Hey, how was your trip, Chief?" Bradley asked.

"Exciting and productive." I gave them a brief rundown of the harrowing chase in Mexico after I tricked Gutiérrez into giving me his fingerprints, as well as his DNA.

"The DNA evidence won't hold up in court," Bradley pointed out.

"I know. I was more interested in getting the fingerprints. They probably won't fly in court either, but they'll tell us if this is our guy. Then we'll have to figure out how to prove it."

I paused, considering. "I'm thinking about having Bert run the DNA through the system anyway. I promised the man I wouldn't put it *in* the database, but I never said I wouldn't compare it to what's already there. Oh, and we have our victim's real name now, Delores Maria Sonoma Gutiérrez. The bastard recognized her picture, but he didn't even ask what happened to her, or where her body was."

"I think we should keep calling her Tatiana, Chief," Cruthers said in a mournful voice, his broad face sagging. "At least among ourselves. That's the name *she* picked."

I glanced at the crime scene photos and nodded.

A knock on the door. Ernie stuck his head in. "Definitely got a match, Chief, with Sheriff Pierson's crime scene. Not as sure about the print on our victim's car door handle. Might not be enough points of similarity to hold up in court, but we think it's a match."

"So he's our guy," I said, "or at least he was there. But I'm betting he wielded that sap and was trying to force her to cough up the kid, but he lost his temper and killed her."

Something else was niggling at my brain. I couldn't seem to lasso it and bring it to the forefront. I still felt a little foggy. Which reminded me...

"Ernie, there's a partial bottle of wine on my counter and a wineglass in the sink. I need the wine in them analyzed. I think it has some kind of sedative in it." I tossed him my apartment key and he left the room.

When I turned back to the detectives, four sets of eyes were staring at me. I sighed and filled them in on my visitor last night.

"It's amazing that he didn't hurt the kitten," Collins said, his usual enthusiastic smile missing in action.

"She most likely heard him out in the living room and started yowling," I said. "So he let her out and... Wait, why didn't she yowl when he closed her in the other room?" I snapped my fingers and pulled out my cell phone.

"Yeah, Chief," Ernie answered after only one ring, road noise in the background.

"Check the kitten's kibble and water. He may have drugged her as well."

"Also look for catnip," Collins called out. "It puts cats in their happy place and they don't care about much else."

"You got it," Ernie said.

I disconnected, as Collins was saying, "I hope they didn't drug the kitten. Cats can't metabolize human sedatives."

I stared at him, willing my pounding heart to settle down. Pipsqueak had been fine this morning, I reminded myself.

His boyish cheeks pinked. "I volunteer at an animal shelter. I love cats."

"You want one?" I asked, and immediately wished I hadn't.

"I can't. My wife would kill me. We already have four."

I resisted the urge to shake my head. *Four cats?*

I turned to the other two. "Find out where he's landing his plane."

"Oh, that reminds me," Cruthers said. "I hit pay dirt on the first try with that list you sent. He went to flight school in Monterrey in his early twenties, but dropped out toward the end and never applied for his pilot's license."

———◆O◆———

Special Agent Wellbourne still hadn't said a word. She followed us out of the conference room. I hung back with her as the double Cs walked toward the bullpen. Bradley followed my lead.

"Uh, Chief," Wellbourne said. "Could you have someone bring me up to speed on this case? I'm feeling a little lost."

"Sure. Let's go to the crime scene. I wouldn't mind taking another look at it myself. Bradley, you drive. Your car's bigger." Okay, that was lame, but I wanted to get all three of us away from 3MB so we could talk safely.

He cocked a curious eyebrow my way but didn't say anything.

Once we were settled in his car, me riding shotgun and Wellbourne in the back, Bradley said, "No offense, Agent, but why are you still here? I thought you were just helping out with sweeping up the rest of the trafficking ring here in Starling."

"I, um..." Wellbourne stammered.

I interrupted and filled Bradley in on the young woman's real reason for sticking around. "But the official word to the others is that she's helping out with Tatiana's case."

Movement in my peripheral vision. I glanced over my shoulder.

Wellbourne had her pad out. "I have a list of all your personnel. Can you give me your take on their honesty?"

"Start with the uniforms," I said. "Bradley can tell you more about them. I don't know most of them all that well yet."

She ran through that list, with Bradley giving a percentage of certainty as to how honest he thought each one was. Sometimes he added a comment or two. It was useful for me, hearing his take on our officers. The only uniform he gave a one-hundred percent for honesty was his sister, Officer Gloria Barnes.

I hid a smile.

Then they started on the sergeants. "Armstrong's been in the department longer than I have," Bradley said. "He's a bit..." he trailed off, apparently searching for the right word.

"Irreverent," I said.

He chuckled. "Yeah, but I'd give him ninety percent."

I would've said ninety-five, but maybe that was only because I liked the guy. Nice guys weren't necessarily honest guys, however.

Bradley pulled his car off onto the shoulder. We'd arrived at the Sofki Bridge.

We walked along the pedestrian sidewalk on one side. Mid-morning, it was deserted and the traffic was relatively light.

We crossed to the other side. Bradley had brought a couple of orange traffic cones he'd pulled out of his trunk.

Do magic trunks run in the family?

He placed the cones on an angle to funnel the few cars in that lane into the center one. Still we stayed on the narrow shoulder, in case some driver wasn't paying attention. Bradley pointed to where we thought the various cars had stopped and explained Ernie's hypothesis regarding the sequence of events to Wellbourne.

She nodded a lot and took notes.

Back in Bradley's car, we headed for 3MB, and Wellbourne asked about the other watch commanders.

When they got to Sergeant Lewis, I said, "He has a serious attitude problem. I don't know if it's burnout, or because he now has a female boss—"

"Nah," Bradley said, "he's always been that way."

"What way?" Wellbourne asked.

"Cynical..." Bradley trailed off, stared out the windshield. "He always believes the worst about people. Not much compassion for victims, and even less for criminals, even ones who've only committed minor crimes.

"But he's a decent cop, does his job," he quickly added.

"How would you rate his honesty?" she asked.

Bradley shook his head slightly. "Not sure. I've never seen any signs that he's dishonest. But I'm afraid my instincts about him are clouded by the fact that I don't like the guy."

"Same here." I turned in my seat to look back at Wellbourne. "All this is confidential, by the way. I don't want to have it coming back to my department that we've been badmouthing our own people."

Wellbourne's tan and freckled cheeks turned bronze. 'Of course not, Chief."

"Sorry. Didn't mean to sound like I was accusing you of being a gossip."

"No, no," she said. "You've got a right to be distrustful. I can't imagine what it must feel like to discover you've got bad cops on your own team."

Bradley glanced in his rearview mirror, made eye contact with her. "It's not fun."

He looked back at the street ahead, then over at me, his eyes a bit wide. "And I just thought of something. Before Lewis sat for the sergeant's exam, he was one of the patrol officers in the section of town where those call houses are."

"Shit," Wellbourne said, "Oh, sorry, ma'am."

"No need to apologize," I said. "My ears aren't sensitive, and that's pretty much my sentiment as well."

She and Bradley started discussing the detectives. He gave Cruthers ninety-five percent.

I was nodding agreement when my phone rang. Caller ID read *Jenny Coleman, DCF.*

I answered with mixed emotions. "How are you doing, Jenny?"

Bradley and Wellbourne continued their discussion, but in lowered voices.

"I'm fine." Jenny's tone was borderline terse. "Any news on the DNA and fingerprints?"

"DNA processing will take awhile, but the fingerprints—and this is confidential, by the way—they put Gutiérrez at both crime scenes. We think he's our killer, or he ordered the hits. Either way, he was there."

Jenny sighed. "Are you going to extradite him?"

"We don't have enough evidence for that yet."

A beat of silence. "If the DNA says he's Alejandro's father, and you can't prove he's a criminal, we may have to turn the boy over to him."

My fist clenched around the phone. *Over my dead body.*

"Isn't it enough that he tried to kill us?" I said.

"We have no proof that those hooligans were his men." Her tone was definitely terse now.

What'd I do to you, lady? Then I snorted softly. *Besides almost getting you killed, that is?*

"Keep me posted." She disconnected.

A couple more pieces fell into place. That's why Gutiérrez didn't try to stop us on his own property, but rather sent his men after us. Then, if we did get away, we had no proof that the thugs who chased us were his people. And he had a backup plan, to come to Starling and get the test kit back before it could be processed—or so he thought.

My phone rang again. *Emil Herrara,* its screen informed me.

"You're popular today," Bradley commented from the driver's seat. I realized he and Wellbourne had fallen quiet, having finished the list.

I answered the call with, "Judith Anderson," rather than *Chief.*

"How are you today, *mi amiga*?" Emil's smooth baritone said in my ear.

"Not too worse for wear after our exciting day yesterday. How are you?"

"I am well also. *Gracias* for asking." His voice was like warm maple syrup.

I shook my head. *What the hell's wrong with me?*

"I know it is not my case, but since it cost me a tire..." he trailed off.

"The fingerprints were well worth the trouble of getting them. They've positively linked Gutiérrez to one crime scene, and to a partial at another one. The DNA will take a lot longer to process, though."

"And the *niño*, he is okay? You have him some place secure?"

"Yes, in a safe house with his foster family, and with guards, outside of the city."

"*Bueno.* I could tell you were a most competent woman the very first moment I saw you. And I repeat the invitation to show you around Monterrey," he chuckled softly, "under less strenuous circumstances than yesterday."

I chuckled as well, smiling. A warmth spread through me. "I may very well take you up on that, when this case is resolved."

"It will be my absolute pleasure. In the meantime, let's keep in touch."

I wasn't sure if he meant about the case, or... "Yes," I found myself agreeing.

"*Adios*, for now," Emil said.

"*Adios.*" I disconnected, still smiling, and reached for the AC controls on Bradley's dash. "What have you got this set on? It's hot in here." I glanced toward him.

He was watching me, one eyebrow cocked, that half-smile of his on his face.

The warmth spread to my cheeks. My chest tightened. Annoyed, I snapped, "Eyes on the road."

"We're stopped at a red light."

"Oh." I looked up. Sure enough...

I sat back, resisting the urge to fan myself with my hand. I dared not look back at Wellbourne. Hopefully she'd missed the undercurrents in our exchange.

The light changed, and Bradley accelerated through the intersection.

CHAPTER
TWENTY-SIX

Cruthers and Collins lay in wait for me and Bradley in the bullpen at 3MB. Wellbourne had peeled off to study the murder board again.

Collins was practically bouncing up and down, his smile back in place. "We found where he lands his plane, Chief. In a back field of a farm up in Clover County. He pays the farmer a hundred bucks each time."

"And he keeps a car there," Cruthers added, "in one of the guy's barns."

I nodded and waved them toward my office. Barnes followed us in. Once we were all settled—Collins in the comfy chair since he was the star of the moment—I gestured for the double Cs to continue.

"Collins came up with an idea to lure Gutiérrez here," Cruthers gave his protégé a grin, "where we can arrest him and get fingerprints and DNA that will hold up in court. But it all hinges on how carefully he examined the DNA kit from your gun box. If he pulled it out and destroyed it without realizing it hadn't been used, then the plan should work."

Collins frowned. "But if he did look at it more closely, he'll likely figure out that it's a trap."

"The worse that will happen, though," Cruthers said, "is he'll refuse to go along with what we propose."

"Which is?" Bradley asked.

"The chief calls Gutiérrez," Collins said, smiling again, "and tells him the DNA kit was accidentally misplaced."

Which he will know is true, although it was no accident.

"But we showed a photo of him to the boy," Collins continued, "and he identified him as his father. So if he can come here and the boy recognizes him in person, DCF will start the paperwork to turn the kid over to him."

"We watch to see if he files a flight plan," Cruthers added. "If he does, we meet him wherever he's landing. If he doesn't, we're waiting for him in that farmer's field."

Bradley nodded. "We'd have to keep an eye out for him making a reservation on a commercial flight as well."

I leaned back in my chair. "The plan has good bones, but let's flesh it out some. Maybe Jenny Coleman would be the better person to make the call. I suspect Gutiérrez isn't feeling all warm and fuzzy toward me just now. And he'll be less suspicious of a set-up, if the invite comes from her. But how do we explain that we have a photo of him? We didn't take any photos while we were there."

"Might be another reason to get Ms. Coleman to do it," Barnes piped up from her perch against the doorjamb. "She can play dumb if he asks where the photo came from."

"Good point," I said. "Any other holes in the plan you all can see?"

A moment of silence as everyone pondered that, then heads slowly shook around the room.

"I'm thinking," Cruthers said, "that even if he did realize he got the wrong kit, he might come anyway. He seems pretty desperate to get the kid. And once he's on American soil..."

I nodded. "Okay, we try for tomorrow. Barnes, how about you and Bradley go over to DCF and talk to Jenny. She's more likely to cooperate that way. I'm not high on her list right now, since she thinks I almost got her killed."

"You *did* almost get her killed," Bradley said, with that lopsided grin of his.

"Yes, and you have my permission to tell her I feel bad about that."

Everyone stood and trooped out of my office. "Oh," Cruthers stopped in the doorway, turned back toward me, "I have a call in to that accountant of his. I pretended to be with DCF, like you said. I'll let you know when he calls back."

I called Sam and filled him in on the plan. "You okay with us invading your county?"

"Of course," he said. "I'll pull in some extra deputies and put that field under surveillance even if we don't think he's landing there."

"Thanks."

"Uh, remember the other day, when I said I would like to take things to the next level?"

Butterflies danced in my chest and stomach. "Yes?" I tried to keep the anxiety out of my voice.

"Um, well, it is Friday. If you're up for it, I could grill us some steaks tonight on my deck, have a nice relaxing dinner, and see what happens."

Flashes of my father laughing at breakfast, then getting drunk that evening and beating the crap out of my mother.

I shook my head. Sam didn't even drink, except for the occasional beer or glass of wine.

"Or we could just have the relaxing dinner," he backpedaled. I'd paused too long.

"No, uh, I mean yes. A relaxing dinner sounds good. We've both been stressing out over these cases lately."

"And after? I don't want to rush you, but I'd like to know...uh, what might or might not be happening."

My chest warmed with one feeling, while my cheeks flared with another. *How could I even consider flirting with Emil Herrara, when I have a good guy like this interested in me?*

Sam cleared his throat. Again, I'd paused too long.

"Or we can wait," he said, "and see what–"

"Yes," I heard myself saying. "*After* sounds good too."

A sigh. "Good, good. Um, about seven?"

"Seven," I repeated, my eyes suddenly stinging.

"God willing and the bad guys behave, I'll see you then."

I disconnected and sat back in my desk chair. Why the hell did I feel like I wanted to cry?

Maybe because you're falling for this nice man. My mother's soft voice inside my head.

"Yeah sure, Mom," I said out loud.

My stomach turned queasy with guilt and grief. She'd said it so many times when I was a teen. All she wanted was for me to find a nice man who would make me happy. Then she'd pause and add, "And grandkids. I want grandkids." But neither of those things had happened.

"You would have made a terrific grandmother," I whispered, then knuckled the grit out of my eyes.

Was I falling for Sam? Maybe...probably.

Then why was I attracted to Emil?

I snorted softly. "Can you say *sabotage*, boys and girls?"

Jenny used her own cell phone but she made the call from our conference room. Barnes, myself, and Bradley were present. Cruthers was back at his desk, on the phone with Gutiérrez's accountant, who'd returned his call as we were heading for the conference room. And Collins was working on a tactical plan for each location we would need to cover. Wellbourne had volunteered to help him.

Jenny took a deep breath. "Here goes." She placed the call.

We'd debated about putting her phone on speaker, but any strange noises in the background might make him suspicious.

Jenny greeted Gutiérrez. "I might have good news, Señor, but first the bad news. The DNA sample, um, it got misplaced."

A short pause. "I don't know."

A longer pause as she listened. She looked up at me. "Yes, I thought she was more competent than that as well."

I gave her a small smile, and she actually smiled back.

"Here's what we're proposing instead," she said. "I'm afraid my agency can't afford to send me down to Mexico again, so we showed Alejandro a picture of you and–"

Another pause. Gutiérrez had cut her off, as I'd suspected he might.

"I don't know that either, Señor. I guess the detective snapped a photo when we weren't looking." She glanced up at me again, full out grinning now. "Yes, that *was* rather sneaky of her."

I grinned back and mimicked taking a picture with my phone. The humor seemed to be helping her stay calm.

"Anyway," she said into the phone, "he definitely identified you as his father, and he seems excited about seeing you again. If you could possibly come to us, and if he recognizes you in person, then we can start processing the paperwork to turn custody over to you."

Another pause. "Not all that long. A day or two. I was satisfied with your answers during our interview, and I have someone checking your finances as we speak."

A short pause. "Tonight?"

Oh, no. Sam!

I must've shaken my head slightly, because Jenny said, "Well, we were thinking tomorrow." Her eyes were on me.

I waved a hand and mouthed, *Tonight is good.*

"But yes, I think I can set it up for this evening. What time would you arrive?...Seven."

I groaned internally but nodded.

"Seven is fine. Let me give you the address for our offices. I'll arrange to have a playroom available, a more welcoming environment for the boy than my office....*Buenos días* to you too, Señor Gutiérrez."

She disconnected, sat back and blew out a huge sigh.

"You did great," I said.

She grinned. "I was a member of the drama club in college. I guess I've still got it." We laughed softly together.

Cruthers quietly opened the conference room door and stuck his head in.

I waved him in. "It's okay. We're done, and he took the bait. Although he's coming this evening, so not much time to set things up."

He stepped into the room, Collins behind him. "The accountant confirms that Gutiérrez has family money," Cruthers said, "but he sounded nervous. When I pressed him, he said something a little strange, that the *first half* was about to run out. But then he said that Gutiérrez also does consulting work, for which he receives substantial fees."

"Consulting on what?" Bradley asked before I had a chance to.

"Gutiérrez never told him that." Cruthers paused, shook his shaggy head. "Again, he was pretty nervous. Either there's something else going on that he wasn't telling me, or he's really intimidated by this guy."

"Or maybe some of both," I said. "Gutiérrez *is* pretty intimidating."

"And his employees are even more so." Jenny gave a mock shudder—at least, I thought it was mock. "Especially the ones carrying rifles."

"'The first half is about to run out.'" Bradley made air quotes. "What does that mean?"

"Good question," I said. "Thanks again, Jenny, for helping out."

She rose from her chair. "No problem. I need to get this resolved as well, for Alejandro's sake." We said our goodbyes and she left the room.

I'd turned the murder board around when we'd first come into the room, so as not to upset Jenny. Now I gestured toward the blank back of the white board. "Barnes, would you do the honors? Guys, what do we know for sure, or we're pretty sure of, regarding Gutiérrez?"

"He admitted to being our victim's husband," Barnes said, and started writing on the board.

In my head, I went over the interview in Mexico. "He also admitted to being in Jacksonville a month ago, and to knowing that Starling exists."

"He owns a plane," Cruthers said. "Employs a pilot but also knows how to fly himself."

"The old farmer," Collins piped up, "he said the plane has landed twice in the last week, but he was vague about dates."

"One of those dates is probably the day he attacked Donna Glaser and Patterson," I said. "He matches the descriptions they gave us."

"And he used a sap on them," Cruthers added. "The same weapon used on Tatiana and Ms. Baumann."

"And probably Juarez," I said, "but the pathologist isn't as sure of that."

"I'm thinking about what he said in front of Patterson." Bradley shook his head. "Why would he work so hard to get the kid back if he's not all that fond of him?"

"He might be more interested in him as an heir," I said, "rather than having an actual relationship with the boy."

"So, what did he say to Patterson?" Cruthers and Collins said in unison.

"That he needed to find the '*puta*'s brat,'" I said.

Cruthers sneered. "What a loving father."

I held up my left hand to tick off fingers. "Okay, we've got motive." Index finger touched index finger. "Tatiana ran off with his son and heir."

I touched my middle finger. "Opportunity. He was in the area, and could secretly come and go via that plane."

Index finger to ring finger. "Means...his weapon of choice, a sap."

"It's enough to arrest him," Bradley said. "Not sure it would be enough for a jury to convict."

"We need to pin down that farmer on dates," Collins said.

I nodded. "We will, but first we need to set up our trap and make the arrest. Let's go, folks."

Everyone trooped out of the conference room. I headed to my office to call Sam with the disappointing news about our dinner date. Barnes followed in my wake.

"I'm gonna pull you off of Pirolnik for tonight," I said. "Just leave that rookie, Thompson with him. I don't think he's at great risk anymore."

She jogged a couple steps to catch up. "Thanks. I was gonna ask if I can be in on the takedown of this bastard."

"Sorry to disappoint, but you haven't been getting much sleep lately. My thought was to send you to the safe house as one of the guards for Alejandro and Ada's family. That way, we can reassign one of those evening shift uniforms to this operation."

"Crap. But I understand. We're spread awful thin."

"Yes, and I want someone that I know is good on Alejandro tonight. Why don't you go home and catch a nap, then head over there at four-thirty."

She was beaming at the compliment. "You got it, Chief."

Sam and I were getting to spend the evening together after all—huddled behind some bushes on the edge of a farmer's field. It had rained earlier. Cold drops plopped down on us from the live oak above.

One trickled under the collar of my jacket and dampened my shirt. I had put on the sneakers I keep in my car, but hadn't wanted to take the time to go home and change clothes. Fortunately, this was not one of my favorite pantsuits. The odds of it surviving this evening's activities were iffy.

Ten uniforms, five mine and five Sam's deputies, were scattered inside the edge of the woods. Once Gutiérrez stepped on American soil, we'd close the net.

My phone vibrated in my pocket. It was Cruthers, texting to say that no flight plan had been filed by Gutiérrez's pilot. And Foster had reported that he wasn't on any passenger lists for incoming flights to Jax airport, but JSO had several plain-clothes cops covering the exit from the security area, just in case.

I relayed all that to Sam, adding, "So it's looking like he's gonna be landing here. The double Cs are heading our way now."

"The double who?" Sam said, his eyes still on the field.

"Cruthers and Collins. Don't tell them I called them that. I usually only think it."

He flashed me a quick grin, then returned his gaze to the field.

"Um, what you were telling me about the other day," I said, "you know, about your partner, Glenda. When did all that happen?"

"A long time ago. I was in my late twenties. Why?"

"Just curious. You said you fell apart for a while. Was there alcohol involved?"

"Yeah, but I didn't let it get totally out of hand. I didn't want to lose my job. It was all I had left." He glanced my way.

I gave him a fake smile and turned back toward the field myself. "Are you a mellow drunk or a mean one?" I pumped a little laughter into my voice, as if I were only making conversation to pass the time.

Another quick glance. "I usually sat on my couch and drank until I passed out. I guess you'd call that mellow. What's this all about, Judith?"

"You're not the only one with demons in their closet."

"I kind of assumed that." His tone was carefully casual.

The sun was going down behind us, the trees' long shadows stretching out across the grassy field.

"I think I'll tell you about them another time though," I said. "Gutiérrez should be landing soon, to allow time to get to Jenny's building by seven."

He nodded, then his body stiffened. "I think I saw something, over there in the woods." He gestured toward the other side of the field.

I squinted at where he was pointing. Sure enough there was a flash of light. My heart rate kicked up a notch.

Sam keyed his radio. "Hey, does anybody have a flashlight on?"

A round of answers came back, all negative.

"Come on." He moved out of our hiding place but stuck close to the edge of the field, trotting along in the shadows.

I was right behind him, my ears straining for any sound of a plane's engine. It would not be good if this guy landed while we were out of position.

A couple of minutes later, we arrived at about the spot where we'd seen the light. Faint tracks in the grass led into the woods. Sam's hand went to the butt of his gun in its holster. I drew my Glock.

Above those tracks, a thick wall of foliage blocked our view. Sam grabbed a branch to push it aside. It came loose in his hands. "These are cut branches, meant to hide something," he whispered.

My heart went into overdrive. We pushed the branches out of the way and followed the tracks through some underbrush, scanning for anything out of place.

And suddenly something very out of place loomed in front of us—a huge green lump.

A small airplane, covered by a tarp.

CHAPTER TWENTY-SEVEN

One corner of the tarp was flipped up, exposing a small section of the plane's windshield. It must've caught the light of the setting sun.

We made sure the two-seater plane was empty. Then we tromped as quickly as we could back out of the woods. "I thought something was off with that farmer earlier," Sam said, "when I asked about the last time he'd heard from Gutiérrez."

"He could've gotten here hours ago." *Barnes!* My throat tightened. I'd sent her to the safe house. If Gutiérrez had figured out where it was...

I pulled out my phone. *Damn, no bars.*

"Or he came last night and never left," Sam said.

He took off across the field. I ran to catch up.

He was on his radio. A staticky voice responded to whatever he'd said. He glanced over as I fell into step beside him. "I'm leaving four deputies here, in case he comes back before we catch up with him, but I think the rest of us should get to the safe house."

I nodded. "My thoughts exactly," I huffed out, struggling some to keep up with his longer stride. "Gimme that for a moment."

He handed over the radio, and I instructed my people to follow Sam's truck.

When we got to where we'd hidden the vehicles, most were occupied, engines running. Sam and I jumped into his truck and he peeled out.

I held my phone in my hand, impatiently waiting for bars to appear. When they finally did, I called Barnes. It rang three times, then went to voicemail.

What the hell? Why wasn't she picking up?

I called the watch desk. Armstrong answered. "Sarge, I need every available officer at the safe house *now*. Gutiérrez had already landed before we got there. He may be going after the boy as we speak."

"I'll send reinforcements. Patterson and Barnes are there now. I had sent Officer–"

"Wait! Patterson?"

"Yeah, he called, said he was going stir crazy, so I sent him to the safe house. Figured he was in good enough shape to sit around with a gun in his lap. And that would free up somebody–"

"Okay, okay," I said impatiently. "Get people out there asap." I disconnected and sank back in the passenger seat.

"What's the matter?" Sam said. "I mean, besides the obvious."

"I'm not sure. The detective who was attacked, he just got out of the hospital yesterday. And he's calling the watch commander, telling him he's going stir crazy, asking for something to do."

"That's a little odd. Why wouldn't he call Bradley, his boss? And he needs the doc to sign off before going back on duty."

"There's all that too. Armstrong's a new watch commander. He probably didn't think about the need for the doc's release. But what's really bothering me is that Patterson is not usually that dedicated. Indeed, he can be downright lazy. And he *just* got out of the hospital, under strict orders to rest for at least a week. So why's he saying he wants to be put to work?"

Sam glanced my way, his face grim.

My phone rang. Caller ID said *Derek*. I was tempted to ignore it, but I answered, "Chief Anderson."

"Hey Chief, I've got more to report on your computer."

"Make it quick. We're kinda in the middle of something."

"Definitely signs that Chief Black was also paying off another cop, but I can't figure out who. He refers to the cop only by the initials, L.O. But I can't think of anybody in the department with those initials."

"L.O.?" I said.

"What?" Sam said.

"Oh, it's something else I had Derek working on. You got anybody in your department with the initials L.O.?"

Sam thought for a moment, then shook his head.

Into the phone, I said, "Did you check personnel records? Do we have anybody who worked for us in the past with those initials?"

"I haven't checked yet, but I will."

"Okay. Thanks." I disconnected.

"What's all that about?" Sam asked, his gaze glued to the road. It was now dusk, making it hard to see on tree-shrouded country roads.

I sighed. "Long story short, we're checking out some possible bribes in the past to Chief Black, and by him to at least one other cop in the department."

Sam snorted. "Why am I not surprised?"

"L.O., L.O.?" I shook my head. "What's our ETA?"

"Three minutes."

"What else could L.O. stand for, if they aren't initials?" My mind was free-associating on those letters. What could they mean?

"Lazy one!" Sam shouted.

"Shit! Patterson! And he's at the safe house."

The truck surged forward as Sam floored it.

Sam parked in a nearby farmer's lane and we jumped out of his truck. Without waiting for the others who were pulling in behind us, we ran toward the safe house.

Sam was on his radio, telling our people to spread out and surround the property.

The safe house was a Cracker-style farmhouse on a two-acre lot, what was left of some old homestead. Most of the rooms showed lights, but no outside floods. That seemed off to me.

I stopped at the edge of a line of trees, a hundred feet from the house, and texted Armstrong. *How long ago did Patterson call you?*

Sam had stopped beside me. He was huffing softly. The sound was somehow reassuring.

Half hour, Armstrong replied.

It was a thirty-five minute drive, roughly, from Starling to here. So who was where was anybody's guess. If he'd driven fast, Patterson might be here. If he'd called Gutiérrez at the airfield with the address, *he* might already be here.

He may have already come and gone. I cringed at the thought of what carnage we might find in this house if that were the case. Gutiérrez was ruthless.

Armstrong texted back. *I'm almost to the house myself. Where do you need me?*

Around back, I answered. *He may have one of his men with him.*

I tried to text Barnes as we snuck toward the house, staying in the line of trees. The text didn't go through, even though I had two bars. Not great, but it should've been good enough.

But it wasn't. *A jammer?* My heart hammering, I picked up my pace, Sam at my side.

We made it to a corner of the building, then slipped along toward the front porch. "Motion detectors should be turning on floods about now," Sam whispered.

But they didn't.

We'd reached the front door, one of us on either side. I reached out and tested the knob.

It turned in my hand.

Heart in my throat, I nudged the door open and swung through it, off to the right. Sam took the left. "Clear," we both breathed softly in unison.

A light shone from a doorway on the left. "The kitchen," Sam whispered.

We crept in that direction. Through the open doorway I could see Barnes, sitting in a chair. Relief washed through me. Then I realized her arms were pulled behind her back.

Sam and I burst into the kitchen, guns raised, eyes scanning.

Patterson sat slumped on a stool at the breakfast bar, his pistol trained on Barnes. He jerked upward and dropped his gun on the bar. "Thank God!"

A tugging sensation in my chest. I glanced up the stairs. I really wanted to go check on Alejandro and Ada and the rest of her family. But we only had minutes, at most, to set our trap.

Patterson had told us he'd been forced to call Armstrong to get the safe house's address. "Gutiérrez came to my place and threatened my daughter."

"He said he'd kill her?" I asked, a sickening mixture of rage and sympathy churning in my stomach.

"Worse. That he'd take her one day on her way to school—and I'd never know when that might happen—and he'd sell her as a sex slave."

My stomach heaved. I swallowed hard.

"I sent her out of town with her mother, but I wasn't sure that would get them out of his reach so..." He trailed off and shuddered. "I went along with him, agreed to leave the door unlocked, turn off the outside lights, and disable the other guard." He shook his head. "But I wasn't going to let him take that kid. Barnes and I were going to jump him when he got here."

"We weren't able to get any calls out," Barnes's words rushed out. "And we were afraid that if I got in my car and drove off to find a better signal, well, maybe he would see me and know something was off. And Patterson would be the only one here to protect..." She paused for a quick breath. "So we figured we'd pretend that I was tied up, then–"

"Go upstairs," I interrupted, "and guard the family, *with your life*." The last part wasn't really necessary. Of course Barnes would guard them with her life. But I wanted her to know it was an important job, one that needed to be done even if it did keep her out of the excitement down here.

And hopefully out of danger.

Only the slightest of hesitations before she took off for the stairs.

Sam was holding up his radio. All that came out of it was static.

"Jammer," I said.

"And if we go outside to signal the others," he said, "and Gutiérrez is nearby, he'll see us."

A deep breath. I turned back to Patterson. "You still willing to be the bait, if Gutiérrez gets past our people?"

Patterson's Adam's apple bobbed in his neck, but he nodded.

"You stay out here," I said, "tell him you disabled the other guard and drugged the family. They're all upstairs, and the boy's asleep in the back room down here, which is where we'll be." I gestured to Sam and myself.

"Uh, can I have my gun back?" Patterson asked.

"No." I believed his story about Gutiérrez's threats, but I also believed he was a dirty cop.

I looked at Sam. He gave a small nod and led the way through the living room and into a large rec room in the back of the house.

I turned on one small lamp, on a desk near the doorway. Sam stood behind the door, and I slipped back into the shadows, crouched behind an overstuffed armchair, my Glock in my hand.

Minutes ticked by. Finally voices in the kitchen, three of them. Yup, he'd brought one of his thugs.

I held my breath.

Gutiérrez's voice, louder. "You go get him. Bring him out."

Damn! Should've known he wouldn't walk right into a potential trap.

A shadow moving down the dark hallway and Patterson appeared in the doorway. "Hey, Alex," he said, his voice fake cheerful. "Come see your papa."

Sam pulled him into the room and behind him. Then Sam started down the dark hallway, half crouched, his gun extended.

Heart pounding, I followed, Glock in hand.

Just before we reached the lighted kitchen, Sam stopped, looked at me and mouthed, "One, two, three."

We burst into the kitchen, yelling in unison, "Police. Don't move!"

The two men in the room froze for a nanosecond. I stared at them, mouth open.

Gutiérrez's arm flicked down. A black object appeared in his hand.

"Look out!" I yelled, as he swung at Sam.

Sam's arm came up. He yowled in pain, fell to the floor. His gun skidded away.

My heart stuttered in my chest. Keeping my Glock aimed at Gutiérrez, my gaze swung back to the other man. He was pointing a pistol at me.

"Drop the gun, Judith." Emil Herrara's expression was sorrowful. "We don't want to hurt you."

CHAPTER TWENTY-EIGHT

The kitchen door flew open. Armstrong plowed through it and into Emil. They went down. Emil's gun skittered across the floor.

Gutiérrez raised his arm, sap in hand, over Armstrong's head.

I pulled the trigger.

The impact of the bullet knocked Gutiérrez off his feet. He screamed like a stuck pig.

I smiled grimly, even as my stomach roiled with worry for Sam.

Armstrong had Emil subdued. He hadn't put up much of a fight.

I bit my lower lip to keep from running to Sam, approached Gutiérrez instead. A circle of red had blossomed on the shoulder of his white shirt, but his eyes were open.

Patterson ran into the room.

"Help me with him," I said, "then go out and tell the others what's going on, and call for an ambulance."

While I covered him, Patterson rolled Gutiérrez over and cuffed him. The exit wound on the back of his shoulder said the bullet had gone on through. Probably minimal damage.

Damn shame! I consoled myself with the knowledge that his ego was no doubt severely wounded. He'd been shot by a woman.

Barnes came down the stairs, gun in hand.

Letting her and Patterson deal with Gutiérrez, I ran to Sam. His eyes were open, but a bit glassy. "D'w get 'im?" he muttered.

"Yes, we got him," I said, gently stroking the side of his head that wasn't bleeding.

"Good. Then get me some painkillers quick," he said in a clearer voice. "I think my arm is broken and it hurts like hell."

I almost laughed out loud.

I glanced around the room. Barnes had grabbed a kitchen towel and was putting pressure on Gutiérrez's wound. His eyes were closed, his face contorted. And Armstrong had hoisted Emil to his feet, hands cuffed behind him.

Emil stared at me with those liquid brown eyes. "I'm sorry, Judith," he said softly.

One of the perks of being chief—you get to choose who you'll interrogate.

Cruthers and Collins were at the hospital, waiting to have a go at Gutiérrez, once his wound was treated.

I didn't dare get near the bastard just yet. I doubted I'd be able to control my anger. The sight of Sam falling to the floor, blood running down his face, kept replaying in my head.

His arm was broken, but it was a good thing he'd gotten it up there in time. Gutiérrez had been aiming for his temple, which could've been a fatal blow. As it was, the edge of the sap had only grazed his scalp, producing a lot of blood but doing no real harm.

I'd turned my Glock over to Wellbourne. The FDLE would investigate, but I had no doubt it would be ruled a good shoot.

Now, Patterson was cooling his heels in a holding cell. And Emil was across the table from me in our smaller conference room, cuffed to his chair.

Barnes leaned against the closed door, pad in hand, even though I had a recorder going.

"And here we thought you were a clean cop," I said.

Emil sighed. "I was when your Detective Cruthers met me in 2020. Hell, I was yesterday when *you* met me."

He stared past my shoulder, then sighed again. "I have been divorced for many years," he said in that syrupy baritone that now made my stomach turn. "A foolish marriage, young love. But it produced my son."

I tapped fingernails on the table. "I don't need your life story."

Emil gave me a weak smile. "I don't make a lot of money," he continued anyway, "and my son is in college. He has always wanted to be a doctor. It's his life passion. I'm barely managing his tuition."

I gave him my best stone-faced look.

He leaned forward, as far as his cuffed hands allowed. "When my sergeant and I went back to Gutiérrez's *hacienda*, he asked to speak to me alone. He made me an offer I could not refuse. Enough money to put my boy through medical school, or he would..." Emil stopped, cleared his throat. "He said he would have José killed."

My insides churned with mixed emotions. If Patterson hadn't told me of a similar threat earlier, I might not have believed Emil. And now, damn it, I felt sorry for him.

He shook his head slowly. "I thought I had the solution to my problems. He only wanted his son back, after all. He did not trust the American bureaucracy. And he promised no one would get hurt."

And you conveniently overlooked that we believed he'd murdered his wife, and that he'd tried to have us killed.

"Why did he bring you with him?" I asked.

"We came last night, in his plane. We most likely landed before you did in Jacksonville."

My anger spiked again. *You didn't answer my question, asshole.*

Then it hit me. "The gun case. You were the only one who knew I'd put the DNA kit in there. You told him where to look."

"No, I was the one in your apartment. I volunteered to get it, told him I would say I had come to seduce you if I got caught. I didn't want you getting hurt." He said the last part more emphatically.

"I'm touched." Sarcasm dripped from my voice. "Again, why did he bring you with him?"

"I'm not sure. But I suspect it was to cement our deal. Once I had committed a crime for him, I couldn't turn him in without losing everything."

I stood. "Thank you for not hurting my cat."

"I would never harm such a tiny creature."

I gave him a curt nod and moved toward the door.

"Judith..."

I stopped but didn't turn around.

"I am sorry," he said, his rich baritone a little choked. "I have many regrets, but most especially that I have betrayed your trust."

My throat tight, I left the room.

When I stepped out of the conference room door, I almost collided with Sam.

He had a patch of white gauze taped to his left temple, and that arm was in a sling, but he was the most beautiful thing I'd ever seen. I pinned my arms tightly at my sides to keep myself from throwing them around him.

I gestured down the hall, toward the bullpen, and my office beyond. "I thought they were keeping you at the hospital overnight?"

Sam fell into step with me. "I decided they'd observed me long enough."

I shook my head. *Men!* But then I admitted to myself I would've done the same thing. Especially when there were criminals to interrogate.

"Anything yet from Gutiérrez?" he asked.

"Not that I've heard. But I'm assuming he'll demand a lawyer."

Sam shrugged his good shoulder. "I think we've got enough to nail him anyway."

I wasn't as sure. He might blame everything on his dead underling, Juarez. But I kept those doubts to myself.

We entered my office, and Sam closed the door. When he stepped over next to me, a residual hint of his woodsy aftershave drifted my way, combined with undertones of male sweat. I didn't mind the combo one bit, but it was getting hot in here.

I took off my jacket and tossed it on my chair, while acknowledging to myself that the heat wasn't due to the small room. I straightened my short-sleeved blouse, clamped down hard on my feelings and cleared my throat.

Sam's sleeve brushed my bare arm. I jumped slightly. The corners of his mouth twitched. He'd done that on purpose.

I wanted to laugh and kick him at the same time.

A knock and Bradley stuck his head in. He looked at me, then at Sam, a ghost of his half-smile on his face.

I glared at him.

His face smoothed to neutral. "What do you want to do with Patterson?"

"Did you take his statement about tonight?"

"Yeah, and I suspended him, for now."

"Then put him in a cell."

Bradley raised an eyebrow.

"He and I have other things to discuss," I added.

He didn't push for more, just nodded and left.

"I put in a call to Herrara's supervisor in Mexico," Sam said. "He's being very helpful. His people are searching Gutiérrez's *hacienda* as we speak. And he apologized for his subordinate's behavior, said he had thought Herrara couldn't be corrupted."

So did Herrara.

Sam sidled even closer, looked around to make sure the bullpen was empty. "Can I kiss you?"

"That's probably a bad idea."

He opened his mouth, but I added, "I doubt we'd be able to stop there."

He grinned. "You're probably right." He reached out and closed the blinds nearest the entrance to the bullpen.

I closed the rest of the blinds and came back to his side. He wrapped his good arm around my back and pulled me in close. "I needed this," he whispered, "to know it's real, that we both survived."

My arms snaked around his waist, and I laid my cheek against his stubbled one. We sighed in unison. We stood that way for several minutes, absorbing each other's reassuring presence.

A light knock on the door. We stepped apart.

"Come in," I said.

Bradley stuck his head in again. "Sorry, Chief, but Patterson is asking for you. He's a basket case, wants to call his daughter."

"Take him to the conference room and let him have his phone. I'll be right there."

Bradley nodded and quickly closed the door.

"Are you going to charge Patterson," Sam asked, "with accessory to attempted kidnapping?"

"I'm gonna leave that up to the State's Attorney's office. The suspension is for dereliction of duty. He should've called me or Bradley instead of going out there to try to take down Gutiérrez himself. He could've gotten a lot of people killed."

Including Barnes and those children. I shuddered.

"And then there's the matter of whether or not he's a dirty cop." I pulled open the door. "I'll call you later?"

Sam gave me a warm smile but shook his head. "I'm gonna stick around for a bit. See if I can get a crack at Gutiérrez when your guys are done."

Patterson was indeed a hot mess, his hair disheveled, his face sweaty and pale under his tan.

Bradley had cuffed one of his hands to his chair. In the other, he held his phone. "It's okay, sweetie, I'm okay. I'll see you soon...No, it's all over. We got the bad guy." He disconnected.

"But it isn't all over for you," I said, pulling out a chair to sit across from him.

Barnes slipped into the room. "Spoke to Ada Johns. They opted to stay at the safe house for tonight. The kids are all finally asleep, including Alejandro."

"Good." I turned back to Patterson.

"Do I have to go through it all again?" he said. "I told Bradley everything that happened. He said I'm suspended. I'm grateful you're letting me keep my badge."

"We'll see about that." I leaned back in my chair. "You know, I still have Chief Black's old computer, and I found some hidden files on it."

Patterson froze. "Files?"

"Black thought he'd erased them," I continued in a conversational tone. "But Derek is truly a genius. He was able to retrieve most of them."

The man blanched.

"Did you know that Chief Black called you Lazy One behind your back?"

Patterson looked like he was about to faint.

"Barnes, get him some water, please."

She went to the water cooler in one corner of the conference room, drew him a paper cup of water.

He gulped half of it.

"I've been wondering," again, the conversational tone, "why did Black keep the files in the first place?"

Patterson closed his eyes, blindly putting the cup on the table. Some water sloshed out. He didn't seem to notice.

I leaned forward, hardened my voice. "If you come clean now, I'll ask the assistant state's attorney to go easy on you. What were the payoffs for?"

He sighed, opened his eyes. They were red-rimmed. "I knew about the hookers and the call houses. Occasionally, we'd get a complaint from a neighbor for noise or strange people coming and going, and Chief Black would send me."

He closed his eyes again. "I'd go through the motions. One time, I saw one of Butler's men with a girl who had to be underage. He was obviously handing her off to a john."

He opened his eyes and leaned forward some. "I arrested all of them, mostly to rescue the girl. She swore she was nineteen, but she looked real scared. Kept glancing at Butler's man. I wanted to call DCF, but Black told me to put her in a holding cell. The next morning, she was gone, and so were the other two. I didn't dare ask Black what happened, but that week he handed me an even fatter envelope than usual."

His free hand scrubbed his face. "I told myself they must've gotten out on bail, but the case file had disappeared too. Up to that point, I'd believed it was a victimless crime, that the women were willingly prostituting themselves. But that girl didn't seem all that willing. And she looked sixteen, not nineteen."

He paused, sipped more water. "But I was in too deep by then. Black used the files as insurance, in case I grew a conscience, he said. If he went down, so would I. And I was saving the money for my daughter's college."

What is it with these guys? They think they can justify taking bribes because it's for their kids?

Another sip and Patterson put the empty cup down. "About six months ago, Black told me to find a woman, that she was wanted for stealing jewelry from her employer. He gave me a description of her, and a detailed one of the car she was driving. But he didn't want to put out a BOLO, because she was the daughter of some state politician, so he wanted to be discreet. Said she'd been spotted heading north, and that he'd already cleared things with the Georgia state police if I had to go into their jurisdiction."

Patterson took a deep breath. "I caught up with her just before the border. But when I turned on my siren, she drove faster. Her car ended up in a ditch. I hauled her out and cuffed her. She kept crying and begging me not to take her back. Those were her exact words, 'please don't take me back,' which I didn't quite understand at the time."

He stopped, swallowed hard. "She was maybe twenty, if that much. About an hour later, some guy I'd never seen before was taking her out of the holding cell. Again, she's crying and begging, 'Don't let him take me.'"

Hmm, could that guy be the enforcer Dot's looking for? Maybe later I'd see if Patterson could describe the guy. For now, I didn't want to give him any bargaining chips.

"I started to intervene," he was saying, "to find out what was going on, but Chief Black came up and told me she was being extradited. That she was wanted for murder in another county. I watched her being dragged away, with a bad feeling in my gut."

His free hand went to that gut, then covered his mouth. Barnes nudged a nearby trash can over next to his chair.

Is he acting, or really feeling sick?

And it hit me. This was why he'd been so dedicated to the case, had been taking more initiative. He wanted us to stop Butler and find the women, to ease his conscience.

After a moment, Patterson lowered his hand. "It wasn't until recently that I fully admitted to myself I'd been helping sex traffickers, that I'd handed that woman right over to them." His eyes had filled with tears.

I might have felt sorry for him, but I was already using up all my sympathy for that poor woman.

"Did the bribes keep coming after Black retired?" I asked, my voice hard.

Patterson's head jerked up. "No."

"Did anyone approach you, offering bribes to keep looking the other way?"

He shook his head.

"Bradley's already got your badge and gun?"

He nodded.

"Good." I stood up. "Patterson, you're fired."

He gaped up at me. "But you said–"

"I said I'd ask the ASA to go easy on you regarding criminal charges, and I will. But there's no room on my police force for a dirty cop. We don't get to choose which crimes we deem victimless, and obviously in this case, it wasn't. Barnes, find Bradley and tell him to book Patterson for accepting bribes."

His head dropped into his free hand. He let out a strangled sob.

I turned to walk out of the room. At the doorway, I had another thought. I turned back. "Patterson."

His head came up.

"How come cell phones and radios were being jammed tonight, a good twenty minutes before Gutiérrez got there?"

He blinked. "Uh, I don't know."

"Where's the jacket you were wearing earlier?"

"Uh, Peters took it when I went into the cell."

I hustled to the holding cells. Officer Peters sat at a small desk, doing paperwork.

Ignoring Emil, who occupied one of the cells, I asked her, "Where's Patterson's jacket?"

She produced it and I felt the pockets. Nothing there, but farther down near the jacket's hem, a solid bulge.

"Glove?"

Peters handed me a latex one.

I put it on, and with difficulty got my hand in the pocket. There was a tear in the bottom of it. Enlarging it some, I got three fingers through it and managed to get a hold on the object. I carefully pulled it out.

Black box with multiple appendages on one end. A jammer.

Did Patterson know it was there, or had Gutiérrez somehow slipped it into his jacket? I suspected the latter.

Without being asked, Officer Peters produced an evidence bag.

I took the jammer to Bert, who was still in his small lab, processing items from the safe house.

Then I headed back toward my office. Something was niggling at my brain, something Patterson had said.

Barnes caught up as I was entering the bullpen. "There you are."

"Yes, here I am," I snapped, and immediately felt guilty. "Sorry, it's been a long day."

I stopped short as the niggling thought showed itself. *The car!* Chief Black had given Patterson a detailed description of the woman's car.

"And our day's about to get longer." I whirled around. "Bradley!"

CHAPTER TWENTY-NINE

Back out in the hall, Bradley was leading Patterson away in the opposite direction.

"Hand him off to a uniform," I yelled. "We've got another arrest to make. Striker."

Bradley raised an eyebrow but said nothing. He hustled Patterson down the hall.

Sam came out of the men's room. "What's going on?"

"Come with me. I'll fill you in on the way. This affects your case too."

We piled into my car, Sam in the passenger seat, Barnes in the back. Bradley followed us in his car. We needed to cover two places—or maybe more. There was also the junkyard.

In the rearview mirror, I made out someone in Bradley's passenger seat. Barnes's radio crackled. "Tell the Chief we got two more uniforms coming along."

Armstrong's voice. He was Bradley's passenger.

"I told them to requisition one of the new unmarked cars," the sarge added.

"They came in?" I called out over my shoulder, in the direction of Barnes's radio.

"Yeah, just today."

"Excellent. You all take the repurposing center–"

"Uh, Chief," Bradley's voice, "why are we chasing down Mary Striker tonight?"

"Not her," I said. "Her husband. He's the missing member of the trafficking ring. At the center, have the uniforms cover the back, where Striker's workshop is. They likely have some people answering the phones, even in the middle of the night. Don't let anybody leave!"

"Got it!" Bradley and Armstrong said in unison.

"The Strikers' house is in the north section of Starling," Barnes said from the backseat, her gaze on her phone. I swung my car onto Bennett Street, one of the main north-south corridors through the city.

"What the hell's going on?" Sam said, but there was no rancor in his voice.

"Remember, the new head of the Jax FDLE wanted us to wait to raid the call houses?"

"Yes, but you never told me why," Sam said.

"Sorry. It was need-to-know. We were asked to wait because they were still trying to track down a member of the ring who didn't come to that breakfast meeting with the big boss. Someone they had reason to believe stayed in the shadows, and whose main job was to track down women who got away."

"And you think Striker's husband is that tracker?" Sam said.

"More likely he provided info to Butler who, in turn, sent out his thugs." *Or, in at least one instance, a police officer—Patterson.* "The ring was statewide, so in some cases, Butler might have alerted his cohorts in other parts of Florida."

"Turn right up ahead, Chief," Barnes said.

The houses on the cul-de-sac were large and mostly dark, including the Strikers' residence. Only one light shone through the curtains of a window toward the far end of the house. The master bedroom?

Standing to one side of the front door, hand on my Glock, I knocked. Barnes was behind me, Sam on the other side of the door, his good hand also on his holster.

I knocked a second time. Another light came on, in the window near the door.

"Who's there?" A woman's anxious voice.

"Chief Anderson, Mrs. Striker," I called out. "I know it's late but we need to talk to you."

"Wait a minute." The porch light came on. The snick of a deadbolt being turned and the door opened. Mary's hair was disheveled. She wore a terrycloth robe reminiscent of my own, only hers was pink.

"What could you possibly want at this hour?" Her tone was irritated on the surface, but underneath was anxiety.

"Can we talk inside," I said. "We don't want to disturb your neighbors."

She hesitated, then opened the door wider and stepped back. We entered a spacious living room, and she gestured toward a sofa.

I ignored the invitation to sit. "Is your husband home?"

She shook her head. "He got a call. His mom, she's had a heart attack. He, uh, raced out of here to go to her."

My heart rate kicked up a notch, but I kept my voice calm. "I'm sorry to hear that. How long ago did he get that call?"

She clasped the neck of her robe together, stared at the ceiling. "About fifteen minutes ago. You just missed him. He's catching a one o'clock flight to Baltimore, then on to Boston from there."

I glanced at Barnes. She discreetly began fiddling with her phone.

"I guess he didn't have time to pack much," I said. "Just a carry-on?"

"Oh no, he had a regular-sized suitcase with him."

If I'd still had any doubts, that would've removed them. He'd probably packed the bag the day Butler was arrested, and odds were good it had more than clothes in it.

"He said he didn't know how long he'd have to stay up there, to, uh..." Mary's face was a bit ashen now. Her gaze darted back and forth, from my face to Sam's. "What's going on?"

My phone pinged in my jacket pocket. I pulled it out. A text from Bradley.

Workshop cleaned out. All tools gone.

"What aren't you telling me?" Mary demanded. Then her hand flew to her mouth. "Was there an accident?" She swayed a little on her feet.

"No, not an accident." My phone vibrated again. This time, it was Sam, who was standing right beside me.

Drives a red F-150. BOLO's gone out. About to order roadblocks for Georgia border.

I gave him a slight nod.

Now, what to do with Mary? I doubted she was helping her husband, but she could be. And even if she wasn't, she might call and warn him. I couldn't risk it.

I could have Barnes stay with her, but with Sam partially disabled, I needed backup. And I knew damn well he wouldn't stay behind to babysit Mary.

Her eyes met mine. They were now shiny with tears. "Please tell me what's going on."

I shook my head. "We need you to come with us."

Mary blinked twice. "I'll get dressed."

"No time, I'm afraid." I took her by the upper arm. "I'll fill you in while we drive." I led her toward the front door.

"Where are we going? The police station?"

"Where's your phone?" I asked, ignoring her questions.

"In the kitchen," she tried to pull us in that direction.

"Good. It's staying there." I hustled her out the door.

Barnes closed it behind us, and I handed her my keys. "You drive." She jogged to the car.

"Shotgun." Sam took one jogging step and winced. Cradling his injured arm with his other hand, he power-walked after her.

But Mary had firmly planted her slippered feet on the porch. "I demand to know what's going on."

I glared at her. "Your husband has been helping Butler catch the women who got away."

Her mouth fell open, and she let me pull her toward the car. "But..." she spluttered.

I crammed her into the backseat, slid in after her. Barnes already had the car running.

Mary was insisting I tell her what I'd meant. I held up a hand to silence her. "Sam, what road would you take north, if you were running from the law?" I was betting north so that he'd be out of the state as quickly as possible.

"Head for State Road 121, Gloria."

Barnes nodded and made a U-turn in the middle of the street. There are advantages to compact cars.

I called Bradley and quickly filled him in. "Ask Foster to cover the airport, just in case."

"I checked the flights already," Barnes said. "There's no flight at one a.m., nor anywhere close to that time, that's going to Baltimore."

"I doubt he's actually flying, nor is he going to his mother's." The latter was for Mary's benefit. "Bradley, you and Armstrong split up, each take a uniform with you. You search along Route 301 for a red 150 pickup. Tell Armstrong to haul ass to I-295." Jacksonville's beltway.

"Copy that," Bradley said.

"Sam's got Striker's license plate number."

I tuned out Sam's voice as he gave the number to Bradley, and turned back to Mary.

She had stopped fussing. Her face was pale. "You're sure about...what you said."

"I wasn't, until he ran. He cleaned out his workshop at the center, by the way."

Mary turned slightly away, stared at the back of Barnes's head. Light from oncoming headlights glinted off a wet cheek.

My chest hurt. I tried to shove aside the feeling. But my throat closed and my eyes stung. This woman had been trying to do good...

I shook my head.

"I think I know what set him off," Sam said. He handed his phone over the back of his seat.

On the screen was the website of Starling's local paper. The banner headline read *Local Ringleader in Trafficking Network Makes Deal with State's Attorney.*

Shit! How'd they get that info?

"Can I see that?" Mary said.

I turned the phone toward her. Her eyes were now hard as she glared at the screen, her mouth a grim line.

Sam's phone rang, making me jump a little. I answered it. "Chief Anderson."

"Oh, uh, I was tryin' to reach Sheriff Pierson."

"He's here." I put the phone on speaker, held it between the two front seats, and leaned forward. "What've you got, Deputy?"

"Red truck approached our roadblock on 121, slowed some, then veered left onto County Road 10."

"Take this next left." Sam pointed ahead. We were practically on top of the crossroad already.

Barnes hit the brakes and swung the car to the left. It almost went into a spin.

"He's trying to cut across to 23," Sam yelled over the screech of tires. "But 10's a dirt road." The car straightened out and its headlights revealed a narrow asphalt lane.

I rolled my eyes in the dark car. *Ten's a county road but it's unpaved? Only in Florida.*

Sam leaned toward me. "I saw that, Anderson," he whispered, with a slight chuckle. Then louder, "I think we can cut him off. Charlie, we got a roadblock on 23?"

"Yes, sir," the deputy said.

"Good. Stay alert, in case he circles back toward you, when he realizes 23 ain't the road to freedom neither."

"Yes, sir!"

I disconnected, and resisted the urge to laugh out loud as adrenaline buzzed through my veins. This was why I was a cop. Yeah, I wanted to catch the bad guys, see justice served. But this... I sucked in a deep breath.

"He can't go all that fast on 10," Sam was saying, as Barnes barreled along, way faster than we should be going on *this* narrow road.

I hung onto the hand grip above my window.

"Here," Sam yelled. "Go right!" Tires squealed again and I almost fell into Mary's lap. I righted myself and glared at Sam.

He was looking back over his shoulder, grinning at me. "We're on State Road 23 now."

A tense couple of minutes later, I spotted a sign for the junction with CR 10 up ahead.

We rounded a curve, and Barnes slammed on the brakes. The car fish-tailed. More squealing tires.

My hand flew again to the grab handle, as I mentally calculated how much new tires would cost me. I was pretty sure the tread was gone by now.

In front of us, our headlights flashed off of a back window and lit up the slanted red tailgate of a truck. Striker had apparently taken the turn from 10 onto 23 too fast. He'd gone off into the ditch on the opposite side of the road.

The shadowy figure of a man in the ditch, with what looked like a jack. His head jerked up, eyes the red of a feral animal caught in the light.

Barnes jammed the car into park and threw open her door.

Sam jumped out of the passenger side, gun drawn. "Sheriff. Don't move!"

I drew my Glock while catapulting from the backseat. "Starling Police!" I added.

Mary was sliding over to get out after me. I flipped the switch in the door's frame that engaged the childproof locks and slammed the door.

Sam advanced, his gun hand raised. But with his injured arm in its sling, he couldn't steady the gun. His aim might be off if he had to shoot. "Put your hands on your head," he yelled to Striker.

The man complied.

Mary was banging on the back window of my car, yelling for me to let her out.

Not happenin'.

The passenger door of the red truck flew open. A figure bolted from it.

His bulk said he was the junkyard owner.

Barnes took off after him.

I hesitated, glanced at Sam.

"On your knees, Striker," he yelled, then to me. "Go!"

"But you can't handcuff him one-handed."

"No, but I can sit on him if need be. Now go!"

I bolted after Barnes and the shadowy figure ahead of her. He dove into the woods beside the road.

Damn, he's fast for a middle-aged fat guy!

Barnes was almost to the spot where he'd disappeared. She veered off and disappeared into the woods as well.

When I got there, my phone light revealed a narrow deer path. Branches pulled at my clothes as I ran down it.

I caught up with them in time to see the guy stop in a clearing. He turned and swung his arm out.

Moonlight glinted off something metal, aimed at Barnes's head.

CHAPTER THIRTY

Barnes ducked under the swinging tire iron and drove her shoulder into the man's midriff.

"Uuff." He stumbled backward and fell into a palmetto bush.

She landed on top of him, then scrambled to a sitting position on his stomach. He flailed his arms, tried to grab for her holster.

I had no idea if her gun was in it or not. I didn't see it in her hands. I raced over beside them.

She reached for her Taser. "Stop struggling, or I'll zap your sorry ass."

He stopped struggling.

She jumped up, rolled him over, and sat on his legs as she cuffed him. It took both of us to haul him to his feet.

"Uh, have you seen my gun?" she said, her voice embarrassed. "I dropped it when I ducked."

I laughed. "And here I was about to commend you for your excellent apprehension skills, Rookie."

With the help of my phone light we found the gun, and escorted Mr. Junkyard back to the vehicles.

Striker was lying flat on his stomach, hands behind his head. Sam stood over him, gun in hand.

Mary had apparently managed to crawl out of the backseat and exit the car via the passenger's door, which hung open. She stood several feet away, arms crossed over her chest. In her bedraggled robe and slippers, she should have looked pathetic.

But her back was ramrod straight, and the rage on her face almost made me feel sorry for her husband. Almost.

Barnes put our prisoner in the back of my car, and I went over to Sam.

"Get my cuffs, will you? Two of my deputies are on their way to transport these bozos for us."

I nodded, and gingerly reached for his handcuffs case on his belt. Grinning, he wiggled his eyebrows suggestively, and I swallowed a chuckle. Then I leaned down and cuffed Striker's wrists.

When I straightened, Mary was less than two feet away. I braced for her to grab for Sam's gun.

But that wasn't her goal. She stepped around Sam, cranked back her foot and kicked her husband in the ribs, hard. Her cursing was almost drowned out by his yowls of pain.

Barnes jumped forward to restrain her, but it wasn't necessary. Mary turned on her bedroom-slippered heel and, head high, limped to my car.

We opted to leave Striker sitting, cuffed, on the cold ground, until the deputies arrived to transport the prisoners. It seemed a bad idea to have both him and his wife inside my small car at the same time.

<hr />

Sam and Barnes stayed in the car while I walked Mary Striker to her door. I checked that the house was secured, then came back to the living room. She had dropped onto an armchair and wrapped her arms around her torso.

I perched on the edge of the sofa. "Sorry we had to drag you off like that without even letting you get dressed."

She shook her head. "I understand. You had to stop him." Her face was ashen, her eyes sad.

"You gonna be okay?"

"Yes. Gonna be...eventually."

I nodded. "I'd like you to come in tomorrow, for an interview and to give us your statement. Of course, you're not required to say anything, since he's your husband."

She gave me a feeble smile. "Oh, I'll be happy to tell you anything you want to know, and I'll be seeing a divorce lawyer right after I talk to you."

I returned her smile with a tired one of my own. "When the dust settles from all this, let's talk about how the police department can support the center's efforts, help you safely be more open about what you do."

She nodded again. "That would be good."

I stood to leave. At the door, I looked back. She was still sitting in the armchair, staring into space and clutching the neck of her ratty robe.

I did believe that she would be okay eventually—she was a survivor—but it would likely take awhile.

Sam and I had agreed that his deputies would transport our prisoners to 3MB for now. "We can wrangle over jurisdiction later," he'd said. Technically, the junkyard owner was his, since he lived in Clover County and was arrested there.

"With any kind of luck," I said, "the state will take them off our hands. It's their case. We've got enough to do tying up loose ends with our homicides."

"But I want to talk to these guys first," Sam said, as we walked to SPD's holding cells, "before the FDLE comes to claim them. See if they know anything about Caroline's death."

"Or Tatiana's. Wanna flip for first crack at Striker?"

"Wait up, Chief." Bert Deming's voice from behind us.

I turned. "You still here?"

"I was finishing up logging in evidence from the plane and the safe house when I heard you were chasing more bad guys. Figured I'd stick around. Wanna know what's in Striker's suitcase?"

I glanced at Sam. "Fifty dollars says it isn't clothes."

He shook his head. "Not taking that bet."

"Good move, Sheriff," Bert said. "It was full of cash, plus a gallon-sized plastic bag of jewelry. I assume his wife's."

"Man, he really is a son of a bitch." Sam turned to me. "You can have first crack at him."

"Not if you want him."

"No, no. Ladies first. I insist." He winked.

I shook my head but smiled. It was a running joke between us, pretending to pass the hard work off onto the other.

"There were boxes of tools in the back of his truck," Bert said. "Ernie's waiting for the tow truck, but he sent me photos of the skid marks. Looking at them, I'd say the weight of the tools probably caused his accident. He took the turn too fast and the back end just kept right on going sideways into that ditch."

"So his greed was his undoing," I said.

Sam laughed. "Nice irony in that."

Bert was smirking.

I thanked him and we resumed our journey to the holding cells.

Officer Peters had been posted to keep the men from talking to each other. They exchanged wary looks as she and I re-cuffed them and hauled them out of their cells. She had the junkyard owner by the arm.

"You go with the sheriff to the conference room," I told her.

"I'm okay," Sam said.

I resisted the urge to roll my eyes. "Bradley's waiting for me by the interrogation room. You take Peters."

"This way, sir," the officer said to Sam, tugging Harry forward.

Ten minutes later, everything was set up in interrogation. Striker had been Mirandized and was now sitting across from me, cuffed to the ring in the table for that purpose. And the video equipment was rolling, with Bradley in the observation room.

I opened my mouth.

"It was Butler's doing," Striker blurted out. "I didn't want to be any part of it. He approached me, offered me a ton of money, but I said no."

Again, I resisted the urge to roll my eyes. At this rate, I was gonna sprain an eye muscle.

"But then he threatened to hurt Mary."

So we can add liar and wimp to your list of endearing traits, I thought but didn't say. Instead I asked, "You didn't think to call the police?"

"Well, yeah, I thought about that. But Mary was so bent on keeping the center a secret, even from the police."

"You thought she'd prefer having the women she was trying to help be dragged back into slavery?" I couldn't quite keep the incredulous tone from my voice.

He hung his head. The body language looked genuine enough, but with this guy...

"I guess I let greed get the better of me."

"It wasn't enough to have your rich wife outfit the workshop of your dreams and buy you a spankin' new truck?"

"I bought the truck with my own money," he said defensively.

"You mean with Butler's blood money."

Get a grip, Anderson. I wanted to slug this guy, but I needed to back off or he'd stop talking.

I slowly took in a deep breath and sat back in my chair. "Tell me how it worked."

"At first, he'd only go after the ones we'd given cars to. I'd provide him with a detailed description of the car, including the bogus plate number. And I'd tell him when she was getting the car. So he'd know to watch her close around that time. He'd have one of his men tail her but they were to wait until she was out of Starling. Then he'd ship the woman to somewhere else in the state."

So that's how Butler knew exactly what car to look for and when. One of his "staff" had been following Tatiana, waiting for her to leave town. But her husband got to her first.

"Why wait until she was out of the city?"

"We didn't want Mary and her people catching on. Butler figured if the center didn't exist, somebody else would fill the void. Better the devil he knew, he said."

"I'd watch who you're calling a devil."

His face fell. "Yeah, I know." He dropped his gaze to the table. "Mary's an angel."

I paused, thinking about that. Why would Butler allow Mary's operation to continue unhindered?

"Butler was willing to let some of the women get away?" I asked.

Striker's eyes darted off to the side. "Yeah."

"Really?" I threw as much disbelief into my tone as I could muster.

He swallowed hard, his Adam's apple bobbing in his neck. "Well, at first. But then he started pressuring me to give him their new names and the bus or train they were leaving on. I told him if every woman got caught, Mary would find out eventually. He said not if he waited until they were well outside of Starling before he picked them up."

And there was my answer. If the women took off on their own, he'd only catch up with some of them. But if he let Mary's group help them, thanks to this piece of shit in front of me, he could snare every one of them.

My stomach roiled. Then he'd sell them to or trade them with other traffickers in the network, and Mary and her group were none the wiser.

Striker looked around, swallowed again. "Could I have some water?"

I nodded, signaling Bradley. "Someone will bring it in a moment."

Striker stared past my shoulder at the mirror behind me. "I started trying to get more of the women to take cars. I pointed out that they'd have transportation when they got to their new homes. It was safer for me that way. Every time I had to get into the records to find out the info Butler wanted, there was a risk I'd get caught."

"I thought Caroline Baumann was the keeper of the car list, so how did you find out who got what car?"

"Well, I could get Mary talking, over dinner, or whatever, get enough details to figure out who was getting what. And I knew what date I had to get them ready by."

It was really hard to keep a neutral expression. *You are truly scum. You used your wife's pillow talk to...Grrrr.*

"I needed more cars," Striker was saying, "so I paid my friend Harry a cut to find them for me. When I told him I needed to leave town, he insisted on coming with me. I figured I'd better let him. He's not the brightest bulb in the package. If I left him behind, he'd probably say the wrong thing and blow my cover. I was hoping it would look like I was just leaving my wife."

"Harry knew what you were doing?"

"Well, not all the details, but yeah. We've been friends for years."

"How did you get the info on the women if they opted for bus or train tickets?"

"Mary doesn't like keeping records for long. She's paranoid they'll fall into the wrong hands."

"Her paranoia was obviously justified." My tone was acidic.

"Well, yeah." He shrugged. "Caroline kept the info on who was going where, along with the plane or train info, locked in a file cabinet inside her locked office. After a woman was on her way, her file was destroyed. I had a key maker in my workshop. It was easy enough to borrow Caroline's keys one time and make a copy."

"So we can add pickpocket to your list of talents."

He half grinned. "Yeah."

Oh how I wanted to put a fist through his face.

Clamping my teeth together, I counted to five. Then another thought had my stomach hollowing out. "Did anyone else besides Butler ever approach you for information about the cars and the women getting them?"

Striker shook his head, looking up toward the ceiling and to his left.

I'd asked my friend Kate one time if there was any truth to the theory that people looked in one direction when they recalled a true memory and in the other direction if they were lying. She'd said no, that theory had been debunked by research. If people were practiced at lying, you most likely wouldn't be able to tell that easily.

This guy might be practiced enough to fool his wife, but I'd bet my next paycheck he was lying.

He dropped his gaze, made eye contact. I stared at him.

Finally, he cleared his throat. "Well, there was this guy, he came into my workshop one night when I was working late on a car. He was Hispanic, not tall, but big." Striker puffed out his chest and shoulders to illustrate. "He had a gun. At first, I thought he was going to rob me. I told him I didn't have any money in the shop. But he pulled out a picture and asked me if I'd ever seen the woman in it. I shook my head, even though I'd recognized her."

Striker paused, sighed. "I gave him the cover story, that we were a charity that reclaimed things and repurposed them. We gave fixed-up cars to people too poor to buy one." His eyes darted toward the ceiling again, this time to his right. "He was pretty scary but I didn't tell him anything about Tatiana."

I wasn't surprised that the woman in the photo was Tatiana. I'd seen that coming. I pulled out my phone and scrolled through photos, found the closeup of Juarez's face that I'd taken in the sinkhole. "Is this the man?"

Striker blew out air. "Is he dead?"

"Yes."

"Thank God."

"You're glad he's dead?"

"Well, I'm, um, not glad he's dead. But like I said, he was pretty scary. It's not surprising that he came to a bad end."

"And you're sure you didn't give him any info?"

A quick eye dart to the ceiling, then he shook his head.

My stomach was queasy now, my chest tight, as I asked the next question. "You didn't happen to mention to him about Caroline Baumann and her laptop, did you?"

His eyes went wide and his face blanched. He shook his head more vigorously.

I clasped my hands together on the table to keep myself from grabbing his shirt front and slapping him silly. "I think you did," I said, in a low, firm voice. "I think you sicced him on Caroline so he'd leave you alone. Or did he pay you?"

Striker was shaking his head continuously, eyes darting around the room.

I stood up. "How much did he pay you?" I yelled.

Striker's face crumpled. He tried to cover it with his hands, but the cuffs wouldn't let him. "Five grand," he whispered.

I strode to the door. I had to get out of there before I strangled this guy. I'd certainly known plenty of criminals who used people as badly as he did, but they were truly evil. This guy was just plain self-centered, which somehow made his complicity in the evil worse, in my book.

Bradley was standing outside the door when I opened it, a paper cup in his hand.

"Give him his water, then take him back to his cell." I shoved past him, sloshing some liquid onto his jacket sleeve. I kept moving.

"Chief, you okay?" Bradley called after me.

"No." I did not look back.

CHAPTER THIRTY-ONE

I needed to get some fresh air and tamp down my anger. I went down the fire stairs and out the back door of the municipal building. The evening air was chilly, but nothing my suit jacket couldn't handle.

Walking city streets at two in the morning might not be the wisest thing. But then again, in my current mood, I'd pity the poor mugger who tried to take me on.

I shook my head. I couldn't seem to eject Striker's face from my mind's eye.

Why were people so often *not* who they seemed to be?

Chameleons had nothing on guys like Striker and Butler—and my father. They could change their demeanor to fit the setting, convince others that they were all sweetness and light. But they had a dark side, or in Striker's case, an incredibly greedy side, that they hid well.

Then there were people like Emil Herrera, who seemed to care about doing what was right, but eventually caved to fear and/or temptation.

Was I holding people to too high a standard? Did I really know for sure that I wouldn't buckle if someone found the right threat? I doubted anyone could tempt me with materialistic rewards, but if they threatened someone or something I loved...

I was yanked out of my reverie by a low cough behind me. I whirled around, reaching for my Glock, which wasn't there.

A homeless man sat cross-legged on the sidewalk, his back against a cement-block building. He cleared his throat. "You got any spare change, ma'am? I ain't had nothin' to eat today." His voice was hoarse.

I froze for a second, then reached for my wallet. Heat creeping up my cheeks, I pulled out a twenty-dollar bill. "Please spend it on food," I said, as I handed it to him.

"Of course, ma'am." His surprised expression seemed genuine. "Thank ya kindly."

I headed back toward the municipal building, shaking my head. And sometimes that whole thing could work the other way. Someone seems like a threat, but isn't. They're only a hungry, homeless man.

As I stepped off the elevator on the third floor, someone, partway bent over, barreled past me. I blinked. Was that a *chair* he had on his back?

Officer Peters raced past him, then turned and shot him in the chest with her Taser. He went down.

Out of my peripheral vision I spotted Sam coming out of the conference room. He was cradling his injured arm and limping slightly.

Barnes had come running from the bullpen. She looked down at the man, whose face I couldn't see. It was obscured by the chair now lying on top of him. "So you managed to get yourself zapped after all," she said.

Ah, that's who he was. Harry, the junkyard owner.

"Barnes, Peters," I gestured toward Harry, "help him up and get him loose from that chair. And bring him to my office. I'm calling the ASA to see if I can get him a deal."

"You're offering him a deal?" Sam roared. "He just upended a table on me."

I turned toward him. "Did it hit your arm?" I was truly concerned, but I was still gonna offer Harry a deal to testify against his friend. I wanted that slimeball Striker behind bars for as long as possible.

"No, I jumped back in time, but then I fell on my keister." He rubbed his butt with his good hand, a chagrined expression on his face.

And I almost laughed out loud.

"Come on to my office," I said to him. "I'll explain while they get him disentangled." I called back over my shoulder, "And Barnes, make a note to have the conference room table bolted down."

It was after three a.m. before everything that could be done tonight had been done.

We'd decided it was unwise to leave Harry and Striker in cells next to each other. Sam had called one of his deputies to take Harry out to the county jail.

It didn't matter where we housed him now. The ASA's district included both city and county, and she'd agreed to a deal. In exchange for testifying, Harry would get off with an obstruction of justice charge, a misdemeanor, and would pay a hefty fine—every penny he'd received from Striker and then some—but no jail time. And his former friend would be charged with accessory to kidnapping, false imprisonment and human trafficking, one count of each for every woman he had helped Butler recapture.

Plus two counts of accessory to murder. The ASA wasn't sure she could make those two charges stick, but either way, Striker was going away for a very long time.

Sam and I were about to step onto the elevator, when Bert came around the corner.

"You're *still* here?" I said.

"Yup, Ernie just came in with Striker's truck. We're both jazzed, so we're gonna pull an all-nighter and go over it. Don't worry. We won't put in for overtime. We'll take tomorrow off instead, if that's okay?"

"That's fine. And Bert, thank you. We all don't say that often enough. Your job is important, crucial even."

He beamed and ducked his head. "Um, we found a laptop under the back seat of the plane. I couldn't get it to open so I gave it to Der–"

"It's mine." I breathed out a sigh of relief. "But yes, let Derek look it over."

Bert nodded. "And I almost forgot, Ernie found Rohypnol in the wine, and a dish of milk in the kitchen had minute traces of Benadryl. Whoever broke into your place knew something about cats. I looked it up. That's the only human sedative that you can give to cats with a relative amount of safety, and even then only in tiny doses."

"Thanks." The elevator dinged and the door opened. I managed to stifle the shudder until after we were on it. That bastard Emil had put roofies in my wine, and he'd drugged my poor innocent kitten! I wondered if he'd stood in my living room, researching on his phone how to sedate cats, while I lay helpless in my bed. I shuddered again.

"You okay?" Sam sidled over and put his good arm around my shoulders.

I blew out air and lied. "Yeah."

After making an exaggerated show of looking around—as if we weren't alone inside an elevator—he leaned down and kissed me. Tenderly at first, then he deepened the kiss.

I let myself melt against him as warm tingling feelings invaded my body.

The elevator bell dinged at the first floor.

I broke the kiss. "You know, that going-to-the-next-level thing you talked about," I said in a husky whisper. "I really want to do that, soon."

The doors opened.

I pulled away. "But not tonight. I'm going home to my cat. I'm exhausted."

Sam looked crestfallen, but then he chuckled. "I'm pretty exhausted myself."

At my car, he gave me a chaste kiss on the cheek. "Say hi to Pipsqueak for me."

Between our separate but equally crazy schedules, it was almost two weeks before we managed that evening on Sam's deck.

It was a warmer than average late November evening, and we had a nice bottle of Cabernet Sauvignon going. Between the wine, warm socks and a sweater, I was pretty comfy stretched out on a chaise lounge.

Sam, his arm still in a sling, manned the grill. The sight of him—in jeans and a navy flannel shirt—combined with the hot-grease fragrance of sizzling steaks made my mouth water.

"Hey," I said, "you'll never guess what came back today."

"What?" He poked at the meat with a big fork.

"Gutiérrez's DNA results—from the new sample, taken after he was arrested."

He pivoted toward me, eyes wide. "Really? That was fast."

"The FBI ran it through their lab, gave it priority. Turns out he *is* the hit man who's been knocking people off with his sap in the Southwest."

Sam returned to poking the steaks. "Not Juarez?"

"Nope. Juarez was his leg man. He did all the preliminary stalking, figuring out the victim's habits, et cetera. Then Gutiérrez swooped in, caught the victim unaware, and did his thing with his sap. He wore gloves and his ski mask in most cases, but there was some trace evidence from a few of the cases that had his DNA on it."

I sipped wine. "A few hairs on the floor, in one case, and black wool under the victim's fingernails. The detective on that case now thinks she managed to yank off his ski mask. But there was hair from several people on her floor. She was a hairdresser, pregnant with her rich boyfriend's baby and threatening to tell his wife. At the time, the detective ran the DNA from all the hairs but nothing popped. He didn't give it another thought then, just went with the explanation that she probably fell and hit her head on the edge of her shampoo sink."

"Until you provided Gutiérrez's DNA," Sam said, grinning over his shoulder. He expertly flipped the steaks and put the fork down on the picnic table, already set for dinner.

He came over and sat in a lawn chair beside me, took a swig from his wineglass he'd picked up from a side table. "That explains the email I got from the State's Attorney's office. They're filing the charges but they're holding off on prosecuting Gutiérrez for Caroline's and Juarez's murders. I guess the ASA figures the multiple killings out west take priority."

I nodded. "Since those are murders for hire and in multiple states, he'll be facing federal charges for them. Did he admit to anything regarding Juarez?"

Sam shook his head. "No, but the assumption is he either got pissed because Juarez failed to find his son or he became a liability once he'd been arrested. He might have led the police back to Gutiérrez."

"Or even flipped on him."

Sam sipped more wine, staring at the sun setting behind a row of trees at the back of his property.

"The charges she'll be filing are as long as my arm," I said. "Besides the murders, there's attempted kidnapping, the threats against Patterson's daughter, the assault on Donna Glaser and Patterson, and on you. Even the assault on Pirolnik, since Gutiérrez no doubt ordered that."

"But with Juarez dead, that one might be hard to prove. Oh, and you forgot flying an airplane without a pilot's license."

I gave him a half smile. "Sad that she's holding all those charges in abeyance, but we'll get our crack at him eventually. Cruthers checked in with the accountant again. Once he'd reassured the man that Gutiérrez was behind bars, the guy became a spigot. Turns out Gutiérrez did want Alejandro because he was his heir, but it wasn't just ego. His father had a clause in his will. Gutiérrez only got half the money from his estate. If he produced an heir by the time he was forty-two, the other half would be released to him, but if he didn't, it would go to charity. And the heir had to be legitimate and living with him."

"Did the accountant know that his client was a cold-blooded killer?"

"No, but he wasn't surprised. He said Gutiérrez refused to tell him what type of consulting work he did. He just sent him a cashier's check for several hundred thousand dollars every few months, to add to his investment funds."

I took another sip of wine. "And cold-blooded is the right term. There were other ways he could've supplemented his inheritance, but my psychologist friend, Kate thinks he enjoyed killing, that he got off on the power and anger release it provided."

Sam nodded. "One thing I haven't figured out. How did Gutierrez know that his wife and kid were here? Once they fell into the hands of those traffickers, they could've ended up anywhere in the country, or the world, for that matter."

"In Mexico, he admitted, reluctantly, that he'd had business in Jacksonville recently. His last two hits were in Louisiana and Mississippi. I think he was expanding his business, and he had a hit in north Florida, maybe even in Starling. Juarez came here, doing his reconnaissance thing, and he spotted Tatiana in the park."

"A coincidence then," Sam said.

"More like dumb luck."

"So some poor schmuck in the area, with a price on his head, has gotten a reprieve."

"Yeah," I said in a grim voice, "until his supposed loved one finds another hit man."

"Sorry." Sam looked chagrined. "Didn't mean to kill the mood."

I let out a bark of laughter. "What mood? We've been talking murder and mayhem for the last ten minutes."

Sam grinned, and somehow that made my chest warm. This guy got me. He wasn't threatened by me, he didn't need to compete with me...he just got me.

"So what happens to Tatiana's little boy?" he asked, his face sobering some.

Now, I was the one grinning. "Guess who's adopting him?"

"His foster mom?"

"Nope, Pirolnik and Donna Glaser. She's moving into his guest room. Jenny Coleman said that single people are rarely used as foster parents, and singles also have more trouble adopting. Gabe asked her if the couple had to be married to each other. She said technically there was nothing in the rules saying they did, so he and Donna applied together, to foster the boy for now, and eventually adopt him."

Sam's eyes sparkled in the fading daylight. "An unorthodox arrangement, but it should be good for all of them."

"Jenny Coleman said she has to go through the process to end Gutiérrez's parental rights first, before he can be adopted. It helps that Alejandro was born on American soil, in a private clinic in Arizona. That makes him a U.S. citizen."

"A happy conclusion to a very sad event," Sam said.

"We don't see enough of those in our line of work."

He nodded and stared off into space for a moment. "You know, that taking it to the next level thing. It doesn't have to be tonight."

I chuckled. "Sam, I appreciate that you've been taking things slow, but we've been doing..." I gestured with my wineglass, "...whatever this is we've been doing for almost two months now."

Sam turned toward me, grinning. "Good, then dessert tonight will be very sweet indeed."

A sizzle and pop from the grill. "But first the steaks." He jumped up, went over and turned them again.

He came back and sat. "Just a couple more minutes."

"Seriously, I do thank you for going slow. Most men wouldn't be that patient. Uh, I've got trust issues."

He gave me a look that said loud and clear, *You think?* Out loud, he said, "Well, you're not alone there. I've gotten quite picky in recent years. Picky enough that I've been celibate for a long time. I figured staying that way a little longer was worth it, if I got this right and didn't scare you off."

I snorted. "If I ran away scared, it would've been more about the crap in my psyche than anything you might do."

"You're not alone there either." He took another sip of wine.

I shook my head. "I've been giving this a lot of thought lately. Our profession doesn't exactly improve our trust in humankind. We see too many people who seem good on the surface, but when you scratch that surface, they turn out to be scum bags, or worse."

"But sometimes," Sam said quietly, not looking at me, "you scratch and only find more goodness."

"Yeah, that's the other thing I've been thinking. If I never get to know anybody well enough to scratch the surface, then all I'm going to ever experience are the bad people I see at work. That's a quick path to total cynicism and burnout."

He turned toward me. "So how have you kept from going down that path before?"

I took a deep breath. "I had friends in Maryland, most of whom I never really acknowledged as friends. One is my former partner, Dolph, and I met Kate and the others through him. They're all good people, through and through. They used to irritate the hell out of me because they'd sometimes stick their noses into my cases, but I realized after I moved down here that I missed them. They kept my view of humankind more balanced."

He leaned over slightly, bringing his face a bit closer to mine. "Tell me more about Kate and your friends."

I sighed softly, staring up into his eyes. "Another time. Tonight–"

He cut me off by gently pressing his lips against mine. I love how his kisses start off sweet and tender, then deepen into something more passionate.

A flicker and a pop. I opened one eye.

"Uh, Sam!"

"What, sweetheart?" he whispered, his voice husky.

"Your grill's on fire!"

⸺◆⸺

AUTHOR'S NOTES

If you enjoyed this book, please take a moment to leave a short review on the ebook retailer of your choice. Reviews help with sales and sales keep the stories coming. You can readily find the links to these retailers at the *misterio press* bookstore (https://misteriopress.com/bookstore/)

This is Book 2 in this series. Book 1 is *Lethal Assumptions*, and Book 3, a Christmas novelette, will be out in November, 2023. Book 4, *Felony Murder*, will hopefully be out in late 2023 as well.

This book was proofread by multiple sets of eyes, but proofreaders are human. If you noticed any errors, please email me at kass@kassandrala mb.com so I can have them corrected.

Heck, email me anyway. I love hearing from readers!

And you may want to sign up for my newsletter at https://kassandr alamb.com to get a heads up about new releases, plus special offers and bonuses for subscribers. You will receive a free novelette, *The Tell-Tale Bark*, the prequel to the Marcia Banks and Buddy cozy series, AND a free novella, *Sweet Sanctuary*, the prequel to my Kate Huntington Mysteries. The C.o.P. on the Scene Mysteries are a spinoff from this series. Judith is a secondary character in that series, first showing up in Book 4, and playing a more extensive role in most of the books after that.

Also, *misterio press* now has a readers' group on Facebook (https://w ww.facebook.com/groups/misteriopressmysteries/) where we chat with readers and also offer giveaways, contests and other goodies. Please stop by and check it out!

Bear with me as I spread around some gratitude and then I will share some tidbits of background information.

First a big thank you to my sister authors at *misterio press*, Kirsten Weiss and Vinnie Hansen, who helped shape this into a better story with their feedback. Also my unending gratitude to my wonderful editor, Marcy Kennedy, and to my husband who always does the "final" proofread. I put final in quotes because I have a tendency to mess with things right up until the story goes into final production, and sometimes I inadvertently introduce new errors. So any boo-boos you found are my fault, not his.

I am having so much fun writing this new series, although I'm finding that police procedurals require a lot of research, especially if one is not in law enforcement. I try to look up procedures and such and/or ask real-life LEOs, but there will be times when I inadvertently make assumptions that turn out to be wrong. Any LEOs reading this book, if I screwed something up, please email me at the address above and let me know. I do want to get it right.

One of the things I had to research was whether or not LEOs can take their guns on a commercial airplane. They can. But the gun has to be packed a certain way (as described in the story) and has to be in their checked luggage. And they declare them when they check the luggage at the airline's counter.

That is all that is required for taking their guns with them within the U.S. In reality, though, to take guns into Mexico, a U.S. LEO would need to get advance permission from the Mexican Secretariat of National Defense. But I decided not to complicate the story with those bureaucratic details.

One of my best moments so far as a writer was when I read an early review of one of my Kate books in which the reviewer compared my writing style to that of JA Jance. I was thrilled, since she is one of my favorite authors. I especially love her Sheriff Joanna Brady series. There are two references to that series in *Fatal Escape*. One is direct, when Sergeant Bradley mentions that he spoke to Sheriff Brady of Chochise County in Arizona about the homicide in her county that may be one of a pattern of murders for hire.

The other is indirect. I have borrowed Joanna Brady's nickname for her two detectives whose last names both start with C. She calls them the Double Cs, and I couldn't resist having Judith, in her own mind at least, refer to Cruthers and Collins as her double Cs. I do hope that Ms. Jance takes this borrowing of the label in the spirit intended, as a tribute to her wonderful characters. I actually feel like I know Joanna personally!

To the cat lovers out there, yes, I know that one shouldn't give even Benadryl to a kitten as tiny as Pipsqueak. I did not know this however, until my editor, Marcy pointed it out, that Benadryl is the only sedating human medication one can give to cats and then only in tiny doses, and not to very young kittens. I originally had the intruder slip roofies into the kitten's milk. But after Marcy set me straight, I decided to include the info about other sedatives being dangerous to cats, but stretched reality just a tad by having Pipsqueak survive a small dose of Benadryl unscathed.

And lest some fellow Floridians decide to take offense at the comment about how poorly Florida's teachers are paid, this state is ranked 48th out of 50 when it comes to the average teacher's salary. Although some politicians like to claim that we are ninth.

The city of Starling and Clover County are fictitious locations, but Jacksonville obviously is real, and their law enforcement agency is called the Jacksonville Sheriff's Office (JSO). The FDLE is a real agency as well, although my fictitious character, Dot Wilder, is *not* the Special Agent in Charge of the Jacksonville region. Also the elderly ME in charge of the District Four Medical Examiner's Office is a figment of my imagination.

The Mexican state of Nuevo Léon and the city of Monterrey are also real places. And there truly was a drought in the area in 2019 that caused the Rio Grande to be unusually low that year.

I hope you are enjoying this series as much as I am and will stay tuned for the next installment. In the meantime, if you haven't already read my other series, they are listed at the front of this book.

ABOUT THE AUTHOR

Kassandra Lamb has never been able to decide which she loves more, psychology or writing. In college, she realized that writers need day jobs in order to eat so, being partial to eating, she studied psychology. After a career as a psychotherapist and college professor, she is now retired and can pursue her passion for writing fiction.

She spends most of her time in an alternate universe with her characters. The portal to that universe, aka her computer, is located in Florida, where her husband and dog catch occasional glimpses of her.

Kass has completed the ten-book, traditional mystery series, The Kate Huntington Mysteries (set in her native Maryland, about a psychotherapist/amateur sleuth), plus four Kate on Vacation novellas (with the same main characters). She is also the author of the Marcia Banks and Buddy cozy mystery series, about a service dog trainer and her sidekick and mentor dog, Buddy. There are thirteen stories in that series, which is set in Florida.

And her new series of police procedurals stars Lieutenant Judith Anderson from the Kate Huntington series as the main character in the C.o.P. on the Scene Mysteries.

To read and see more about Kassandra and her books, please go to https://kassandralamb.com. Be sure to sign up for the newsletter there to get a heads up about new releases, plus special offers and bonuses for subscribers (and free stories).

Kass's e-mail is kass@kassandralamb.com and she loves hearing from readers! She's also on Facebook and hangs out some on Instagram. And she blogs about psychological topics and other random things at https://misteriopress.com.

Kassandra also writes romantic suspense under the pen name of Jessica Dale.

~~

Please check out these other great *misterio press* series:
Karma's A Bitch: Pet Psychic Mysteries
by Shannon Esposito
Multiple Motives: Kate Huntington Mysteries
by Kassandra Lamb
The Metaphysical Detective: Riga Hayworth
Paranormal Mysteries
by Kirsten Weiss
Dangerous and Unseemly: Concordia Wells
Historical Mysteries
by K.B. Owen
Murder, Honey: Carol Sabala Mysteries
by Vinnie Hansen
Full Mortality: Nikki Latrelle Mysteries
by Sasscer Hill
ChainLinked: Moccasin Cove Mysteries
by Liz Boeger
To Kill A Labrador: Marcia Banks and Buddy
Cozy Mysteries
by Kassandra Lamb
Steam and Sensibility: Sensibility Grey
Steampunk Mysteries
by Kirsten Weiss
Never Sleep: Chronicles of a Lady Detective
Historical Mysteries
by K.B. Owen
Bound: Witches of Doyle Cozy Mysteries
by Kirsten Weiss
At Wits' End Cozy Mysteries
by Kirsten Weiss
Payback: Unintended Consequences
Romantic Suspense
by Jessica Dale
Steeped In Murder: Tea and Tarot Mysteries
by Kirsten Weiss
Travels of Quinn

by Sasscer Hill
Blogging is Murder: Digital Detective
Cozy Mysteries
by Gilian Baker
Maui Widow Waltz: Islands of Aloha Mysteries
by JoAnn Bassett
Plus even more great mysteries/thrillers in the *misterio press* bookstore.